FLEDGLING

COPYRIGHT

FLEDGLING

MOLLY HARPER

DANCING WITH ILL-TEMPERED UNICORNS

I once believed that the hardest thing I would ever face would be a mountain of dirty laundry or polishing every piece of silver in my employer's house, and then I was sent to finishing school.

"Ladies! Ladies! Why these glum expressions in the face of such delightful work?" my dancing instructor, Madame Rousseau, called as I sagged at the waist and braced myself against my knees just to catch my breath.

The spring sun beat warm upon my back as I struggled to force air into my lungs. The grass of Miss Castwell's expansive south lawn was silky and warm beneath my bare feet. The breath I drew in was scented with the waxy sweetness of white and purple hyacinth blooming on the edge of the knot garden. Behind us, Miss Castwell's Institute for the Magical Instruction of Young Ladies loomed like a cursed fairy tale castle, the late afternoon light lending the green-gray stone an eerie, ethereal light.

Madame Rousseau, a reed-thin woman with sepia skin, clucked her tongue disdainfully at the class full of sweaty, winded students. Miss Rousseau never got tired. She never got winded.

Her thick black hair never slipped from its neat chignon. And she never ceased to be disappointed by our insistence that we needed to breathe *and* feel the blood circulating through our limbs. I was in very real danger of flopping forward and meeting the earth face-first. Even Callista Cavill, an awful girl who prided herself on being the unshakeable model for all that was elegant in our class, was beet-faced and shaking.

"This vernal circle is an intermediate dance at best, ladies, though its purpose is the truest and purest in intents. Summoning a unicorn is a blessing for Miss Castwell's. It definitely seals our magical boundaries for the year. It's your duty to these glorious halls and all they have granted to you to throw yourselves whole-heartedly in this exercise!" Madame Rousseau scolded us. "How shameful that this class has so little love for our venerated school!"

"Does she think we do not know that *none* of the other classes have been able to summon a unicorn this spring?" Alicia McCray hiss-whispered in my left ear, propping herself on the ground with her palms to prevent face-planting. "Because it's tricky work at best! And unicorns might prefer the presence of magical maidens, but sudden movements can make any animal nervous! So doing the dance in triple time is what some people might consider counterintuitive!"

My other best friend, Ivy Cowell, was bent in a similar L-shape to my right, sweat giving her chestnut skin an almost iridescent sheen. Ivy made several attempts to raise her hand before I shoved my shoulder under hers and helped hold her arm aloft. "Perhaps, Madame Rousseau, if you didn't ask us to do the dance at such a quick tempo, our performance might be adequate."

Ivy had a gift for both understatement and diplomacy.

"Ridiculous," Madame Rousseau sniffed. "I have written several papers on this very subject. Summoning rituals are even *more* effective at an increased speed. I've tested this on spirits, nymphs, *and* merfolk. Do you have any idea how difficult it is to summon a merman when he doesn't want to be called?"

Madeline Sato, one of those most dedicated dancers in the school, groaned under her breath. "I think she is trying to murder us."

Alicia wheezed in agreement, her tiny, pale shoulders heaving. "It's the only reasonable explanation."

"That will teach you to tell your mother that you're ready for the 'full educational experience' offered by Castwell's," I huffed, laughing until I realized how much it made my stomach muscles hurt.

"I just wanted to be able to take my classes with you two," Alicia hissed. "I've felt very well over the past few months, but I'm nowhere near my full strength. I thought I would be taking an easy potions course or even belomancy, which you know both know I hate because flinging an arrow at a target is *not* a reliable way to predict the future. But I was willing to put up with it for the pleasure of your company. I did not expect to have to run around a lawn at *triple time,* sweating through my clothes. I am not amused."

I snickered, my shoulders shaking into Ivy's. The truth was that it was very easy to sweat through our Castwell green physical activity gowns, thin, light muslin dresses with short puffed sleeves and shin-length skirts. Because we were so scandalously dressed (and unicorn historically shunned masculine company), all the male staff had been directed to the other side of the campus so they wouldn't manage to — *gasp* — glimpse our exposed ankles. Male visitors had been banned for the next two hours. We might be learning to do magic with enormous knives while conducting social terrorism, but Miss Castwell's took the reputation of its students very seriously.

Ivy, bless her, continued to try to reason with Madame Rousseau. She placed her hands upon my back, and I tried not to grunt too loudly as Ivy used me to push up to a standing position. "But has the theory been proven with unicorns, Ma'am? They're notoriously skittish creatures."

Madame Rousseau narrowed her eyes at Ivy's flushed face and considered for a moment. "Fine! Ladies! Assemble, we will perform the dance at double time."

The class groaned quietly in unison and straightened, stumbling back into formation.

"You tried," I said to Ivy. "It's more than I was able to do. I was too busy stubbornly clinging to consciousness."

Ivy chuckled as several older girls keyed up violins and a guitar. Poor Theodora Brandywine had the bad luck to be extremely proficient at the most unglamorous instrument of all ladies' musical options — the snare drum — and was expected to keep time. Sighing, the petite girl tapped a double-time tempo against the skin of the drum and the other girls joined in a lively spring tune.

We skipped in tight concentric circles until the music sped up even further, and we darted in and out of each other's formations, making floral patterns that could be seen from above. Now that we were moving at a more reasonable speed, I wasn't worried about hitting the right spot on the ground or not tripping or holding my arms straight and my shoulders back. There was simply movement and breathing and the rare joy of being able to run — a rarity for any proper young lady of Guild Guardian society.

The song repeated on and on in a dizzying cycle, and suddenly there was a collective gasp behind me, and I turned to see a pale graceful shape moving out of the woods surrounding the school. We continued dancing, as instructed, but at a slower pace, welcoming the unicorn into our midst. As my side of the circle moved toward the trees, I could see the unicorn more clearly — long elegant legs with delicate ankles, a shining coat of creamy gold, and an ivory horn as nearly as long as my arm.

It was one of the most beautiful things I'd ever seen in my young life, and yet, my stomach churned at the gleam of its mane and the clip-clop of its shimmering hooves. The dragonfly on my hands, a living metal tattoo that marked me as the Translator of the Mother Book, vibrated with an emotion I'd never felt from it — dread. The mark was trembling with anxiety, and there was no rational explanation. Unicorns were loving beings who only wanted the best for the maidens who called them. We should be thrilled to have called one so easily.

The Hollowhorn

That fear overrode any glow of peace and hope we were told to expect in the presence of a unicorn. All I felt were revulsion and dread and a prickle of cold sweat under my arms. I hadn't felt this out of sorts since last term, when the late Miss Morton had nearly drained my magic and life away in misguided attempt at world domination.

"I don't feel well," I whispered hoarsely to Ivy, who was staring dreamily at the unicorn as she moved. The wind picked up and a softer, wistful melody piped over the musicians' efforts. Eventually, the players gave up and simply stood there, staring as the unicorn moved closer.

No, *we* were moving closer to the great beast, our formations becoming misshapen and sloppy. Yet, Madame Rousseau said nothing.

Something was wrong.

The slow lilting song grew louder, and my legs felt like one of Mum's aspic jellies underneath me. I fell forward, dropping to my knees on the lawn and the other girls simply stepped around me, moving closer and closer to the unicorn. I swallowed thickly around the nausea that was making my stomach roll. Now that I was finally still, I could get a long, steady look at the unicorn, and I could see tiny perforations in the unicorn's horn, spiraling up to the tip in a pipe formation. I realized the haunting melody was coming *from* the unicorn itself, from its horn.

Oh, sweet Circe's rounded cheeks. We hadn't summoned a unicorn.

"Stop!" I yelled, stumbling to my feet. One of Callista's cronies, Millicent DeCater, broke from the dancing circles and drifted toward the creature with her arm outstretched. "Millicent, stop!"

"It's so beautiful," she mumbled, her voice dazed and her blue eyes glassy.

In my remedial magical zoology reading, I'd learned that hollowhorns were a malicious, bloodthirsty cousin to the unicorn. The holes in their horns caught the wind to make music, attracting poor dumb woodland creatures that were too mesmer-ized to object as the hollowhorn fed on them.

Which explained why Millicent was the first among us to come forward.

"Madame Rousseau! It's a hollowhorn! We *must* stop the music and get away, quickly!" I cried, tugging at Madame's long green sleeve. But she ignored me and shrugged me off as she glided gracefully across the lawn.

I surged towards Ivy, who ignored me completely as I shook her. "Ivy! Wake up!"

But Ivy's usually luminous brown eyes were too dulled by adoration for the poisonous music in her ears. She strained away from me, testing what little upper body strength I had as I caught Alicia around the waist. I dragged both of them away from the creature. "Alicia! Please! Would both of you just snap out of this, for pity's sake?"

But they did not snap out of it. If anything, my creating distance between them and the monstrous horse seemed to make them more determined to reach it!

"HELP!" I yelled, turning to the building, while I struggled against my friends' pulling. "Somebody please! Help!"

Why wasn't I affected by the music like the others? Why was I alone in this? This felt like a child's bad dream, fear and panic and helplessness all rolled together. The oily grip of fear sliding along my mark didn't exactly help me focus. I wrung my hands out, as if I could force more magic into the tips of my fingers.

I reached for my ritual blade, Wit, and cast the spell sigil for "silence," a bright blue symbol staining the air. The lilting music continued. In fact, the hollowhorn seemed to send me a filthy look, as if it didn't appreciate my attempts to interrupt his perfor-mance and mealtime.

Letting loose of Alicia, who then flopped face-first on the lawn with the force of her yanking away, I drew a sigil for *alarm*. To increase the degree of difficulty, I did this while stomping on the hem to Alicia's gown, slowing her progress as she crawled on the grass towards the hollowhorn. I flung my arm towards Headmistress Lockwood's office window and the glowing red symbol flew like a hawk toward the glass. Vaguely, I heard a shattering sound as I darted around Ivy and planted my shoulder against her chest to keep her from shoving me along towards certain doom. I turned and saw that Millicent's paper-pale fingertips were almost touching its evil velvety nose.

"Millicent, stop!"

Unfortunately, there were too many girls between me and Millicent.

"I'm almost sorry about this, Millicent," I murmured, throwing something of a "hallway curse" — a livid pink spell that would never be taught in the classroom but whispered among the students far out of the hearing of the teachers. If a student wanted a rival to injure her ankle — not permanently, mind, just long enough to keep her from dancing with a particular boy from the Palmer School for Young Men — she would cast the Glass Ankle Curse. Said rival would immediately sprain their ankle so severely that she would think she'd attempted ballet on a buttered floor.

The pale pink sigil hit Millicent in the left leg, and she crumpled with the ground with a sickening *pop*. None of the girls seemed to notice. The pretense of dancing had stopped, and they were simply stumbling towards the hollowhorn. The monster's eyes, the flat gray of a gravestone, glanced down at Millicent's prone form with interest while she moaned over the state of her ankle.

Breathing deep, I cast the Stone Shield sigil to put a magical barrier between Millicent and the creature. My arms ached with the effort of it, but it simply bounced off of the awful thing and faded into the lawn. The hollowhorn's haunting, sinister song played all the while.

Was the creature simply too malevolent to be affected by good magic? Or was it that I wasn't strong enough to affect it? I was only a student, a powerful student of course, but a student all the same. I desperately wished for an adult — any adult — to see this bizarre scene out of a window and come to my aid. As grateful as I was to be free of the hollowhorn's thrall, it seemed to be a great burden to put on the shoulders of someone who was in so many remedial classes.

I blinked fast, wiping sweat from my brow and trying to focus on priorities. Millicent was on the ground, immobile — thanks to my spell — and very vulnerable to attack. My friends were getting closer and closer by the step. Madame Rousseau was no help whatsoever, and there was no help forthcoming from any other quarter.

I nodded, licking my lips. "Right."

Drawing a quick silver sigil on the air, I threw a Certain Sleep Charm at Alicia, who dropped onto the lawn in a heap. I tried the same on Millicent, and Jeanette, and even Ivy, but I was still mastering the charm, and Alicia was so much smaller than the others. She was easier to dose and curled onto the grass like a sleeping kitten.

"Think think think," I whispered to myself, sweat dripping down the back of my neck as I reviewed every spell I'd learned from the Mother Book. But all I could think of was a potion to prevent toadstool warts, which didn't strike me as particularly useful at the moment.

What was the most powerful spell I knew? The one that had saved us from Miss Morton last year. With all the will I had left beyond the haze of panic and exhaustion, I drew the most dangerous symbol in the Mother Book.

Unmake!

The dirty green light sputtered out of my blade and died before it could form the sigil. I tried it again.

Unmake!

Nothing. Not even the sad little emerald light this time. It seemed that I needed the support of the friends who helped me cast the spell last time, and they were currently trying to pet an evil unicorn.

The tip of the creature's spiraled horn dug into Millicent's shoulder. She screamed, though she sounded more surprised than pained that this beguiling beast had betrayed her so. Millicent's complexion, usually so rosy, paled ever so slightly as if the monster was draining her of her life, and while Millicent seemed to be slowly waking from the music's spell, she wasn't able to crawl away from the hollowhorn.

Because I'd injured her ankle... which may have been a mistake.

The creature whickered and pressed its horn deeper into Millicent's shoulder. Millicent cried out as her skin turned an unhealthy grey color. The hollowhorn pulled its soft white lips back, revealing sharp fangs with serrated edges like a shark's teeth. They were stained with the blood of previous meals. It lowered that awful mouth towards Millicent's wound and licked at it delicately with a forked blue-black tongue. Millicent screamed as if the contact burned her.

I glanced toward the building and saw Headmistress Lockwood making her way across the lawn but not fast enough. She didn't realize what was happening or else she would have run as fast as she was capable in her voluminous Castwell green skirts. My friends were still drifting towards the hollowhorn as if they wanted to be next on the menu.

I glanced down at Wit in my hand. It was a powerful magical

instrument, but it was still a knife. It was carefully forged steel and enchanted to stay as sharp as any dagger could be. I balanced its weight in my hand and wondered how much damage it could do to such a creature. I held the blade by its tip, throwing Wit like I was throwing an arrow on the belomancy range.

Unlike the lessons on the belomancy range, I managed to hit something. The force of Wit shattered the creature's horn, the substance cracking like porcelain, as the blade embedded itself in the hollowhorn's forehead. Those awful grave stone eyes focused on me, as if it couldn't believe I'd done something so very rude. Its glossy white legs folded under its dead weight, and it dropped to the ground. As the hollowhorn's eyes rolled back into its head, it breathed out one last angry groan.

My classmates wilted collectively. I let out a breath I didn't realize I'd been holding and propped my hands against my knees. Sweat dripped down my face and soaked into the neckline of my gown. Ivy gasped, grabbing my arm.

"What just happened?" she asked me, shaking as if to clear cobwebs from her head. "What's wrong with everyone? Why is Alicia napping, and why is there a dead unicorn on the lawn? Why does my chest hurt? Did you *tackle* me?"

"No." I sighed. Relief rushed through my tense limbs and it felt like I could breathe properly for the first time since dance class started.

I cast a sigil to wake Alicia, who suddenly took in a huge gulp of air and shouted. "Slime mold!"

I paused while helping her to her feet. "What were you dreaming of?"

"Botany," Alicia said, frowning. "It was the most boring dream I've ever had. Painful, really. I'd prefer a nightmare. What happened here?"

Madame Rousseau blinked rapidly, and her expression shifted

from dazed to extremely offended that we were out of formation. "Ladies, what is this? Why has the music stopped? And your lines? Has not one girl in here ever heard of proper posture? Were you all raised to be slouching sloths?"

Madame Rousseau's eyes went wide as she caught sight of the fallen hollowhorn, but she turned her back to it and cast what appeared to be a shielding spell over her shoulder because the carcass disappeared from sight. The girls blinked at the illusion but in their disorientation focused on the brisk instructions coming from her mouth. "Miss McCray? Who gave you permission to take a nap in the middle of class? And Miss — Miss DeCater? What has happened to your ankle? Oh, my dear girl, do not try to stand on it. It's quite swollen."

Leveling a long, speculative look at me, Headmistress Lockwood interjected, "Ladies, you are dismissed. Please return to your rooms and dress for dinner, which begins in one hour. Miss Reed, please stay, I'd like to speak to you and your usual cohorts in chaos, as well."

Headmistress Lockwood was a tall, compact woman with iron grey hair pulled back into a severe knot. While she had a surprisingly delicate features, her dark eyes were always stern and alert. It was as if she was as eager to catch her charges misbehaving as she was to protect us from all threats, known and unknown. She would not respond kindly to the hollowhorn's intrusion on our peaceful campus.

Callista and her friend Rosemarie had enough composure to call "Oooooh," as if to mock my predicament, but Headmistress Lockwood snapped, "Miss Cavill, please help Miss DeCater stand and take her to the hospital wing."

Callista's expression shifted from smug to annoyed in an instant, but as someone who spent most of her time trying to prove to the faculty what a darling she was, she could hardly protest something as thoughtful as taking one of her closest friends to seek medical attention. She pulled Millicent to her feet and none-too-gently guided her across the lawn.

"Cohorts sounds a little cold," Alicia grumbled under her breath as we helped her brush the grass from her light brown curls. "I prefer to think of myself of a partner or at least a fervent accomplice."

"I think she was prioritizing alliteration over word choice," I assured her. "You are the author of most my ill-advised plans."

"Thank you," Alicia preened while Ivy laughed.

As the other girls filtered away from the now-invisible spectacle of the dead hollowhorn on the lawn, their expressions baffled and tired, Madame Rousseau called, "And do not despair over the condition of your persons. Remember, ladies do not perspire. We glow with the dew of our exertions. Be proud of your work today!"

Alicia burst into giggles but hid it with a fit of coughing.

"What happened here?" Ivy asked again.

"An evil unicorn tried to eat our dance class… which sounded far sillier than I thought it would before I said it aloud," I mused.

"A hollowhorn?" Madame Rousseau scoffed gently, giving me an indulgent smile. "Miss Reed, I assure you a hollowhorn would never venture onto school grounds, particularly when we were trying to summon their mortal enemy."

Headmistress Lockwood sniffed and waved her hand, undoing Madame's glamour. The silver-white body faded into view, its gold and ivory horn in pieces on the ground. "While I would normally agree with you, Madame Rousseau, the evidence seems to speak for itself."

"But why would a hollowhorn come here of all places?" Madame Rousseau demanded.

"What if we were trying to summon them with a song played

at the wrong tempo?" Ivy asked, nodding toward where the musicians had abandoned their instruments in their daze to get back to the school building. "Using a violin made of blackthorn wood, which is known for its appeal to more sinister creatures?"

"That's Emily Benisse's violin," Alicia noted, with a yawn. "It belonged to her great-grandmother, Charlotte. She was so excited to play it with the band for the first time."

"Charlotte Benisse was known for her skill at parlaying with the most frightening of creatures," Headmistress Lockwood muttered, deep in thought.

Madame Rousseau's mouth dropped open. "You must know, Headmistress, I never intended for this to happen. And sweet little Emily wouldn't hurt a dormouse. She would never dream of luring a dangerous creature to her classmates on purpose."

"Of course not," Headmistress Lockwood sniffed dismissively. Born with a permanently exasperated expression, she exuded a dismissive air without really trying. "Though, I believe I will keep the violin in my office for the time being. Emily can use her practice instrument until further notice."

"I'm sure she will see that would be best," Madame Rousseau agreed. "I believe I will retire, ladies, after I return these instruments to the other musicians."

As Madame Rousseau gathered the drum and guitar from the grass, Headmistress Lockwood turned to me with an arch look. "Miss Reed, I appreciate your quick thinking in seeking help in your predicament, but could you have found a way to do that without breaking my office window?"

I turned to see the shattered pane of glass at the headmistress's office hanging in the frame by a tiny sliver. Then that sliver snapped, and the glass fell two stories in a shower of glittering destruction.

"I may have thrown that spell a little harder than I intended, ma'am," I admitted. "I'm sorry."

Headmistress Lockwood waved her own blade, a long black dagger with silver twisted into the handle, and the glass returned to its original state. "I suppose you did do the school a service by not allowing a cursed creature to devour fellow students."

I nodded. "Thank you."

"But you did break my window. And Millicent DeCater's ankle, using a curse not sanctioned by the school."

"It's not broken, merely sprained… enthusiastically," I insisted. "And I thought an ankle injury would be easier for you to explain to her parents than her being digested by a hollowhorn."

Headmistress Lockwood seemed to mull that over for a moment. "Fair enough. For your grace under pressure and devotion to the well-being of the students, you will be rewarded with the shattered remains of the creature's horn… once the groundskeepers clean up this mess."

My brows raised. The horn she was offering me was a powerful magical ingredient, valuable for purging the effects of malicious spells. I could sell that powdered horn to one of the purveyors on the Magical Mile and save quite the little nest egg for myself. It would be the difference between survival and destitution should my situation at Raven's Rest ever change.

"Thank you, Headmistress," I said, curtseying. "Should we to send it home to Aunt Aneira for safekeeping?"

"No," Headmistress Lockwood said, in the flinty tone she always used when speaking of her longtime rival and old school chum, Aneira Winter. "I would rather keep the powerful magical item where I can see it, under the school roof."

"Yes, ma'am," I agreed, careful to keep my tone glum. Ivy elbowed me lightly, but I ignored the nudge.

"Now, you should help Misses Cowell and McCray back to their rooms to dress for dinner."

"Yes, ma'am." I tucked my arms into Alicia and Ivy's elbows and walked toward the school.

"And Miss Reed?"

I paused to return my gaze to Headmistress Lockwood, who was *smiling*. It wasn't a wide grin by any means, but it was a more mirthful expression than I'd seen from the woman in months of knowing her. "That was an excellent bit of marksmanship. Your belomancy instructor will be very pleased."

"Oh, that's praise I do not deserve, Headmistress Lockwood."

Ivy elbowed me in the ribs and out of the side of her mouth, muttered, "Accept the praise."

"Thank you, ma'am," I amended.

Headmistress Lockwood frowned down at the hollowhorn carcass and dismissed us with a wave. "That's enough, ladies. Go dress for dinner."

Alicia sighed as we turned towards the Castwell's building. "You couldn't just let her think you'd done something impressive for one moment?"

"It *was* praise I didn't deserve," I insisted as we passed the knot garden.

"How could you say that?" Ivy demanded. "You withstood the temptation of that creature's evil stupefying music. You defended your classmates from said creature using a single blow from your blade. You hit the hollowhorn dead center in its forehead. That was very difficult."

I pursed my lips. "Yes, but I was aiming for its neck."

2

THE MOTHER BOOK DISAGREES WITH ME, VEHEMENTLY

"Do we know any spells to cure blisters?" Alicia asked as we limped down the narrow, high-ceilinged corridor to the dorm wing. The floor-to-ceiling Castwell green wallpaper reflected on the black-and-white tile floor, giving the whole hallway an otherworldly glow.

"Madame Rousseau says blisters build character," I said. "Right now, I'm much more concerned with the 'dew of my exertions.' I do not smell dewy."

"None of us are walking out of here smelling like a rose," Ivy groaned.

"Speak for yourself. Those of us who are ladies manage to control our baser functions," Callista sniped as she slipped by. I could only imagine that she had unceremoniously dropped Millicent at the hospital wing and *run* away before she could be asked to be supportive of her friend in any way. "By the way, COW-ell, you sound like a cart horse clomping about when you promenade."

"Well, you sound like an imbecile when your mouth opens. We all have our burdens to bear," Alicia shot back.

Alicia had no gift for diplomacy or understatement.

"I suggest you move along, Callista," Ivy said. "Alicia, dear, you know that it's unkind to find a battle of wits with the unarmed."

Callista's blue eyes narrowed and her thin upper lip curled back from her teeth, but instead of speaking, she whipped her head around and stomped away — sounding a bit horse-like herself.

"She never changes," Ivy noted.

I rolled my eyes a bit because my ladylike restraint had met its limits for the afternoon. "And never learns."

"Well, if she did, I would be rather disappointed in her inconstancy," Alicia said, tucking her arms into ours as we made our way past the oil portrait of our frowning founder, Emmeline Castwell. "But I am going to have to remember that 'battle of wits' comment for later. I noticed you still remain silent in her presence."

"I promised Mrs. Winter I wouldn't antagonize her, and that includes aggressive wordplay," I sighed as we climbed the sweeping main staircase, filing in behind the other tired girls. "And aggressive spell-casting. And aggressive salt-passing at meals. Mrs. Winter gave me a very comprehensive list of what counted as antagonizing her. And then Mr. Winter added a few Mrs. Winter hadn't thought of. Callista and her mother are just barely intimidated enough to keep mum about Mary's scene at the masquerade ball. Any provocation and Callista may decide that the threat of Mrs. Winter's wrath isn't enough of an incentive to behave like a decent human being."

Far from her floral claims, Callista had always been a thorn in our collective side. She'd bullied Ivy mercilessly since they'd started classes at Miss Castwell's. She'd tried to turn me into her little lapdog, attempting to harness my social cache as Mrs. Winter's niece and the Translator to her advantage. Alicia probably had it the worst of all three of us because Callista still had delusional hopes of somehow persuading Alicia to her side in Callista's lofty goals of courtship with Alicia's ridiculously attractive older brother, Gavin — which was why Callista tolerated Alicia's impertinence.

Fortunately, Gavin had other ideas about who he wished to court and had been visiting me at the Winters' home, Raven's Rest, for several months. We weren't officially courting, as Mr. Winter, who for all intents and purposes was my uncle and legal guardian, hadn't given his permission. And, frankly, Gavin's mother didn't like me very much. Gavin had recently graduated — early — from Palmer's and was helping his uncle run McCray and Company. And Mrs. McCray believed he should focus his efforts the office and with her at home. We were, however, in a nebulous pre-courting stage where Gavin was allowed to visit me with chaperones and was allowed to send me gifts and letters, as long as said chaperones screened them. And yet, given the reactions of the other Castwell girls when those gifts and letters arrived, ours was a scandalous affair.

There was a good deal of giggling, so much giggling.

"You couldn't have at least *nudged* Callista towards the evil unicorn?" Alicia mumbled. "Technically, it wouldn't be murder. Merely pointedly failing to save her."

"You've become a very sinister individual since fall term," I told her.

"Would it be terrible for me to skip the dressing for dinner process all together and just eat dinner from a tray in my room? In my nightgown?" Ivy asked. "While I soak my feet in a tub with peppermint oil? And study our potions notes? Surely 'evil unicorn' is justification enough for dinner in bed."

"It would be incredibly clever for you to do that, but Headmistress Lockwood caught on to girls doing that last year and banned all dinner trays on dance lesson days unless you are actively vomiting or bleeding from the head," I sighed. "I feel that people have spent an inordinate amount of time explaining rules to me recently."

"Where's the trust, I ask you?" Alicia asked as we neared my room. "You break a curfew or two, enter forbidden areas of the school, disintegrate a teacher, and suddenly you're considered a problem student."

"Should we be worried about recent cursing from an evil unicorn?" Ivy asked. "In terms of residual magic or vulnerability to other evil horned animals — evil stags and evil gazelles and evil narwhals and such? And why weren't you shambling toward certain horn-related injury along with the rest of us?"

"I have no idea," I said, holding up my hands. "Maybe because of the mark? Or perhaps my connection to the Mother Book? Or because I'm smarter than the two of you?"

They burst out laughing.

"All right, you didn't have to laugh quite so loud at that. You're both simply terrible people," I said, making them giggle. "Also, change of subject, just to make you both feel guilty for teasing your friend who loves you, Auntie Aneira sent me some charmed bath salts to use after dance lessons. She didn't make it clear what the salts did, but she did say that I wouldn't look like a 'shuffling street urchin' and bring shame upon Winter House after using them — which I found promising."

Alicia snorted. "All my mother sent me in the last mail call was an extremely guilt-laden missive telling me that I *will* be joining the family on the annual holiday to Scotland immediately after school closes, even if Mother has to tie me to the luggage rack of the carriage."

"Scotland in summer sounds rather lovely," I responded.

"Oh yes, picturesque, sweeping landscapes, stunning views of the Loch of Amethysts, blah blah blah," Alicia muttered. "But holidays with my mother generally mean a months-long slog of Mother chasing me around to stop me from 'over-exerting myself' as if I'll shatter like painted china if I sit down too firmly."

"I'm suddenly very grateful that my family has never been on holiday," I said, nodding.

"Well, I'm sure Auntie Aneira could arrange a tour of the continent if you ever feel the need," Ivy snickered. "And do not think I didn't notice how you manipulated Headmistress Lockwood's dislike of your aunt into keeping the horn close, here at school."

"What did Mrs. Winter *do* to Headmistress Lockwood when they were at school together?" Alicia asked, her eyes wide.

"I believe she implied that Headmistress Lockwood was too prideful about her appearance to be taken seriously as a student," I whispered while my friends made cringing faces. "Which is why the headmistress adopted such a severe aesthetic all these years later. And I do not like to use the word 'manipulate,' but I couldn't let Headmistress send the horn home. Auntie Aneira would never let me sell it. She'd rather display it in Raven's Rest as a demonstration of my accomplishment."

My friends were the only people at Castwell's who knew that my "auntie," Aneira Winter, was actually my Guild Guardian. While I was enrolled under the name Cassandra Reed, the orphaned distance niece of the powerful Winter family, I had been born a Snipe, a member of the servant class to families like the Winters.

Generations before my birth, magical people had been quite alarmed at the technological progress that us mundane people had managed to make during the Industrial Revolution. While they enjoyed the luxury of steam-power and some machinery, magicals from around the world agreed that industrialized non-magicals would eventually create weapons beyond magic's ability to protect them. My papa said they also were deeply concerned about our inability to have arguments that didn't escalate into wars, which seemed fair. Although, stepping out of obscurity to inform non-magical populations that they would be taking control of the planet seemed like an over-reaction.

The armies of the newly formed Coven Guild melted the gates of Buckingham Palace and informed the non-magical monarch that her reign was over and the Guild would now protect us from the escalating threat of our own technological innovations. The non-magical governments tried their best to put up a defense, but when the opposing forces can disintegrate buildings and people, it isn't exactly a fair fight.

Over the years, the world devolved into a more feudal society where non-magical families — Snipes — were assigned to magical families for employment. Conditions for Snipes were by no means cruel. We were paid a fair, living wage for our work. The Guardian government wrote laws to protect our health and safety, but the unwritten laws were very clear. Guild Guardians ran the world. They made the decisions that shaped law, society, the economy, and magic itself. And thanks to that magic, the potential of their lives was unlimited. As long as they were accepted into the right research guilds after graduation, they could study metallurgy, crystallography, botany, glamours, any number of magical occupations.

Snipes stayed Snipes. We cooked and cleaned and served tea and did any number of physical chores that could probably have been accomplished through magical means, but Guardians preferred to keep their energy to loftier pursuits.

Snipes did not have magic, or so I had been told every day from birth. We simply did not have it in our bodies, and I believed that right until the moment I levitated one of Mrs. Winter's favorites vases in her parlor out of sheer panic and threatened the very fabric of magical society. I was given a false identity and placed here at Castwell's for safe-keeping rather than being turned over to the authorities for whatever fate they deemed necessary. I was one of the lucky ones.

I approached my suite door marked with the Castwell's quill and blade crest and reached for the doorknob. The door swung open, and Jenny, my newly assigned lady's maid, nearly bowled me over.

"I'm so sorry, Miss!" Jenny cried, curtsying deeply. Her cheeks were flushed, and her blond curls were mussed around her delicate heart-shaped face. Her thin arms were burdened with an enormous basket of linens she'd taken from my bed as part of her daily chores.

"It's alright, Jenny. You didn't know I was coming in," I assured her. "Are you well? You look a little flushed. And I say that as someone who looks like she was a struck by a sudden land-bound hurricane."

Jenny shook her head. "I'm quite well, Miss, thank you. I'll just take these downstairs, and I'll come back to help you dress for dinner."

"I would insist that I do not need help, but I do not think I can lift my arms," I told her.

"I can see that, Miss."

"Miss Reed defeated an evil unicorn in single combat," Alicia told her solemnly.

Jenny's brow winkled, but instead of arguing, she simply gave a blank well-trained-servant smile and said, "Of course, she did."

Jenny bustled down the hall and we three shambled into my room, an elegant suite done in shades of green, from the drapes to the counterpane to the green-tinted marble fireplace mantle. I took *Wit* out of my reticule and drew the blue symbol for silence against the door, preventing anyone from eavesdropping at the door. Unlike the spell I'd attempted on the hollowhorn, it worked. *Silence* was a spell I'd come to value more and more since Alicia and Ivy had learned about my origins. It felt good to be able to share that part of my life with them, to hold nothing back. That did not, however, mean I wanted the whole school to find out, bringing ruin on my parents and the Winters, not to mention, an arrest and worse for me.

"Your new lady's maid seems very ... excitable?" Alicia said, dropping onto my canopied bed. Phillip, my blue-green familiar of undetermined feathered origin, chirped indignantly from his perch. Phillip hated it when people sat on my bed. For a bird, he had an unreasonable hatred of rumpled covers. "Is it a permanent condition?"

"She does always seem to be in a hurry," I admitted, digging into the chest at the foot of my bed to pull out a large jar of Mrs. Winter's miraculous bath salts.

"Why did your old maid get re-assigned?" Ivy asked as I poured a bit of the peppermint and eucalyptus scented salts into two small glass jars. "Oh, that smells fantastic."

"Susan wasn't re-assigned. She got married to her sweetheart back in the Warren. The wedding was held right after her birthday. Her father wanted her to wait until she was at least nineteen, which was a matter of some discussion between them from what she told me," I said. "They moved to a situation in the south, somewhere near Surrey."

"Oh, how lovely!" Alicia cried. "I hope she'll be very happy."

I nodded as Alicia took her own portion of salts. "It was a love match, which is a bit rare for our ki- Snipes."

"It's rare for the upper class, too," Ivy reminded me gently. "Marriages are carefully brokered between families to maintain the balance of power, to make new allegiances. It's all strategies and wealth and *breeding*. My parents are treated like scientific oddities when they admit that they were a love match. My grandmother is practically embarrassed when she mentions how happy they are, as if Mother should have had some other, loftier goal in mind."

"I think it's wonderful that your parents love each other so completely," I told her. "My parents — I supposed they're perfectly civil to one another, but I cannot ever remember them sharing a laugh or a kiss or even a moment that wasn't occupied with what they had to do to get through the day. I know they were matched by the Winters and some branch of the Mounfort family, who thought they would make a good fit as head groundskeeper and gardener of Raven's Rest, but I wonder if they ever felt anything more for one another than polite friendship. I wonder if they were ever happy to be married, or worse, if they were happy, was it my birth and the problems that came along with me that made them less so? It couldn't have been easy, the constant worry that they would be caught, a Snipe family harboring a child with magic and what that could mean for them. And I know that Papa disagreed with making me take the suppressors, when Mum insisted I should. He hated lying to me about those pills. He hated lying to me about why I was so sick all the time, even when Mum said it was for the best. What if that was an argument they never stopped having? What if that's what wore them down to what they are now?"

Ivy smiled sadly and patted my arm. Alicia, on the other hand, sighed loudly and said, "How in the world do you have the energy to be so maudlin after what some would consider an act of heroics? Is it some after-effect of listening to that hollowhorn's music to be the world's longest-suffering martyr?"

I was so shocked I laughed out loud while Ivy made scolding noises at Alicia.

"Well, honestly!" Alicia cried, dodging a pillow Ivy sent flying at her with the wave of her hand. "Are you going to take the blame for everything that's ever gone wrong the history of England, or just your tiny corner of it? Yes, it must have been very difficult and very frightening for your parents to be in that position, but it's not as if you asked to be born with magic. It's not as if you set out looking for it."

"But —" I started before Alicia cut me off with a sharp hand gesture.

"Do you think I asked to be born as I was?" Alicia asked pointedly. "Do you think having to bind my power to keep me from the very source of my magic and life force was something my parents did lightly? According to Gavin, they argued about it extensively, but they did it because they loved me and it was what was best for me. And if it caused tension between them, that was theirs to resolve. It wasn't something I caused or could change. It simply was."

My cheeks flushed with shame. Alicia suffered from a condition known as reverberation. When any practitioner used magic, the body suffered gradual damage from energy drain of casting spells. Most practitioners were able to heal from this damage quickly and continue to use magic without problems. In reverb patients, their magic seemed to echo inward and instead of healing, the damage would fester. Many patients like Alicia had their magic bound so they were limited to small spells, and the disconnection from their magic left them under-sized and sickly-looking, much like I had been. Then again, we tinkered with the wards placed on Alicia during our confrontation with Miss Morton the previous year, resulting in some rather remarkable feats of magic. Gavin had tried to replace the wards, but they were less effective than before. Alicia was able to cast more easily. She'd grown nearly a foot in six months, and she was developing curves.

Rather than looking like a skinny child of nine, she looked much closer to our age.

"You're right," I admitted. "I'm being self-indulgent. I wasn't thinking of the parallels of your situation. I'm sorry."

"Feel guilty for the deeds that you can claim as your own. Everything else? You do not carry that weight on your back. You'll end up with great rounded shoulders like Margaret Macliber."

"That's not fair," Ivy told her, though her shoulders were shaking. "The Maclibers are a mining family, a branch of the Cavills from the eastern areas of the continent. All of them are built like great stone bricks."

Alicia wiped at her temples with the cooling towel. "True, I should be kinder to Margaret. She suffers enough being related to Callista. Can you imagine having to attend family gatherings with her?"

"I'm sorry. I'm not sure why all that just burst forth," I said, shaking my head.

"Madame Rousseau does claim that dancing is a cathartic process," Ivy suggested sagely.

"Madame Rousseau also claims that we can become great dancers if we only practice until our toes bleed," Alicia retorted. "Sometimes, Madame Rousseau can be a bit mad."

Alicia turned to me, her tone kinder. "And it's possible that you're feeling unsettled because it's been months since anyone has seen your sister. Your parents are getting more frantic. I've seen your face every time Mrs. Winter visits with news of home. Your nerves have to be suffering."

I nodded, not quite sure how I could phrase my feelings about my sister, Mary, and her disappearance after working to topple my carefully constructed persona. I didn't trust myself not to lose my temper when discussing Mary's spiteful words, her obsession with Owen Winter, and how she used it to excuse lashing out at me. The more I thought about it, the angrier I got, and the more the silver dragonfly embedded in my palms vibrated with fury. I could hear a muffled thud like I was listening through water.

"Dearest, perhaps you should calm down," Ivy murmured.

I nodded, but it was hard for me to even speak through the angry clench in my jaw.

The rattling thud seemed to get louder, and the dragonfly hummed on my palms. I closed my eyes and tried to breathe deeply, to expel the anger and distress from my body, but all I could think about was Mary's face when she revealed the truth to Callista at the Winters' annual costume ball, the lack of any hesitation or concern for how that might hurt me. She only thought of herself, just like she'd always thought of herself, playing me for a fool, making me feel guilty for the fact that she was healthier than me, lying to me.

The rattling noise got louder and louder until the locked cabinet over my desk burst open and a large object flew out and flapped around the room like a giant rectangular bird. It flailed about the room, bouncing off of the walls, and then made a beeline for my head.

"Gah!" I yelped, dropping to the floor just as it flew past, careening against my vanity, boomeranging back and smacking my chest. "Ow."

The Mother Book, the resting place for all secret knowledge for centuries written in magical cuneiform that only the Translator could read, had just knocked the wind out of me.

"It's never done that before," Ivy said, edging closer as I struggled to draw in breath.

"Well, it did fly to you when you summoned it," Alicia noted. "But it seemed less intent on crushing your sternum."

"It was responding to your anger, which is a little frightening," Ivy said, peering over my shoulder to look at the page that the book had fallen open to. It showed a page I'd already translated, showing a Revenant, a re-animated dead body enchanted by a Necromancer to do whatever unpleasant deeds a Necromancer raises the dead to accomplish.

"It still looks like absolute nonsense to me," Alicia said. "I recognize that awful picture, but that's it. Is it safe to help you up?"

I shuddered at the illustration's slack jaw and graying skin, slamming the book shut. "This is very helpful, thank you."

I glanced down at the dragonfly mark, now silent and still, and flopped down to the floor. "Do you think a book-related contusion would count as a reason enough to take a dinner tray in my room?"

The other girls chorused together. "No!"

3

ALMOST HOME AGAIN

Raven's Rest was home and yet not. I had spent most of my life in the Winters' ancestral seat but not as a welcome guest in its stark, elegantly decorated rooms. I was hardly recognizable as the Sarah Smith who had dusted and polished and tended this house until my fingers cracked and bled. Still, returning to the enormous grey stone manse, even just for a weekend visit felt as comfortable as sliding into a warm, sweet-scented bath. With the Winters, I could at least drop the Cassandra mask. I didn't have to pretend to be anyone else, and yet my position in the house was unclear compared to my place at school.

I wasn't a servant anymore. I wasn't expected to do more than sit on Mrs. Winter's elegant furniture and display the refined manners I'd absorbed thus far. And yet, I wasn't a member of the family either, no matter what elaborate lie we'd concocted about my deceased parents who were Mrs. Winter's distant cousins on the Brandywine side of her family. It was incredibly uncomfortable in my first few weeks as Cassandra to sit at the formal dining table and take meals with Mr. Winter at the head and Mrs. Winter watching, always watching and evaluating my table etiquette. Every time one of the maids entered to deliver a platter to the table, I had to tamp down the urge to rise and help them. I felt such incredible guilt, sitting there doing nothing while they worked. I had not been raised to be a pampered creature of leisure.

Still, I would see my parents, which was the point of the visit. Because I'd managed to protect my identity and behave in a manner that protected myself and the Winter name, my access to my parents was far less restricted than the total lockdown I'd experienced just after Mrs. Winter discovered my magic. I'd been angry with them for hiding it from me, for lying to me, but now that I'd experienced some of the dangers of the Guardian world, I understood why they'd tried to shelter me.

We'd reached a state where we were trying to answer each other's questions without getting angry or blaming each other for the misunderstandings of the past, and we were all worried for Mary. Yes, I was still incredibly angry with Mary, but I did worry for her. Though she was older than me by three years, she didn't seem to understand how the world really worked. She seemed to think that because she was exquisitely pretty, society would just make exceptions for her. She'd believed for years that somehow, someway, Owen Winter returned her feelings and that someday they would marry and live happily ever after. She wasn't prepared for the machinations of men in Guardian circles. She couldn't predict how they would use her and discard her, and she was too proud to come home to our parents when she had nowhere else to go. As angry as I was with my sister, I didn't want her broken and alone. Just quieter and not so bloody selfish.

I took a deep, calming breath and sat back in the carriage. I wasn't supposed to curse, not even in my head. I smoothed my hands over the pale blue gown I'd donned that morning. I never thought I'd be so happy to wear a color other than green. Though Madame DuPont had crafted each of my school gowns to accentuate my figure and complexion, they were each Castwell green. As I was supposed to be a distant Brandywine cousin, Mrs. Winter had the Brandywine white apple blossoms subtly embroidered on all of my dresses and handkerchiefs. All of the fashionable girls at school did this, sneaking their house sigils in some form into their ensembles to show allegiance to their families and remind their classmates of their place in grand social scheme.

The monotone green gowns were supposed to prevent obvious disparity between the girls, no matter how well-off (or otherwise) the family might be. Still, wearing the same color every day, over and over, became tiresome. Sometimes I had nightmares where I drowned in a sea of spring green cotton waves.

We rolled through the iron gates that separated Raven's Rest from the bustle of Lightbourne. I waited for the crayfire carriage, powered by McCray crystals instead of horses, to pull to a stop in front of the mansion. Timothy, a footman I'd known since I was a child, stepped forward and handed me down from the carriage.

"Hello, Timothy. How is your mother?" I asked as Phillip fluttered out of the carriage and landed on my shoulder.

"She's doing very well, Miss Reed. Hasn't had a cough since Mrs. Winter gave her that ginger tincture."

"I'm so glad," I said, pasting on an uncomfortable smile. I'd forgotten that, like most of the servants at Raven's Rest, Timothy didn't recognize me. We'd known each other for years, since I was first allowed to accompany my mother to the kitchens. Mr. Winter had cast careful spells on each of them to barely recall poor Sarah, the maid-of-all-work who had "passed away" the previous year. My parents and Mary were the only ones left who remembered me as I was, pale and small and unremarkable thanks to the suppressor tablets my parents had fed me every day under the guise of medicine.

My family — the Smiths — were fortunate enough to be assigned to the Winters, who had been Guardians to our family almost one hundred years, from generation to generation since the Restoration. Mrs. Winter never paid much attention to us personally, treating us as particularly useful household articles. They were not cruel or cold employers, merely detached, but they were also detached from each other, focusing on their personal pursuits. Much like the icy grey and white rooms that made up their home, they lacked the effusive warmth that one would see in most servant class families.

Another footman, Amos, opened wide white-washed door, and I stepped into the foyer. Aneira Winter, my "auntie," stood at the top of the curling staircase, the hem of her slate blue day gown draped just so across the first step. I wondered how long she had been posing like that, waiting for my expected arrival. She shot what could only be called an unhappy glance at my feathered companion.

Mrs. Winter did not appreciate the presence of a bird in her lavishly decorated home. Birds did not *live* in Raven's Rest, particularly with Owen's horrible seal-point cat familiar, Horace, living there — not to mention Mrs. Winter's own Egyptian Mau, Bast. Birds were put on display here, in the form of Mr. Winter's fascinating avian skeleton specimens and rare precious egg. The white of shell and bone contrasted sharply against the dark grey silk and black marble.

Like the parlor mantle, the newel post at the base of the sweeping staircase prominently featured a large raven, frozen mid-lunge over a precisely carved apple — the Winter House crest It was an homage to the crest of House Mountfort, the larger mother house that included the Winter family, which showed a set of golden scales with a raven on one side and an apple on the other.

Through the door at my right, I could see the formal parlor's icy gray walls with their blinding white trim and dark furniture. The best black enamel and ivory pieces were kept in this room where Mrs. Winter greeted important guests. It also happened to be the room where I first discovered my magic, levitating that vase in a panic when Mrs. Winter startled me. Every cell in my body begged the expensive porcelain not to hit the floor. To my shock — and Mrs. Winter's — the vase obliged. The sight of that room made me feel oddly nostalgic. I hadn't been happy as Sarah Smith, with my sickly constitution and uncertain future, but life had certainly been simpler.

"Go to your perch in my room," I whispered to Phillip. "Avoid the cats, if at all possible."

Phillip chirped and flew up to the second floor, carefully cutting Mrs. Winter a wide berth. I handed my bonnet and gloves off to Amos and curtsied deeply. "Aunt Aneira."

"Cassandra, dear, welcome home," she said, sweeping down the staircase and greeting me with the barest of air-kisses on my cheek. "We'll take tea in the garden, Jane. Please inform Mrs. Smith that we'd like the usual array. And… the lapsang souchong, I think. Miss Reed could use something bracing after her journey."

"The journey wasn't all that difficult," I said softly as she wound her arm through mine and led me through the double doors to the back garden.

"Yes, but we delicate ladies must give the impression that a mere hour in a perfectly comfortable carriage is an ordeal that we must recover from. Otherwise, men will know that we are sturdy, terrifyingly resilient creatures, and we lose the element of surprise."

"Fascinating."

"Honestly, haven't they taught you this at Miss Castwell's? I must question Lockwood about what they're teaching at that school. The curriculum has clearly suffered since my days there."

I laughed, not too loudly. Young ladies of Miss Castwell's did not guffaw. "Oh, I'm sure the headmistress would love to have that conversation."

"We received a maddeningly vague note from the headmistress about an incident with a hollowhorn this week. Parents were only told that the creature had wandered onto school grounds and no students were injured as a result."

I kept my expression passive as Mrs. Winter closely examined my face. I wasn't sure whether to feel guilty for not telling her about the hollowhorn prize. Mrs. Winter provided handsomely for me, including more pocket money than I'd ever had in my entire life. Yet somehow, I knew I needed to keep that to myself, that eventually the hollowhorn would be needed, so I simply smiled. "Tell that to poor Millicent DeCater, who was gored in the shoulder. I believe she would consider that an injury."

"Oh, I must send darling Millicent's mother a note. That must be so embarrassing for poor Headmistress Lockwood," Mrs. Winter mused. "To have a student injured while under her care. How on Earth did a carnivorous unicorn manage to trot onto campus in the first place?"

With a sigh, I explained Madame Rousseau's misled dancing instructions, the musical class-wide hypnosis, and my own knife-flinging contributions to saving my classmates. Mrs. Winter maintained total facial composure through my tale. After my battle with Miss Morton the previous term — which involved the school librarian kidnapping students staying at the school for the winter holiday and attempting to use our magic and the Mother Book to raise an army of Revenants to overthrow Guardian society — I suppose that, by comparison, tangling with an angry one-horned pony didn't seem very dramatic.

"Really? You were the only student unaffected? How interesting." Mrs. Winter murmured, pursing her lips. "Do you think it has to do with your position as the Translator?"

"It's possible," I conceded. "Then again, Madame Rousseau says I do not have a farthing's worth of musicality in my body, so it's possible I was simply impervious even to evil music."

"Still, I wonder if you might apply this immunity in other areas."

"I would hope that I wouldn't encounter many more malevolent musical creatures," I quipped.

Mrs. Winter chuckled. "No matter, I commend you for your quick thinking and doing credit to the Winter family."

We reached the garden, and I beheld the floral wonderland before me. Spring had come to Raven's Rest to claim her blossomed crown. The ornamental cherry trees wept curtains of candied pink, stretching in a long corridor leading to the flowerbeds. My personal favorites, the shy purple irises, were just starting to peek out from their long, awkward stems. Wind rustled the tumbles of wisteria dripping from the arbor, the whispering sound giving the garden a secretive air. Smooth velvety green grass met the robin's egg blue sky on the horizon, which only proved the wealth and power of the Winters, to own such a large piece of property in the crowded capitol.

The gardens were the one place in the world my father ruled. While Mrs. Winter gave Papa a general idea of what she wanted, she tended to focus on the ground-breaking magical specimens she kept in the walled-in, secure section nearer the house. Papa tended every bloom here like one of his children — better, in fact — as Mum was always the one to take care of us when we sick.

Mrs. Winter led me to a small wrought iron table set with two extremely uncomfortable but elegant chairs. In an instant, the tea tray was set between us by silent, efficient hands. Like most good servants, the new maid, Jane, moved soundlessly and unseen and then disappeared before she was noticed. I had never quite grasped that element of service. I subjected the Raven's Rest occupants to spills and trips before Mrs. Winter and my mother decided I was much more suited to private household tasks. Mrs. Winter nodded towards the silver service, and I brewed a perfectly timed cup of tea for each of us — with lemon for Mrs. Winter and a dash of cream for myself.

"Nicely done," Mrs. Winter commented, sipping her tea. "Now, other than your adventure with the hollowhorn, how have you fared these last weeks? Your scrying messages seem particularly guarded."

"I know it may seem paranoid, but I thought it unwise to include too many details in a message that could be observed by others. The girls are always working on charms and curses to violate each other's privacy. Every time you think you've come up with the most secure way to scry a message, some first-year revolutionizes eavesdropping."

"It's not at all paranoid. It's appropriate caution. For your peace of mind, the girls were doing exactly the same thing when I was a student, so that's nothing new. I would, however, like to remind you that just a few months ago, you would have been considered one of those first-year girls."

I smiled, plucking one of my Mum's lemon tartlets from the tiered silver tray. Mrs. Winter had only selected one of the tiny, paper-thin cucumber sandwiches for herself. "Yes, well, I'm much more experienced now, a veteran really. And I'm the Translator, so I'm practically a graduate."

Mrs. Winter smirked. "Oh, I see we've reached the invincible and all-knowing stage of your adolescence. How delightful."

I laughed. "Hardly. I'm very well-acquainted with my mortality, thank you. I simply feel more comfortable at the school than I did before, and my magic is coming along nicely. I'm no longer required to take remedial classes. I'm no longer afraid to receive my marks at the end of the term, and Miss Entwhistle no longer hovers at the belomancy range. Last week, I managed to charge all of the crayfire crystals to light the third floor without one explosion."

"Yes, your teachers seem very well-pleased with your progress."

"And yet...?" I asked.

Mrs. Winter set her teacup down with a sigh, the Winter symbols of apples and ravens hovering along the ivory porcelain rim. "You haven't Translated a new page in months, at least not one that you've told me about. Mr. Crenshaw has sent me several increasingly accusatory letters, informing me that I'm not allowed to keep the Translator from contacting the Committee."

I scowled. Sebastian Crenshaw was a distant cousin of Mr. Winter's and a member of the Coven Guild Senate Inquiry Committee *and* the Committee for Antiquities and Artifacts — but holding very limited power on both. The Inquiry Committee was the governing body for investigating inappropriate acts by Snipes and Guild Guardians alike. It was an agency charged with investigating groups that could be considered subversive or potentially damaging to Coven Guild society. To add a fly to the ointment, the Committee for Antiquities and Artifacts oversaw use of the Mother Book and, by extension, the Translator. Mr. Crenshaw felt particularly indignant that I'd been chosen as Translator without his direct approval and even more incensed that I did not submit daily reports on every new piece of information the Mother Book revealed to me. I had the distinct impression that only Mr. Winter's position with the Senate and Mrs.

Winter's incredibly intimidating presence kept Mr. Crenshaw from showing up at school and shaking information out of me by force.

"Do try to avoid making that face, dear," she said, gesturing to her own smooth forehead. "Once you establish frown lines between the eyebrows, you will spend the rest of your life casting glamours to cover them, and eventually your face looks like a motionless wax mask."

"The book has not seen fit to reveal anything new to me," I said, sipping my tea. "The only real interaction I've had with it recently was it flying around my room and barreling into my chest when I was angry. Frankly, I'm starting to wonder if it's upset with me somehow."

"Why on Earth would the book be upset with you?"

"I have this impression, which is based on nothing but my own feelings, that the book wants me out looking for the other Changelings and not staying at the school, comfortable, learning magic. I do not think it's going to give me any new revelations until I become more aggressive in my search than just asking you to put your resources to work."

"Oh, do not be ridiculous, my dear," she said, tapping her fingertip against my palm, over one half of my dragonfly mark. "You are the Mother's Book chosen companion and voice to the magical world. It wouldn't have chosen you if it was going to get *angry* with you. I do not even know if the book is capable of being angry."

"If the book can choose me, it may be capable of getting angry. What if finding the other Changelings was the purpose of choosing me in the first place? And if that is *my* purpose, where would I get that idea, if not from the book? If I'm not fulfilling that purpose, what's the point in my having the book?"

"Bringing social cache and credit to Winter House, the house that took quite a risk in hiding your unique nature from the Inquiry Commission — and claiming you as one of our own, I might add. You will make time to find the other children like you when you can," Mrs. Winter reasoned, waving her hand dismissively. "I've made discreet inquiries of my contacts on your behalf within the Senate and the various committees. They are responding slowly with what information they have."

"What information is that?"

"Nothing useful, I'm afraid. Confirmation that, yes, there are rumors that such children exist, but of course, it isn't possible because the very notion throws everything we know about magic into question. One particularly persistent rumor is that there is a training facility for magically gifted Snipe children in a mountain range called the Weeping Sisters — where they are learning to use their magic to protect high-ranking Senate officials."

"Miss Morton planned something similar," I muttered. "Though she never mentioned anything about a mountain. Could you really hide a big facility on a mountain? I've never seen one, but that seems unlikely."

Mrs. Winter patted my hand. "Sometimes I forget how little of the world you've seen. Yes, you could certainly hide a facility inside a mountain. However, the hazards of building such a venture and transporting children and supplies to it would be nearly insurmountable. It's far more likely that the facility is located one remote location like the Isle of Wight — a much more likely rumor that is also circulating — or in America. Who knows what they find to do with themselves in America."

"Yes, it really is a regret that I didn't spend more of my youth scrubbing chamber pots across the continent," I sighed wistfully.

Mrs. Winter made a noise dangerously close to a snicker but covered it with a slight cough. "Well, another rumor states that the Changelings have been sent to a farm in Ireland to magically weaponize potatoes."

"I have so many questions," I said, sipping my tea. "The first of which would be… why?"

"Rumors do not always make sense, my dear. But by comparison it does make a training facility across the ocean seem quite plausible, doesn't it?"

"Quite. Do you expect any more responses from your contacts?" I asked.

"When undertaking an endeavor such as this, patience is more than a virtue," Mrs. Winter reminded me.

"It would be much easier to search for those children if I could speak directly to the government officials and ask my own questions."

"And how exactly would you explain that?" Mrs. Winter asked. "A proper young Guardian lady asking questions no proper young lady would ask?"

"I could tell them I'm gathering information in an attempt to get into one of the more academic research guilds."

"That's actually not a terrible idea," Mrs. Winter mused, then almost immediately dismissed it. "But still too risky. Mr. Winter is seeking re-election to his seat with opposition. He's lost support from some key family members, due to his failure to vote for stronger sanctions against Snipes who behave out of turn."

I pressed my lips into a thin line. It had always irked me that an unfair, totalitarian system had chosen a democratic form of government to maintain itself. Of course, being able to vote each other out of office only increased the strain on Guardian politicians to hold onto those offices. Maintaining power depended on constantly applied social pressure from the wives working behind the scenes. And this new urge among Senators to punish Snipes who pushed back against the government that controlled every aspect of their lives could only be meant to target people like my sister, servants who refused to let convention or reality get in the way of what they wanted — Snipes whose obsessions, whether they be an attractive boy out of their reach or an irksome insistence on controlling their own destiny, made them difficult to manage.

"I would remind you that your primary task at school is forging connections, building a life for yourself after you leave school. You've established a very nice start, with your friendships with young Alicia, and even Miss Cowell's family ties to Mrs. Dalrymple will serve you well. And of course, managing to capture the interest of Gavin McCray was quite the coup, very well done. But now you must focus on pushing those relationships to the next level, expanding your circles of friends into other influential families, not to mention nudging young Mr. McCray into the next stage of courtship."

I muttered, "I understand."

"I sense a 'but' in my near future," she said, dryly.

"*But* beyond my more pressing concerns involving the Changeling children and whatever mad plans Miss Morton had in place, I'm very happy in my friendships with Alicia and Ivy. I know I can trust them with the truth of my nature," I said.

"A decision I still do not agree with," Mrs. Winter noted. "And Miss Morton is no more, if you'll recall. You and your friends disintegrated her at a cellular level. There is no coming back from such a measure."

"I know you are correct. Logically, I understand it. But I saw the madness in her eyes at the end, the hatred she had for Guardian society and the absolute certainty she would bring your entire world crumbling down."

"*Our* world crumbling down," she reminded me. "You are a part of Guardian society as well, Cassandra, and while I am trying to be sympathetic after what you've suffered, your fears are that of a child waking from a nightmare. Miss Morton is gone, along with her plans. You must focus on the dilemmas in front of you, instead of chasing errant broomsticks."

I sighed. "Well, I do not know if I'm going to be able to forge the close connections you want with other girls. And I certainly do not know if I can push Gavin into a more serious arrangement than what we now enjoy. It seems no one can push Gavin to do anything he doesn't want to do, and frankly, I do not know if I want to."

"That seems true enough," Mrs. Winter said, taking a tiny bite of her cucumber sandwich. She chewed thoughtfully and dabbed at her lips with a napkin. "And I'm not saying that you have to become close confidants with half of the student body. Just become passing acquaintances. Reach out, host chocolate parties after hours in your room, offer to help some of the less fortunate students with simpler spells. Let it be known that you are a magnanimous, discerning girl, willing to share your good fortune."

"That sounds terribly pretentious."

"It is, but it's also an excellent way to make friends of equally pretentious girls."

"Well, you make it sound just delightful."

"Promise that you will at least try," she said, leveling those cold blue-grey eyes at me.

"I will," I replied, "if you continue to try to gather more information on the Changeling children."

"When did we reach the point in our arrangement where you believed you could set terms?" she asked archly.

"Somewhere between becoming the Translator and preventing the rise of an undead army?" I retorted.

"I never should have given you lessons in cutting sarcasm."

Mrs. Winter carefully folded her napkin on the table and rose. "Now that we've concluded our business, I believe there are two people who would very much like to speak to you waiting just there. Dinner is at seven. Owen will be joining us whenever he bothers to stir himself and take the carriage home. I've left a new gown from Madame DuPont in your room."

"Thank you, ma'am."

Mrs. Winter patted my shoulder and offered me a rare half-smile. "Do try not to worry so much, my dear."

I smiled back, and she suddenly gestured to her face. "The wrinkles, you know."

I laughed as she retreated towards Raven's Rest and her sacro-sanct parlor. Through the chatter of birds nesting in the fruit trees, I heard familiar voices. I turned towards the house where I could see my parents emerging from the kitchen door. My mum, frizzled grey hair blowing in the breeze, was wiping her hands on her apron. Papa was untying the heavy leather vest he wore over his clothes to protect them from the worst of the dirt.

I let out a happy little cry and ran towards them. Well, I moved as fast as I possibly could, but one of the best benefits of proper ladies' school was that I'd learned to move much faster in those heavy gowns.

Even from a distance, my father looked so much better than the last time I saw him. The healthy flush on his cheeks seemed to be from sun exposure rather than the tiny broken vessels left by years of drinking. His eyes were clear and happy, and he was steady on his feet. It was hard to imagine that he was drinking less with one child pretending she wasn't his and another missing, but somehow, he looked as if a great weight had been lifted from his shoulders. He took my hands before I could throw my arms around his neck, and then doffed his cap. "You don't want any of this garden dirt on your pretty clothes, my lady."

"I'm only pretending to be a Winter, not nobility, Papa."

"Well, you look like a princess. I don't care what you're telling people," he said.

He glanced at the windows.

"Mrs. Winter isn't having any visitors. It's quite safe to hug your daughter," I told him.

He threw his thick arms around me and squeezed me tight, enveloping me in the scent of peppermint and soft spring flowers. It was a smell I remembered from childhood and made me want to stay there in his arms forever. It was a scent that meant I was safe.

"Put her on her feet before you take the breath out of her," Mum scolded and wrapped her arms (nubby grey wool shawl and all) around me the moment I was free. Mum looked, well, still worn down by a life of hard work and little sleep. But her rounded, rawboned face carried fewer lines, and her blue eyes weren't underscored by dark circles. She'd taken the time to arrange her hair in rather attractive coronet on top of her head. I couldn't remember the last time Mum had fussed with her hair.

"You look very pretty, darling. How are things at that school?"

"I am earning good marks and staying out of trouble," I told her, slipping my arms through both of their arms and leading them on a circuit of the gardens. I wanted to see the new developments in the plants, and I wanted to escape any prying eyes or ears in the house. Phillip usually warned me of that sort of thing, but he would probably stick pretty close to my room with the cats roaming the floors.

"Well, that's all we can ask of you," Papa said.

"Well, we could ask that she visit a little more often," Mum noted.

"True," Papa agreed. "But it's a good school, and we should be happy that she's receiving such an education."

"Well, I have been trained in the ways conversational subtext, so attempts at broad hints are futile. I am immune."

Papa shook his head with a false stern expression. "It's a terrible school, and I don't think you should go there anymore."

THOUGH CASSANDRA WAS SUPPOSEDLY HOME to spend time with her beloved aunt and uncle, I spent most of the weekend in the kitchen with my mother. I wasn't allowed to help her with the work. She kept insisting that I was too much of a lady to peel potatoes or whip eggs. I found magical means of doing so, however, adjusting movements of Wit to do both.

I waved my blade like a baton, making the symbol for *flay*, which was a rather murky purple spell, but the potatoes didn't object to the violence, their peels curling through the air like ribbons and landing in a perfect little mound on the table. Wordless magic, simply drawing the symbols on the air with one's blade, was more advanced magic than the spoken spells I'd started with at Miss Castwell's. I was proud to have mastered a quiver full of those spells, even if Mum seemed less than impressed.

"This feels like a waste of magic," she told me, though her eyes watched the peels flying through the air with delight.

"Well, it's my magic, and I'll do what I want with it," I said primly. "Perhaps I have a future in writing magical cooking guides."

"Why would proper Guardian ladies ever need cooking guides?" Mum scoffed, dropping the potatoes into boiling water — without magic.

"You make an excellent point," I noted.

"Just think of all the work I could have saved myself if I'd never hidden your magic from you," she mused.

"It seems a bit early to make jests about it," I told her.

Mum shrugged. I wasn't used to Mum making jokes at all. This strange new attitude from both of my parents felt oddly out of place considering our family's situation. But somehow, I was glad, to see them less anxious. I couldn't remember a time when either of them seemed so easy.

"What are you frowning over?" Mum asked.

"It's nothing," I said, sinking back against the kitchen chair.

"Keeping our tongues still was what caused so many hurts between us, Sarah."

I sighed. "You and Papa, you seem happier, with both of us gone. It makes me wonder if we were so very troublesome that my being away at school and Mary being no-one-knows-quite-where seems like a holiday."

Mum chuckled, wiping her hands on her apron before sitting across from me. She poured a cup of plain black tea for the both of us, using the third best china service. The particular pattern, thorn vines wound with little ravens and apples, was only used it when Mrs. Winter's sister-in-law Ursula Winter came to visit, so Mrs. Winter was perfectly amenable to the staff using it. Mrs. Winter hated her sister-in-law with a fiery passion.

"We have been a little more cheerful as of late because we know that you are doing so well at that school, and for the first time we know that you're safe. Or at least, safer than you were before."

I smiled at her, keeping my expression blank. I'd kept the worst of the details about Miss Morton from my parents. They'd been through enough already. They didn't need to know how unsafe I was.

"And we have had some news of Mary," Mum added.

I gaped at her. "Why didn't you say anything before?"

"I wanted to wait until we were alone so we could talk it over."

"Well, tell me!" I demanded, my tone flinty. "Where was she seen? Where is she now?"

Mum raised her hand and I quieted down. "I asked Edwina, who runs the kitchens at Ironwood Abbey, to ask her girls if they'd seen Mary anywhere, that she'd left home and that we were very worried about her."

I shuddered as I sipped my tea. Mum had activated the Snipe version of scry messaging — Tell Edwina Williams anything. Mrs. William was the biggest gossip in all of England. Word of Mary's disappearance would spread like a dragonfire amongst various households in Lightbourne.

"Bessie Balcher — she's worked for Sophia Benisse as a ladies' maid for years — spotted Mary in a shop on Cromwell Street."

"Working as a shop girl?" I asked, frowning at her. It wasn't unusual for Snipes to work in stores operated by their Guardians, but Mary had never had the patience to deal with more than one person barking orders at her. She barely tolerated Mum barking orders at her. And she didn't have the head for figures required to total up purchases. I'd seen enough "incidents" at school to know that proper Guardian ladies did not appreciate being shorted a single one of their pennies, no matter how many pennies they had.

"No, she wasn't working. She was shopping for ribbons."

I made the most unladylike face possible, and I may have dribbled tea out of the side of my open mouth. "That seems… unlikely. Snipes go to the Warren shops when they need clothes. We don't shop on Cromwell Street."

"*We* don't shop on Cromwell Street," Mum told me. "*You* could shop there easy enough. And Bessie Balcher swears that when she was helping Mrs. Benisse shop for a new set of china, Bessie saw Mary wearing a fancy silk dress, shopping at Tidwell's. Bessie said Mary was loaded down with parcels, as if she was afraid she'd never be allowed to buy another pretty thing again."

"Well, where did she go after that?"

"Bessie said she disappeared into the crowds, before she could see which way she was walking. It wasn't as if Bessie could toss her packages to Mrs. Benisse and run after her."

"That's true," I said, a cold knot of tension easing slightly in my belly.

"Still, it is a relief to know she's safe and well," Mum sighed.

I muttered, "Or at least, she's well-accessorized."

Mum set her teacup on the table, with a half-hearted glare directed at me. "But who could be giving her the sort of money where she is shopping in Guardian shops? And what must she be doing to earn that money? She's clearly not working as a maid. And she's not trained for anything else. Your father thinks perhaps she's taken a position as a ladies' companion."

"Mum, ladies' companions are generally other Guardian ladies. Generally, they are Guardian ladies who come from poorer families or haven't secured a betrothal by the time they've graduated Miss Castwell's or a position with any of the research guilds."

"Yes, but your father doesn't understand that. And I don't want to make him worry."

I sighed. "You're probably right. He seems so well. I wouldn't want to tamper with that. How is it possible that he's getting better when everything seems to be falling apart?"

"Ever since he's seen you blooming at that school, there's a light that's come back to your father, a weight lifted from him shoulders. We'd taken your choices away, and he couldn't live with it. Yes, he worries about Mary, but he also knows that she made the choices that led her to this place. We tried everything we could to raise her well. What she does with what we taught her, that's up to her."

"Would it be wrong to tell Mrs. Winter about this?" I asked. "Perhaps there's some way she can speak to some of the shop owners. If Mary is using someone's account, perhaps the shop could offer up an address. Or Mrs. Winter could use magic to track her. She's very interested in finding Mary and containing the damage she could do."

Mum frowned. "Do you think Mrs. Winter would hurt Mary if she found her before we did?"

"I wouldn't think so," I protested. "Mrs. Winter's not evil. She could have sent me to the Inquiry Commission to be tortured or worse. She might send Mary away. Perhaps to America. Or Australia. Or France."

Mum cringed. "I would hate that. But perhaps it would be better. She could start over somewhere where she wasn't reminded of Mr. Owen or you or any of the things that have made her so unhappy."

I nodded, turning my teacup in my hands.

"I know you're still angry with her."

The dragonfly on my palms vibrated slightly, as if to remind me of the outburst I'd had in my room. "That would be an understatement."

"I won't try to talk you out of that," she assured me. "I just want you to know that I'm proud that you're willing to help find Mary, despite that anger."

I pressed my lips together. "Mum, it's not sisterly affections fueling my efforts. It's self-interest."

"I know. I know the school has changed you and not just your manners and your fancy dresses. You don't let people boss you about like you did before. You don't put what other people want before what you want. You're much more likely to survive in the world thinking that way than you were before."

"So I'm selfish but a survivor."

Mum nodded. "Exactly."

I mulled that over for a moment. My mother was not someone who coddled her children. I couldn't remember compliments or cuddling. When Mum wanted to show us how much she loved us, she gave us second helpings. Her telling me that I'd made needed changes was as close as I was going to get to a pat on the back and a plate of chocolate biscuits.

"How is this going to work, Mum?" I asked. "When I graduate from Miss Castwell's, whatever happens with my life, whether it's joining a research guild or getting married — how am I going to come visit you? How are we going to explain that? If I have a husband, he'll never know you as my mother. If I have children, they'll never know their grandparents. How —"

"Let's worry about that bridge when we cross it," Mum told me. "You're safe for now, and that's all I can ask for."

"And if I'm not safe? If Mary's actions lead to the Coven Guild discovering my secrets?" I asked.

"You're borrowing trouble, love."

I sipped my tea and swallowed the familiar, bitter brew. "That's the funny thing about trouble, Mum. You don't have to borrow it. It just appears whether it's yours or not."

Owen Winter was exactly the sort of boy you would expect from a privileged, powerful family. His features were slim and refined. His auburn hair, a cross between his mother's gold and the darker shade Mr. Winter had before he'd elected to shave it off, was slicked back with smelly sandalwood pomade young men favored. He was dressed in the fashionable suits required for his classes at Palmer's, an exquisitely tailored black frock-coat with a high-creased, heavily-starched white collar and a black-and-silver striped tie. The silver raven tie-pin he'd worn almost religiously had been replaced with a tiny silver Palmer's key and dagger crest.

The Palmer's tie pin had belonged to Mr. Winter and Mr. Winter's father before him. Mr. Winter had seen fit to give the pin to him for Christmas, telling him that Owen had impressed him with his quick-thinking and maturity in helping me blend in Guardian society. Owen had been so touched he'd actually broken his usual mien of haughty disdain and hugged his own father. It had been a disturbing sight, really.

We'd tolerated each other reasonably well in childhood, but an argument over a book when we were nine resulted in bloodshed — Owen pulled my pigtails; I broke his nose with a lucky swing of said book — and we made it a policy not to speak after that. It was a policy we maintained until I was forced into his family under false pretenses. Now, we certainly didn't share a close cousinly relationship, but we were capable of riding in the same crayfire carriage for an hour and enjoying an interesting conversation. The bloodshed was always an option, but we tried not to engage that option whenever possible.

"Ah, the ride to Castwell's, the anticipation of seeing some of the loveliest young ladies Guardian society has to offer," he sighed, rolling his shoulders against the plush black seat cushion embroidered with an enormous silver W. He shrugged. "And then of course, there's you and your friends."

"It's not necessary for you to ride back to school with me, you know," I reminded him. "Also, you should keep in mind that there are fewer coachmen involved in running a crayfire carriage, which means fewer witnesses when I toss you out."

"Haven't they taught you anything about decorum or self-restraint from violence at that school?" he asked, though he was smirking. Owen seemed to get some sort of wicked enjoyment when I threatened him. As an only child from an intimidating family where he received constant praise just for showing up to events with both shoes on, I believed I provided the challenging discourse he'd been lacking most of his life. Or it was possible I simply made funny faces when I was threatening him. He was easily amused.

"Yes, I will keep my little finger pointed up when I toss you out of the carriage," I retorted.

"I thought you would be in a much better mood after a weekend spent with your family," he said.

"I'm in a fine mood, when I'm not trapped in a small enclosed space with certain parties," I told him, staring across the carriage at him with a level gaze. This was the sort of closeness with Owen that Mary would have killed for when we were both Snipes. She'd certainly tried to hurt me when she realized that I would not, in fact, use my new status within the Winter household to bring her and Owen together. And now she was under the protection of someone who was willing to keep her in silk dresses and hair pretties.

Who would do that for Mary? Had she found a job in some place too unsavory for me to even know about? Had she finally found a Guardian beau who would keep her in the lifestyle to which she aspired? And why did I have the feeling that somehow Mary's continued presence in Lightbourne would eventually create problems for me?

Owen's brow furrowed and, in a voice devoid of all derision and sarcasm, he asked. "Are you all right, Sarah? Is something wrong?"

"Merely thinking. So how are things at Palmer's? Why don't your parents spend half as much time enquiring about your education as they do interrogating me about mine?"

"Because my success at Palmer's is considered an inevitability," he said, going back to that glib tone I knew so well. "Even if I wasn't brilliant and talented and one of the brightest stars in my class — which I am — no teacher at Palmer's would dare give a Winter a failing grade. The last one who tried mysteriously swallowed chimera venom."

"When was that?" I cried.

He stared out the window and thought for a moment. "1553."

"Just when I think I have a grasp on how your family operates, you tell me a story like that," I told him, shaking my head.

"Oh please, my parents couldn't be more pleased with your progress, despite your difficulties over the winter break," he said.

"You're the reason my father held on to his Senate seat. How could they remove a man from the Senate when he shelters the Translator in his house? My father actually smiled at dinner the other night when mother mentioned that you mastered water-based divination. My father never smiles. For a moment, I was afraid he was experiencing palsy or an apoplexy. I may be the cherished son, but you're the one they talk about at dinner every night."

"Because my very existence is a threat to their fortune, their standing in society, your father's position in Senate, and your future livelihood," I told him. "Of course, they're going to talk about me. If there was a salamander in your cellar that could burst into flames and burn your entire house to the ground at any moment without warning, you would probably spend quite a bit of time discussing that, too."

"Good point," he noted. "And otherwise, school is going just as expected. I have high marks but not so high that I'm the target of those students who prioritize schooling over the air itself."

"You mean boys who are intelligent?" I asked.

Owen blithely ignored me. "I'm well-liked enough by the students and teachers that I skate by, but I haven't been elected to any sort of position of responsibility. And on a more cheerful note, the boy in the next suite had a nervous breakdown, so I've been able to use his bedroom as my game room."

"What?" I gasped.

"It didn't take much, just a portal spell, and I go back and forth. I installed a gaming table. I'm hoping to add a snooker table before the spring. The faculty should really invest in security measures beyond mere locks on doors."

"No, you — ugh, why did your neighbor have a nervous breakdown?"

Owen scoffed. "Oh, that. We have at least one a year. Pressure at our school is — well, I won't insult you by saying it's greater than the pressure at yours because I've heard Mother's stories — I'll just say it's applied in different areas and in more brutal ways. And we always have one boy who looks to the future, where he's expected to not only master magic but also excel in business and earn enough to support a wife and children and provide for *their* futures. And they crack. It's always handled very quietly. Generally, the boy is taken home to his family for rest, and if they're lucky, they can come back the next term with a tanned face and claim that they were doing independent study in a sunny clime."

"And if they're not lucky?"

"They complete what education they can at home, and they work for their families' businesses, or they retire to a country estate and take up the study of flaming butterflies or some such trifle. Or, in the very worst circumstances, they're sent to a sanitarium and no one talks about in polite company."

"That sounds terrible."

"It is," he said. "But it is rather nice to have the extra space for my gaming table."

I sighed and smacked my gloved hand against my forehead. "Oh, thank goodness. Miss Castwell's."

The carriage rolled down a long white-pebble drive toward Miss Castwell's crescent-shaped building, hung with enough towers and turrets to confuse any bird that dared nest in the eaves. The great grey-green stone walls stood five stories, supporting a roof set with green dragon-scale-shaped tiles. The building's facade cradled itself around an enormous white marble fountain depicting the Maiden, the Mother, and the Crone lifting a stone cauldron together. In the center of that curve rose an enormous bell tower with all four corners supported by heavily carved green marble pillars.

While my Papa kept the lawns at Raven's Rest carefully manicured, the grounds-keeping staff at Castwell's had allowed the woods to creep ever closer to the school building, which may have contributed to the hollowhorn incident, honestly. It was possible that the grounds-keeping staff was less dedicated to their tasks since one of their number, Tom, was used as a Revenant commanded to kill me the previous year. Once an acquaintance was murdered and used as a puppet post-mortem, hedge-trimming probably seemed like less of a priority.

The carriage rolled to a stop. The footman, Timothy, hopped off of the rear quarter and opened the door for Owen who donned his Cahill hat and handed me out of the carriage.

"Thank you for not tripping me," I muttered out of the side of my mouth.

"Mother would never tolerate that sort of disrespect... for your gown."

I snickered.

"It is a Madame DuPont," he sniffed. "And in a very fashionable color — the rose quartz is very *en vogue*. Mother would never forgive me."

I sighed and rolled my eyes heavenward. Phillip flew out of the carriage and landed on my shoulder, chirping indignantly on my behalf. "My bird thinks you're being very rude."

"That's how far I have sunk?" he asked.

"Yes, also I'd like to note that Horace never speaks up for you."

"Just a moment. I'll see to your trunk," he said, in a kinder tone.

Just as Owen began instructing Timothy and Jonas as to the delivery of my things, an extremely outdated chaise and four pulled up to the school entrance. The driver's livery featured the unmistakable prune and tan combination of House Cowell. Ivy's family, who according to Mrs. Winter were richer than Fortuna, didn't believe in spending money for the sake of something fashionable. They'd sustained their financial legacy by remaining sensible, even as they became incredibly successful. If their nearly 80-year-old carriage was still safe and in working order, that's what they would use.

The horses were anchored, and the Cowell servants scrambled to open the door for Ivy and unloaded her luggage, which was promptly levitated up the steps to the school.

"Oh, look, it's your little friend. Daisy, wasn't it?" Owen said, sounding bored. "Didn't she come to Mother's masquerade dressed as a pile of fallen leaves?"

"You know her name is Ivy," I countered. "And no, she was the spirit of autumn, according to her mother."

"Her mother does have the most interesting sense of fashion," Owen's voice trailed off as Ivy was handed down from the interior of the carriage. "Guh..."

Ivy had bloomed considerably since her disastrous masquerade appearance, which had unfortunately resembled an amorphous pile of dead leaves. But since school was not technically in session, neither of us was required to wear our uniform gowns. And Ivy's beautiful dark complexion and hourglass figure were shown to advantage with a saffron silk gown with a tucked waist and a high frog collar. A matching bonnet was pinned into her hair at almost daring angle, bringing attention to her high cheekbones and wide brown eyes.

This was due in no small part to a carefully orchestrated meeting between Mrs. Cowell and Madame DuPont. Mrs. Winter "just happened" to invite Ivy and Mrs. Cowell to tea at Raven's Rest on a day she had a fitting appointment that ran long with Madame. And Madame "just happened" to have a selection of fabrics that would complement Ivy's skin tone far better than the prune-and-tan combination that Mrs. Cowell thought was so very chic. And while she was at it, Madame also introduced Mrs. Cowell to the concept of tailoring a dress to hug one's figure instead of leaving room for one's curves to breathe. Before Mrs. Cowell knew what happened, Mrs. Winter and I had arranged for the creation of ten new flattering gowns in a rainbow of colors, including several in Castwell green. While nothing had changed about my friend on the inside, wearing something that she *knew* made her look beautiful changed the way she walked the school halls. And she was far more likely to snap back at Callista, whereas before she'd merely ignored the ceaseless bullying until Callista and her cronies got bored and walked away.

And there she stood, glowing golden in the morning light, and Owen Winter was speechless. I only wished Alicia could be here to see this.

"Ivy!" I rushed over to kiss her cheek. "That dress! You were right. The saffron was absolutely the best choice. I'm so glad your mother didn't insist on that egg-yolk-colored fabric. It would have been a huge mistake."

"Do you think so?" she said, smoothing her hands over her skirts. "I'm just not used to wearing such bright colors. It feels like I'm wearing some sort of beacon."

"Nonsense. You look like a sundrop," I told her. "Doesn't she, Owen?"

I turned to Owen, who was staring at my friend. Suddenly, his mouth clamped shut from a gaping position. Interesting.

"Ivy, you do remember my cousin Owen Winter don't you? Owen attends Palmer's and has recently acquired some form of selective mutism. Owen, this is Ivy. She excels at crystallography, and she is one of my favorite people in all of England."

Owen was still staring. Ivy's brows knit together.

Sighing, I nudged Owen in the ribs with my elbow. He shook his head and said, "Oh, pardon me. Yes, Miss Cowell, it's lovely to see you again. And my cousin is, of course, correct. That is a lovely gown."

Ivy curtsied. "Thank you."

"Yes, everything is just *lovely*," I said, staring at Owen out of the corner of my eye. "Did you have a nice visit home?"

"My mother presented me with several sketches for summer frocks she thinks will be just gorgeous, in various shades of eye-gouging orange. I may need another visit from your auntie."

I laughed, tucked my arm through hers. She asked, "How was your visit with your… family?"

I glanced around at the other girls filtering into the school entrance from their own carriages. "We can talk about it later."

"I have a gaming table," Owen suddenly blurted out. My head whipped towards him.

For a moment, Ivy's eyes went wide, but she recovered quickly. "Oh, well, that's nice."

"Yes, Owen enjoys cards and darts and is hoping to obtain a snooker table soon."

Owen objected, clearing his throat. "It isn't as if I'm addicted to games of chance. I have many interests. Books. I like books…" His voice trailed off again because he honestly couldn't seem to come up with anything else he was interested in. "Books are good."

"I'm very glad that you can read," Ivy said, looking to me, her brows quirked. "Are you ready to go inside, Cassandra? I think they'll be serving tea in the sunroom soon."

"Yes," I said, shooting an incredulous look at Owen. "I'll be right in."

"Mr. Winter," Ivy said, curtsying.

Owen bowed to her. "Miss — Lady — wumple."

When Ivy was half-way up the school's front stairs I turned to my cousin.

"What is the matter with you? Have *you* had an apoplexy? Or is simply a hex that makes you practically shout random and useless information? And what, pray tell, is a *wumple?*"

Owen shook his head. "I have no idea what you're talking about. I'm fine."

"You just spoke in gibberish. You never speak in gibberish. I am the only one between the two of us that is supposed to speak in gibberish."

"I have no idea what you're talking about," Owen insisted. "I'm fine. Enjoy your week at school, cousin."

Owen boarded the carriage — without bowing to me, a major breach of etiquette — and knocked on the ceiling. The crayfire crystal mounted behind the carriage hummed with energy, and with a crackle of ozone, it surged forward.

Phillip tweeted in my ear.

"I do not understand what just happened either," I said, shaking my head.

I mounted the steps to the school in my flotilla of a dress, a testament to the muscle strength I'd built up over the last few months. A footman, Aaron, opened the door for me, and I walked into the foyer, happy to drop my heavy skirts. I wanted a bracing cup of tea and a bath and to talk to Ivy about what she'd done to reduce my cousin to a gibbering idiot. Owen was often an idiot, but he rarely gibbered.

I heard the sound of a throat clearing behind me, and I turned to see Headmistress Lockwood standing near the visitor's parlor.

"Miss Reed, you have a visitor. You may receive him in the Bouquet Room. Miss Turnwoody will serve as your chaperone."

"Thank you, Headmistress Lockwood."

I walked into the Bouquet Room which I'd once assumed was so named because students received posies from their beaux in that room. I'd been so very, very wrong. Every surface, every fabric, every throw pillow in that room was covered in some floral print. I could only imagine this décor was meant to keep suitors from overstaying their welcome. Eventually being surrounded by that sheer number of flowers became unnerving. A familiar lanky form, carefully folded onto the plump lavender sofa, rose as I entered the room.

"Gavin?" I exclaimed, smiling as I rushed across the room.

"How is the sweetest girl in Lightbourne?" he asked, rising from the sofa.

"Oh, your sister's fine," I told him, laughing lightly.

He scoffed as he bowed over my head. "You know who I meant. There are many words to describe my beloved sister. Sweet isn't one of them."

I laughed. "I'm well, thank you. How are you?"

"Better now that I've seen you."

Gavin McCray shared few physical similarities with Alicia. The height difference alone was staggering. He possessed the high cheekbones and patrician nose of the upper class, with large blue eyes — so different from Alicia's green. He'd been assigned a full-time valet since graduating from Palmer's, so his dark hair was trimmed shorter, and his face was closely shaved. He was wearing a dark, expensively tailored suit with a midnight blue cravat and tie pin in the shape of the McCray silver lamp. His features might have been considered too serious if not for pleased smile. He held out a hand as if he was reaching for my own and said, "Cassandra."

Miss Turnwoody, a plump, pleasant-faced woman who tutored girls on deportment and etiquette, cleared her throat. Her full lips were curved into a censuring line as she shook her head lightly. I halted and schooled my features into a calm mask that communicated no affection or delight whatsoever. Because that was a reasonable expectation for a young woman greeting someone she liked better than the great majority of the world's population.

Gavin shot me a sheepish grin. He bowed, giving me a little wink as his gesture reached its lowest point. I curtsied prettily, my own mouth twitching to contain my amusement.

After years of observing their behavior from below stairs, I knew that Gavin stood out from most young Guardian men. He was incredibly intelligent, which in some cases led boys to conceit, to holding themselves apart from their classmates to pursue their lofty goals — generally some position with one of the men's research guild or the Senate. But Gavin was unfailingly kind and protective of Alicia, another peculiarity amongst his peers. The reason we started speaking in the first place was because I'd made efforts to keep Alicia from being embarrassed when Callista had punch spilled on her at a school social.

We'd met once, when I was still a Snipe. He was rushing to an appointment as I was running back to our house in the Warren to fetch one of Owen's shirts. I hadn't been looking where I was going and was knocked to the ground when I ran into him. Instead of scolding me for touching him, he'd helped me to my feet and used him magic to close the scrapes on my palms. He even let me keep the bit of obsidian he'd used to heal my hands. I'd saved it in a little wooden box in my room, along with some hair ribbons Gavin sent me last term after he met me again as Cassandra, the hollowhorn's broken horn, and Miss Morton's awful Grimstelle owl brooch. I'd never dreamed that one day I'd receive attentions from any boy, much less a Guardian boy from a family so powerful even Mrs. Winter approved.

I'd always told Mary that her dreams about Owen were impossible, and here I was living them. Perhaps that was why there was always a tiny undercurrent of guilt running alongside my anger toward my sister. But none of this was relevant right now as Gavin was standing before me and Mary was out somewhere, shopping her anonymous protector's money.

"I'm sorry I haven't been able to visit more often," he said, taking my hand to help me lower onto the sofa. I arranged my skirts artfully around me, establishing the proper physical distance between us for such a visit. I looked to Miss Turnwoody, who gave a little nod and returned to reading her book — *A Treatise on the Use of Lace Doilies During Ritual Ceremonies.*

"Working for the company is very different from being at school," he said. "I leave for McCray's right after breakfast and sometimes I don't get home until well after dark. I think the kitchen staff are getting weary of keeping dinner warm for me."

"I'm sure that they know they'll benefit from how hard you're working, and they appreciate it. After all, they do not receive their wages if the company doesn't do well," I assured him.

He cocked his head to the right, considering, and his smile grew even brighter. "I'd never looked at it that way. Thank you."

"Are you enjoying the work?" I asked him.

"Yes, I love it. My uncle has shown me magic I'd never dreamed of, and I always thought I was keeping up to date on the developments in crayfire energy! But there's so much innovation in the development laboratories. We've found ways to move much bigger vehicles, far heavier than carriages. We're finding new crystals that require less charging and last longer. We're going to change the world for the better. We'll change the way people travel, the way we deliver goods from one place to another, the way people heat and light their homes. More than we already have, anyway. And I'm involved in every stage! The other people working in the labs, they don't treat me like I'm set apart from them just because my name happens to be McCray. They listen to me and tell me when I'm on the right track, and more importantly, when I'm on the wrong one, they correct me. I feel like I'm learning much more than I did while I was at school."

I couldn't help but laugh at his excitement. One of the things I liked best about Gavin was that he talked to me about his work and his interests and his life at home. He didn't assume that because I was a girl I would be too dim to find his energy magic interesting. He didn't limit our discussions to the weather because it was the polite thing to do. He treated me as an equal, something that was ever more important to me the more time I spent with upper class Guardians. "I'm very pleased for you."

"And I appreciate that you're willing to listen to me blather on about my work when I came to visit you. Alicia says you've been working hard in all of your classes, but I should ask you about dance class in particular?"

"Oh, I'm sure you do not want to hear about that," I muttered. "Alicia's doing very well in her expanded course list, even if she does feel like she's being sent through the laundry wringer every morning."

He shot me a slightly confused look, but said, "I appreciate how you have taken her under your wing. She sounds *excited* when she talks about classes now. That certainly never happened before you arrived at Miss Castwell's."

"Gavin, she was one of my first real friends here. She does far more for me than I do for her."

"Ahem," Miss Turnwoody coughed lightly to remind me that as we were not officially courting, Gavin and I were not on a first-name basis yet. I frowned, but Gavin took this moment of distraction to pull a small silver box from his coat pocket.

"Technically, I'm not supposed to send you anything for Sweetheart's Day because I'm not a Palmer's student. But I would hate for the occasion to go by without me expressing my esteem for you. I thought I should deliver my sentiments a little more personally."

I blinked rapidly at the little gift box. I'd only heard tell of Sweetheart's Day from Owen while serving at the breakfast table, and that was only in the context of his absolute refusal to participate in the ritual because it could raise expectations amongst his female admirers. Sweetheart's Day was a spring tradition at Miss Castwell's occurring in the last weeks of the term. It was one of the few times young people in magical society were allowed to show open gestures of affection and one of the few occasions where the boys of Palmer's were allowed to send Castwell girls gifts without their parents' permission. Of course, the gifts were screened by Headmistress Lockwood and the rest of the staff before they were delivered to the girls. Still, it was a chance for the young people to express *something* to each other without their parents breathing down their necks. Of course, it was also a misguided way for the girls to establish a pecking order, to show how adored they were by some Guardian boy.

I'd never received a token like this before, all wrapped up in a fancy box on a special occasion. I wanted to savor it, maybe even take it back to my room to save it for later, but Gavin's expression was so eager that I slid the silver ribbon through the bow and untied it. The box popped open and a silver charm bracelet floated from inside. My lips parted in delight, and I held up my hand so it landed in my palm.

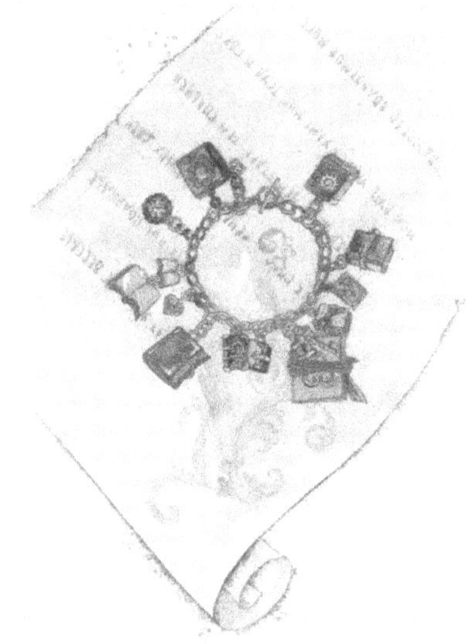

Gavin's Gift

"Oh, thank you." Gavin wrapped the charm bracelet around my wrist and secured the clasp. Instead of the typical charms one found on such baubles — tiny silver animals or flowers or thimbles — each was an evenly sized rectangle, with a colorful scene painted on it. I lifted my wrist and examining them closely. They looked like tiny books. "It's wonderful."

"Tap your finger twice against the charm," he said, smiling at me.

I followed his instructions, and the first charm I touched seemed to explode from its setting into a full-sized volume of Jane Austen's *Pride and Prejudice*.

He carefully unclipped the book from the chain, and I opened it, enjoying the smell of old paper. "I happened to see your cousin at a shop last week. While telling me that he did not like me and did not think I was worthy of you in the slightest, he informed me that if any simpleton wanted to please you with a gift, it would have to be related to reading. I mentioned several times during the course of his insults that I was aware of how much you loved to read, but he insisted that your love of reading was practically unnatural, defining of your personality even. So I thought, what better gift to give you but a library you could wear on your wrist?"

I examined each cover and found copies of *The Illiad, Gulliver's Travels, Jane Eyre, Grimm's Fairy Tales, The Comedies of William Shakespeare,* and *The Tragedies of William Shakespeare.* I supposed combining all of Shakespeare's works into one tiny book would have been too much to ask of any spell.

"These are the original editions," I said, turning the book over in my hands. This was not the heavily edited Snipe editions available in the Warren's bookshop. These were the original works I could find hidden in Mr. Winter's library. This was a precious, almost subversive gift Gavin was giving me. I adored it and him for knowing how much I would love it. And it was possible I adored Owen a little bit for recommending it, but I would never tell him that.

"Well, of course they are," Gavin laughed. "Why would I give you anything else?"

I shook my head, as if I was being very silly. "This is the greatest gift I've ever received. Thank you."

He leaned forward and kissed my knuckles. It did not set the world on fire like the kisses Mary had swooned over in her novels, but it warmed me all the way down to my toes and made me want to kiss him back, preferably his lips, as we had done before over Christmas. Unfortunately, Miss Turnwoody didn't agree and cleared her throat a bit harder. Gavin dropped my hand, and we ducked our heads, laughing.

"Sorry, Miss Turnwoody," I murmured.

"Please try to restrict yourself to the acceptable public displays of affection," she said, turning the page of her book.

Gavin's lips twitched, and he scooted further away from me on the sofa. "School holidays begin soon. I hope that I will be able to see you more often over the summer."

"But your work — Alicia says that your family has come to depend on you," I argued, carefully neglecting to mention his mother.

"My family cannot expect my attention every day, all day," Gavin protested.

I would have said, "You could have fooled me," but I didn't think that would help matters. Owen certainly didn't appreciate the moments I made light of his mother. Mrs. McCray did not like me on principle, the principle being that she didn't like any girl who tried to take Gavin's attention away from his family. Mrs. McCray did not care about my connections to the Winter family. She did not think I was good enough for her darling boy. She did not appreciate the distraction I posed, the competition for Gavin's time and attention. She'd commanded her household staff to prevent Gavin from receiving my letters or from sending his to me. On days when Gavin was scheduled to visit me, she'd created false emergencies at McCray and Company to keep him occupied. According to Alicia, she'd also tried to place a hex on all of the McCray carriages so they would not be able to turn towards Miss Castwell's no matter how the driver approached. Fortunately, as Gavin spent more time in his office, he had taken to riding on horseback in order to get some exercise on his visiting days.

Gavin cleared his throat. "I know that my mother has been… difficult. Mourning my father has been more difficult for her than anyone could have anticipated, but her grief won't last forever. We'll make time to see each other more. I hope that we might reach a more formal arrangement between the two of us someday,

Cass — Miss Reed. I enjoy this time we spend together and our letters."

He took my hand, and my cheeks warmed as I said, "I do, too."

Miss Turnwoody cleared her throat again, glaring at us.

Gavin huffed. "Oh, for goodness sake."

5

MERMAID BOILS AND OTHER MYSTERIOUS RASHES

For good reason, the Art of Healing was a particularly unpopular elective at Miss Castwell's.

While there were witches like Nurse Waxwing, who had dedicated their lives to medical magic and the glory of the The Eir Guild, most proper Guardian ladies considered it far too earthy to learn how to treat minor illnesses and injuries. It was far more fashionable to call for an apothecary. I, however, had the strange feeling that wherever my search for other Changeling children might lead me, I might need to know how to fix the odd broken bone or burn.

It had taken me a while to learn that the classes and ages for Miss Castwell's were a bit blurry. Girls were admitted when their families believed it was appropriate for them to begin their formal education. Class schedules were tailored to each girls' skill and talent, so at 12 years old, a girl could take the same classes as a 17-year-old. It seemed like a terrible idea to me at first, knowing how much it annoyed Mary when she was put in the same lessons as me in the Warren school, but the system tended to keep the younger girls engaged and the older girls' egos in check.

To my surprise, healing was a subject that came relatively easy to me. Having spent years at my father's knee learning plant lore, it was easy enough to concoct magical salves grinding fragrant roots and petals with the mystifying rainbow of powders found in Nurse Waxwing's cabinet. Three days a week, just before dinner, I would follow the nurse through the infirmary with two other girls, checking on any students suffering complaints. The open, high-ceilinged space was painted in detailed murals of a country flower garden, in direct contradiction to the Castwell green that covered every surface of the school. The walls seemed alive with blooming spring plants waving in a false breeze. Non-existent birds chirped from somewhere in the painted trees. Someone had taken the time to paint clouds on the ceiling, enchanted to drift lazily during the day, trailing behind a painted sun that cast warm light against our skin.

Nurse Waxwing insisted this soothing color scheme was essential to the healing process. Over the sharp green scent of herbal remedies, the room smelled of the wholesome, floral scent of warm spring air pumped into the room with a charm Nurse Waxwing devised herself. Millicent DeCater was still recovering from her shoulder wound, napping on chaise lounge near a burbling painted bird bath and under a fluffy green blanket. Nurse Waxwing believed that this was healthiest possible climate for ailing girls. You had to appreciate her effort, considering how far inland the school was located.

This was the end of Nurse Waxwing's maternal instincts. She was a brusque, efficient woman with strong, broad shoulders, severe cheekbones and thick black hair she wore tucked under a white and gold Bellevue cap. She wore a uniform of unrelenting white cotton covered with a white pinafore. She did not see the value in coddling girls in her care or under her instruction, which was evident in the way she left the class scrambling in her lavender-scented wake across the infirmary. A highly detailed caduceus embroidered onto the chest of her apron in golden thread showed that she was a master healer, the survivor of an incredibly frightening series of tests that even the most senior girls whispered of in fear. No Castwell girl had passed the exam in more than ten years.

"Reed," she barked. She was arranging eucalyptus and hyssop in a tall blue glass vase next to a comfortable iron framed bed occupied by a small, redheaded girl named Julia Sitwell. Julia's face was as pale and shiny as new cheese, and she wheezed slightly in her sleep. "I have prescribed this salve to be rubbed on Miss Sitwell's throat twice a day. What is her condition?"

The nurse handed me a small brown glass jar with no label, which struck me as a dangerous way to store medicine. The sharp, herbal smell of the eucalyptus along with the sweet scent of Nurse Waxwing's ever-present lavender perfume kept me from being able to smell the contents of the jar. I took a bit out on my fingers and saw flecks of crushed orange stone. I rubbed it between my fingertips and smelled even more eucalyptus. The stone looked like amber and carnelian, both known to help with breathing problems. That, along with hyssop and rosemary, were used to treat difficulties with breathing, which probably explained why Nurse Waxwing had placed them in a vase by Julia's head. I squinted at the space over Julia's bed and noticed a faint shimmer of yellow. I took Wit out of my sleeve and drew the symbol for *Reveal*, exposing the signature of Nurse's Waxwing's magic. A tent of golden sparks draped over Julia, forming a spell our textbook referred to as a "Breathing Room." All of the essential healthy elements humans needed were intensified within the tent, forcing themselves inside the patient's lungs.

I opened my mouth to answer, but she held a short, stubby

finger in my face and turned to one of the other three girls in the class. "Sato!"

Madeline Sato, the petite first-year girl from my dance class, flinched broadly. She'd been staring off into the rolling grass of the false lawn as she usually did when we were in the infirmary, and once again, Nurse Waxwing had caught her off-guard.

"While you were staring off into nothing, I have given Miss Reed a complete outline for Miss Sitwell's treatment. How should she proceed?"

Madeline's full cheeks flushed bright red. "Er, apply a Flux Charm?"

"Congratulations," Nurse Waxwing said, prompting Amelia to beam even as I cringed inside. Nurse Waxwing dashed that happy expression by adding, "You've managed to kill my patient, who has a dangerous reaction to the Flux Charm which would result in rash, seizures, and swelling of the throat. If you'd bothered to read the patient's chart, as Miss Reed, Miss Montbatten, and Miss Cortina had done, you would have known that."

Poor Madeline's face collapsed like a deflated soufflé. "I'm sorry, Nurse Waxwing."

"Apologies do no good for Miss Sitwell who is now dead thanks to your negligence."

The "dead" patient in question opened one eye — probably trying to determine why there were people standing around her bed declaring her dead.

Nurse Waxwing turned her sharp grey gaze on me. "Miss Reed, what is Miss Sitwell's condition? How should we proceed?"

"Julia is suffering a respiratory ailment, possibly involving an infection of her lungs and throat," I said, throwing Madeline an apologetic look. "Her chart says she's susceptible to bronchial trouble and infections of her sinus cavities."

"Excellent deductive reasoning, Miss Reed," Nurse Waxwing

said. And for a brief, ridiculously optimistic moment, I felt the flush of pride. "You have managed to read the chart."

"Yes, ma'am," I said, pressing my lips together in an embarrassed line. I should have known that was far too close to a compliment to be trusted. "And as for further action, with the Flux Charm being unavailable, you're doing all that you can to improve her condition — the salve, the aromatherapy to open her airways, the Breathing Room. Anything additional might agitate her bronchial system."

Nurse Waxwing turned away from Julia's bed and progressed to the next bed, occupied by Jeanette Drummond.

"Miss Drummond is the unfortunate victim of a potions lab exercise gone awry," Nurse Waxwing said, motioning to the curiously silver boils blooming on Jeanette's chest and arms. The boils formed an iridescent scale pattern that would have been quite beautiful if the itching wasn't making distress so clearly visible on Jeanette's face.

"Given the 'mermaid scale' lesions, we would assume that what element splashed on her skin when her classmate's work station exploded?" Nurse Waxwing asked.

"Selkie's blood?" Sofia Cortina suggested in her soft Spanish accent.

"You are nearly correct, but unfortunately, nearly correct is just enough to kill the patient as treatment for selkie's blood exposure — complete exfoliation with a lemon sugar scrub followed by a calming chamomile bath — is contraindicated with the treatment Miss Drummond needs for exposure to selkie dander, which is highly noxious. Attempting to scrub the dander from Miss Drummond might introduce the dander into her bloodstream through any breaks in the skin, which would result in her death."

"Why do so many answers in this class end with 'you killed the patient?'" Joan Mountbatten asked quietly. Because Joan was more than a head taller than me, with long, willowy limbs and icy-blond hair, her voice sounded as if it was floating down from the ceiling.

I sucked my tongue between my teeth to prevent the snicker from escaping. Nurse Waxwing did seem to accuse of hypothetical murder much more often than one would think possible.

"So now that Miss Drummond has passed on from this mortal coil, would anyone like to hazard a guess at the simple treatment that might have saved her life?" Nurse Waxwing asked.

All four of us remained silent, because we had reached the stage of class where we exhausted with being accused of killing our classmates and preferred to let Nurse Waxwing give us the answers, which was what she wanted to do anyway. She rolled her eyes slightly and told us, "Selkie dander exposure requires repeated bathing in a blend of toadstool spores, tomato juice, hippocampus blubber, and ground seahorse dung."

Jeanette's lips turned into an unhappy line as all four of us took a tiny step back from her bed.

"While the scales left behind are itchy and uncomfortable, they will fade in three days. Miss Drummond simply has to avoid scratching to prevent scarring," Nurse Waxwing said. "And of course, the smell from the curative baths prevents her from returning to class."

Jeanette sighed as we took another tiny step away.

"How are you, Jeanette?" I asked her as Nurse Waxwing led the other girls to the next bed.

"That's a bit of a silly question, given the amount of sighing and frowning I was doing just now," she muttered, adjusting the large green mitts on her hands meant to prevent scratching.

Jeanette was a member of the Drummond family, one of the most prominent Guardian families in society known for ward construction and heavy academic pursuits. As a new student, I'd been far too intimidated to approach her, but after you save someone from being sacrificed in a madwoman's megalomaniacal bid to take over the world, the social strata tended to blur a bit.

"I'm sorry. That was silly. It's just what we're trained to do as polite people."

Jeanette smiled wryly. "I'm sorry. I was snappish. I'm just tired of being asked how I am or what happened. I knew I shouldn't have worked near Callista's station that morning. She's very accident-prone in the potions lab, and it wasn't the first explosion she's caused overheating her equipment. The only thing that made this incident particularly interesting was her addition of moonstone to a potion that required absolutely no stone of any kind. She had to cross the lab, take Madame Thurston's key from the hook on the wall and unlock the semi-precious store cabinet, and take out the moonstone to add it to a potion that didn't require moonstone."

"So you're saying this was not an accident?"

Jeanette laughed, a rare moment from a very serious girl. "I do not put anything past Callista. She's stewing over the fact that you dared to save the class from the hollowhorn and not her, so she's been in a foul mood for days. And she's aiming for a spot in the Athena Guild as well, but her marks are nowhere near good enough. Our Spring Interviews are next year. Disfiguring me to the point where I couldn't show my face in polite society or killing me if Nurse Waxwing allowed you lot to treat me would clear her path."

"I wouldn't put it past her. Also, I prefer to think I would leave you alive if I treated you."

"Well, let's not quibble over details." Jeanette's hands flexed inside the mittens. "I'm more concerned about the courses I'll be missing. I'm in my final year. The divination classes at this level are punishing on the easier days. And I'm already lagging in the class. I'm obviously tops in setting wards."

I smirked. "Obviously."

"But I cannot divine the future to save my life. The science is… well, it's nonexistent. It's guesswork at best and lying at worst. And I cannot bring myself to simply make something up for an exam."

"I'm not particularly good with divination, but I think Alicia McCray is. I could ask her if she might be willing to tutor you."

Jeanette huffed, wisps of her dark hair falling over her grey eyes. "I would be embarrassed that a younger girl has to help me with an advanced subject, but I need this course to graduate and my placement with the Athena Guild is hanging in the balance."

"I'll mention something to her at dinner. I'm sure she'll be willing to help."

Jeanette nodded. "She's a very sweet girl, much like her brother."

"I have no comment on that subject," I said primly.

Jeanette snorted and then groaned. "Now, my nose itches."

"Do you mind if I try something?" I asked. "I would like you to listen to the sound of my voice. Take some deep breaths and close your eyes."

"Nothing can make it worse," Jeanette sighed. Suddenly, her eyes popped open. "Wait, no, that's not true."

But by this time, I'd already tapped my hand against Jeanette's forehead, once, twice, three times, forcing a flutter of activity from the dragonfly on my palm, until a blue glow spread from the spot I touched, across her face. "There is no itching. You are calm and comfortable and will enjoy this time in the infirmary to rest up for your studies because there's no itching at all, just a sense of peace."

"Oh, very funny," Jeanette muttered. "Here, let me slap your forehead a few times for my own amusement."

She glared up at me, but after a few moments an odd expression of relief chased away her irritation. "It doesn't itch anymore."

I whispered, "It's something the Mother Book showed me last year. It's not magic so much as mesmerism. Ancient witches used to use it for anxiety, breaking bad habits, pain relief. It won't interact badly with the medicines you're already taking. You'll just think less about the itching and your classes and just enjoy a nice break from your studies until you can get back to them."

"Thank you," she sighed.

"Just keep that in mind in case I need extra help in advanced ward construction, which I am attempting next term," I said. "And I am expecting terrible marks."

Jeanette snickered, and I scurried to catch up with the rest of the class. Madeline was near silent for the rest of our rounds through the infirmary. After being dismissed, we retired to our rooms to dress for dinner. The other girls chatted amiably, but Madeline was clearly upset, wiping at her cheeks with suspicious frequency. As the other girls peeled off, to go to the rooms on the third floor, Madeline's shoulders were so rounded in on themselves that she was practically concave. She seemed too little to be enrolled at Miss Castwell's, with her slight frame and glossy black hair pulled back into a chignon that seemed far too severe for her young face.

"Are you all right, Madeline? I know Nurse Waxwing's teaching style can be... intense. And unpleasant. It's intensely unpleasant, really." I handed her a handkerchief embroidered with apple blossoms and reed warblers, the bird from which Mrs. Winter had taken my name. I noticed the set of white scales sewn into the collar of Madeline's dress, showing her to be a member of the

Montfort house. The Montforts were considered the premiere healing family among the Mother Houses and considerable pressure was applied to members of that house to succeed in the medicinal arts. If they managed to invent a new treatment or spell to deal with a disease, bringing acclaim to House Montfort? Even better.

Madeline made a wet snort-laughing sound. "I'm hopeless," she sighed, wiping at her cheeks.

"No one's hopeless," I told her. "You're the only one Madame Rousseau doesn't curse at in French during ritual dance. Do you know she called me *le cheval qui claque* the other day? I asked one of the other girls, it means something like 'the clomping horse.'"

Madeline laughed again and sniffed. "My family doesn't exactly boast about my dancing. They're *so* disappointed in my marks. I haven't shown promise in healing arts or potions or even botany. A ninny can excel at botany."

I excelled at botany, but I didn't think that was worth mentioning at this point.

"I haven't been given special permission to attend any of the advanced classes," she said, her tone miserable as the tears slid down her cheeks anew.

"Aren't you in your first term?" I asked, incredulous.

"Yes, but my older sister, Emmeline, was taking *four* advanced classes by the end of her first term."

"Well, that's your sister, not you. Sisters can be very different. Trust me, I know."

Madeline started sobbing, and desperate to distract her, I asked, "Surely, you have one spell that's your specialty. Something you do better than anything else. Can you show me yours?"

She nodded, opening her hand, whispering softly. A plume of green and blue sparks erupted from her palm and shaped itself into a shimmering blue lily bud. The flower bloomed, opening in a wave of dancing color, rotating over her hand until it faded into nothing.

"That's beautiful!" I cried.

Madeline jerked shoulders. "It's just a trick of light. It's not going to heal anyone, is it?"

"If I was very sad and lonely, I cannot imagine anything making me feel better than a lily blooming out of someone's hand. That's a kind of healing. A considerably more pleasant than anything involving seahorse dung."

Madeline laughed. I placed my hand on her shoulder, patting her awkwardly.

"Would you like to come to my room and study after dinner?" I asked. "Alicia and Ivy are going to help me with my crystallography, which is my worst subject. Besides dancing, that is. And I could help you with some of the material we've covered in healing? Despite Nurse Waxwing's faint praise, I am passing the course."

"That would be lovely," Madeline said, nodding.

"I'll meet you here after pudding, all right?"

"Thank you."

Leaving Madeline in the corridor, I opened the door to my room and stepped into a cyclone of swirling gold sparks. My mouth dropped open. I inhaled some of those magical sparks, rendering me speechless as my maid, Jenny, danced about the room, pulling the golden trails of magic behind her hands.

My eye followed the trail of dust, which seemed to be flowing from the cabinet where I stored the Mother Book. The cabinet was locked, as it had been since Miss Morton stole it out of my room for her own nefarious purposes. The key was heavy in my pocket as I watched the book's magic envelope Jenny in a cloud, much like it had embraced me the first time I'd touched it.

I gasped, "What in the world?"

Jenny froze, her arms posed mid-air. The golden glitter of magic faded as it dropped away from her. She paled, and her arms dropped to her side. "I — I'm so sorry, Miss."

She dashed around me and out of the door before I could move my shock-heavy limbs. I stepped out into the hallway and yelled, "Wait!"

But she was already gone.

6

A FUTURE WITHOUT A FRIEND

 tried to follow Jenny to the maids' quarters, through the kitchens, but the head housekeeper, Mrs. Reynolds, stopped me at the door and sent me back up the stairs to my room like a mischievous child. No amount of haughty insistence or blustering would get me past the enormous steaming stoves. Students weren't allowed in the servants' quarters, and there were wards in place to keep us out, she said, none too gently directing me out of her kitchen. I couldn't exactly tell Mrs. Reynolds that I needed to follow Jenny to her room because I'd witnessed her practicing magic. It was a little embarrassing to be thwarted by a stern housekeeper and school policy, but I was bound by Jenny's secret and my own, so I slunk back to my room and stared at my ceiling while my brain tumbled.

What had I walked in on? Was Jenny a Changeling? Was she performing the magic or had the book simply been bored and looking for... someone to coat in golden glitter? The scene mirrored the Mother Book's reaction to me when I was chosen as Translator. Was the book trying to choose another Translator? It hadn't revealed any new pages to me in months. Was it going to choose Jenny instead? On the one hand, it might have been nice to give that burden to someone else. I wouldn't have to deal with Sebastian Crenshaw or the Committee. I could give up all that pressure to improve magical society and focus on the Changeling children. But surely there would be a lot of questions regarding why the book had abandoned me and chosen a random girl. And there would more questions about Jenny and her origins. None of this would result in a long productive life for me or Jenny, but the fleeting moments where I thought I might be able to fade into social obscurity were very pleasant.

It would have been so helpful to be able to talk about this with Alicia and Ivy, but there was always the chance that we could be overheard, and it didn't feel right to say anything when I didn't know Jenny's situation or how she felt about it. If only the mirrors were a safe way to send messages, I might ask Mrs. Winter, but again, it didn't feel right to do that to Jenny when she clearly didn't have the sort of support I did.

As a ladies' maid, she wasn't expected to help serve dinner, but I kept glancing around, trying to spot her amongst the girls serving our roast lamb and potatoes. By the time pudding was served, both Alicia and Ivy were ready to spike my tea with the contents of Madame Ormond's flask — and we weren't entirely sure what those contents were, only that she was much calmer after she drank from it.

"All right, honestly," Alicia said, poking me in the ribs as we walked up the stairs. "You've been silent and broody all night. It's quite similar to an evening spent with my big brother, which I find personally disturbing. I was hoping that spending time with you would provide him with some much-needed levity, not the other way around."

"Just some heavy thinking, that's all," I said. "I'll be right as rain in the morning."

"But not before you master charging crayfire crystals… without making them explode," Ivy said. "We'll meet you in your room in a few minutes?"

I rolled my eyes slightly but gave her a wry smile. "I make no promises."

To my further disappointment, I did not find Jenny waiting for me in my room, only a cold, dark hearth and pointed silence from the Mother Book. Fortunately, I had more than enough experience undressing on my own and building fires, so by the time a faint knock sounded at my door, I'd changed into a dressing gown and built up a toasty fire in the grate. I opened the door to find Madeline Sato standing there with her arms full of books, along with four girls I didn't recognize from the lower terms. They were dressed like me, in their gowns and robes, their hair braided loosely and thrown over their shoulders.

"I hope you do not mind," Madeline said, her smile mildly discomfited. "I brought a few more people."

My mouth dropped open to protest. I'd agreed to help Madeline, but I didn't know these girls. I didn't know their families or their agendas. And for all I knew they were Callista's flunkies-in-training. But then I saw the books in their hands and the eager hope in their eyes, and I realized that company and academics was probably just the thing I needed to keep my mind off of the Jenny situation.

"Please, come in," I said, opening the door. The girls giggled, shushing each other as they rushed into my room. They gathered on the soft green rug spread before the hearth, opening their books and searching for their places. I supposed I should have been grateful that they intended to study, not spend their time gossiping.

My head turned toward the door, where there was another knock. I opened it, expecting to see Ivy and Alicia, but found Joan

Montbatten and Sofia Cortina standing in the hallway. Hopeful smiles wreathed their freshly scrubbed faces.

"We heard something about a study circle," Joan said in her posh accent. For once, she looked unsure of herself, apprehensive. I saw so much of myself in her expression, afraid that she was about to have the door shut in her face.

"I'm having an awful time in History of Houses," Sofia added. "Things are so different here, as opposed to the continent. I can list the Spanish and Portuguese houses down to third and fourth cousins, but English? I get confused by all the Georges and Annes."

"Please join us," I said, ushering them inside. I wondered if I should order up tea and cakes because it was becoming quite the party in my room. Sofia and Joan joined the others, who were already eagerly trading information.

My door was still open when Alicia and Ivy finally turned up, clearly confused by the impromptu social taking place in my room.

"Who are these girls?" Alicia asked. "Do we know this many girls?"

"This is what happens when you talk to people," Ivy told me.

"Let's just get them organized and try to absorb as much information as we can," I said, shaking my head. Mrs. Winter had advised me to expand my circle of friends at school, and this circle was nearly too large to be contained in my room. There was no better way to make those friendships than show kindness where it would be easier to withdraw.

"Madeline, we're going to review basic medicinal botany," I said, sitting next to her on my hearth. I opened our book to an illustration of a plant topped with spindly arms, sprouting tiny white blossoms. "This is hemlock. It is very poisonous. If Nurse Waxwing asks you how to use it to treat patients, the answer is not at all because only a master healer like herself is qualified to administer hemlock for respiratory issues and joint conditions. It's a trick question."

"Nurse Waxwing does seem to love her trick questions," Madeline sighed.

I nodded. "More than she loves any human being. Let's get started."

AND SO BEGAN A NEARLY NIGHTLY ritual in which girls of every class, age, and family would filter into my room after dinner. Girls who were weak in a particular subject gathered around someone who excelled in it. After an hour, the tutors got a break and were then tutored by people adept at their own weak areas. We'd been invited to similar gatherings in the now-graduated Charlotte Rasmurti's room the previous year, though those late-night sessions were more focused on sweets and good-natured gossip. Two weeks in, Jeanette Drummond's rash cleared up, and she joined us, eager to be anywhere but the hospital wing.

Our table in the dining hall expanded, or rather, we added more and more people and eventually scooted so many tables together that Headmistress Lockwood asked us to try to split into two rows. I learned so much about the other girls. Joan Montbatten, despite her chilly demeanor, was bitingly funny and resorted to creative limericks as learning devices once she was tired enough. Sofia Cortina was lonely. Her family had decided that she would make better social connections at an English school with more prominent Guardian families without taking into account our chilly weather or what Sofia politely called our 'less than palatable' food. But as the nights went on, she seemed far more cheerful.

Once Madeline finally relaxed, she grasped concepts easily.

While most of the girls at Castwell's seemed to depend on their family history to buoy them, Madeline's seemed to weigh on her like a stone. Her sister, Emmeline, had been a brilliant student in multiple disciplines, invited to join no less than six research guilds even before her Spring Interview. By comparison, Madeline's talent at dance must have seemed silly to her scholarly family.

I grew closer to the girls I'd known for some time. Helena Mountfort, a far-distant cousin of Madeline's, was far more generous than I would have guessed, willingly tutoring Madeline in the healing arts in exchange for nothing more than the Turkish Delight that Ivy's mother sent from home. Jeanette taught me enough ward construction that I could get through a class without Madame Nyx looking disappointed in me.

I did not see Jenny again, and the study sessions were a good distraction from that worry over the next few weeks. The morning after I found her dancing in my room, a petite blond lady's maid named Rebecca appeared in my room to help me prepare for the day. When I asked about Jenny, Rebecca shrugged with that faraway look Snipes displayed when they were asked something they didn't want to reveal to their Guardians and knew better than to lie about. She said Jenny had been re-assigned to other duties in the kitchens, which made no sense. Once they'd been promoted to the relative ease of working as a ladies' maid, no sensible Snipe girl would want to go back to scrubbing pots and peeling potatoes.

I tried to slip into the kitchens unnoticed, but Mrs. Reynolds caught me time and again, threatening to go to Headmistress Lockwood if I didn't cease and desist immediately. Ivy attempted to tutor me in ward de-construction so I might sneak around the kitchen's protective magic, but I was never going to be as good as her. And while scaling the wall to access the servants' quarters could have been considered an option, I just didn't think I could do it in my voluminous skirts.

As dedicated as we were to our studies, even we took the weekends off, which was why I was so surprised to open my door after curfew on Saturday night to find Jeanette standing there with a glowing orange bottle in her hands.

"Did we have a study session scheduled tonight?" I whispered.

"Shh," Jeanette said, her grey eyes flashing as she ducked into my room.

"Jeanette, as much as I appreciate the visit and the possibly dangerous object you're holding in your hand, what are you doing?"

"It's a magical pot luck," Jeanette said cheerfully. "I invited all the girls 'round."

I had no idea what a 'pot luck' was, but it sounded … involved. And probably messy.

"Not to your room?" I asked pointedly.

"Of course not, my room is much too small," Jeanette said, her tone cheerful as a series of knocks sounded at my door. Eventually the wood was going to wear through from the impact of all the persistent fists.

All of the study group girls filed into my room, each holding some botanical specimen or a murky liquid or a sparkling powder. Alicia was carrying what looked like misshapen purple carrot the size of her arm. Ivy held a small green stone that made a bell-like gong when shaken.

"What is going on here?" I asked Ivy.

"It's a pot luck. A long-standing tradition at Castwell's meant to bond the students in magical learning," Ivy said, fluttering her fingers dramatically. "Each girl presents a magical ingredient without discussing what they're planning to bring, and then the group tries to find a spell they can cast with the ingredients they have."

"So the premise of this bonding experience is that we get a wealth of unknown elements together and try a spell we haven't mastered to see what happens?" I said.

"Yes," Alicia said brightly.

"This doesn't strike you as a *terrible* idea?"

Ivy shrugged. "I do believe this is how Jessica Tipton lost her eyebrows."

"When?" I asked.

"Oh, three years ago, spring term," Ivy guessed.

My mouth dropped open. Whatever spell had been cast at Jessica's pot luck had rendered her forehead unable to regrow hair. The curse was so extensive she couldn't even glamour on a pair of brows. She currently painted them on every morning, using ground charcoal, and she always looked surprised.

"They never grew back, Ivy, not even a little bit," I whispered.

"It'll be fun!" Alicia insisted, her fair cheeks flushing red to match her fiery auburn hair. "It's never anything too dramatic, usually something simple like a glamour or a stirring of air. Common sense keeps the groups from trying anything irresponsible."

I muttered, "Says the girl who, only last year, helped me stop a madwoman from raising a legion of the undead armed with nothing but a book and a positive attitude."

"I concede your point, but everyone is already here, and they're so excited!" Alicia said.

I glanced at the girls, who were whispering and giggling as they inspected each other's offerings. There were very few opportunities for Guardian girls — or Snipe girls, for that matter — to do something silly or carefree. While the Snipe girls were expected to work hard and cheerfully serve every waking moment, Guardian girls were expected to spring from the womb as tiny adults, always poised, always graceful, always seeking opportunities to advance their families. The girls looked so young, squirming like a circle of happy puppies on my hearth. I couldn't take that from them.

I sighed, plopping down on the carpet next to Joan. "All right, let's see what we have."

"Wyvern's blood," Jeanette said, handing me the uncorked orange bottle so I could smell the contents. It smelled like boiled molasses and disappointment. I gagged slightly and handed it back, making her laugh.

"Jade from the Forbidden Mountains of Myanmar," Ivy said, placing the glowing green stone on the carpet.

"Doomed mandrake," Alicia said, presenting the strange purple carrot.

"Star iron," Joan said, offering a jar full of glittering slate-colored powder.

And on it went, until we had an oddly beautiful but completely random collection of items gathered on the carpet.

"What can we do with this?" Madeline asked. "Can you ask the Mother Book?"

"No," I said, emphatically. "I am willing to participate in this strange bonding exercise in the name of sisterhood and camaraderie, but bringing an all-powerful magical tome containing the total magical heritage of the known universe seems like a step too far."

Madeline looked vaguely disappointed but shrugged it off quickly.

"What about Inara's Curse?" Helena said. "You hex someone so wild animals are drawn to them for a full moon's turn. Calista could be finding mice in her bed for weeks. Birds would fly into her enormous hair. If we try hard enough, we might draw snakes from the Americas."

The other girls cackled while my brow furrowed. "It seems like a bad idea to use this opportunity to curse someone, even if they deserve it. It could come back to us in more ways than one."

"I suppose you're right," Helena sighed. "Especially after the incident with the hollowhorn. Our parents might pull us out of school due to pest infestation."

Sofia laughed. "But it would almost be worth it to see the look on her face, no?"

"We could try a love spell," little Lydia suggested, holding open a book with violently pink cover called *101 Love Philtres Guaranteed to Catch a Beau*.

"Too messy. They never turn out the way you think they're going to," Joan said. "And even if they work, the relationships that follow never make for lasting happiness."

"The science is too muddled?" I suggested, remembering her opinions of divination.

Jeanette grinned. "Exactly. Throw that book away before someone gets hurt, Lydia."

Lydia huffed.

"What about a divination spell?" I suggested, crossing to my bookshelf and pulling a textbook labelled *Beyond Portents and Omens*. I giggled when Jeanette groaned. I might have felt guilty, but she did invite all of these people into my room without permission. "Doomed mandrake is a powerful boost for clairvoyance. Forbidden jade, wyvern's blood, and star iron could all be helpful in a relatively harmless fortune-telling spell that won't blow up or result in Lydia's loveless marriage."

"That's not funny," Lydia told me.

I held up my fingers to measure "a little" funny before pointing to a spell called, "A Glimpse of Wisdom."

"That could prove interesting," Helena mused. "What shall we ask to see?"

"Which research guild we'll join," Joan suggested.

"Whether Jessica's eyebrows will ever grow back," I muttered.

Lydia brightened. "Our future husbands!"

"Lydia!" we groaned.

"As if you don't want to know," Lydia grumbled, crossing her arms over her chest.

"Do we have to ask the spell a specific question or can it be more general?" Ivy asked. "Such as, 'what will the future bring?'"

"The more specific, the better," Jeanette said.

"But will we all see the same thing?" Alicia asked.

"According to the book, we will each see a glimpse of our own future. We don't get to see each other's visions," I said.

"So if someone were to marry a disagreeable-looking old man with a pattern of warts on his forehead, no one else will know," Joan said, elbowing Lydia lightly in the ribs. Lydia stuck her tongue out at her.

Once we decided on the spell, putting the ingredients together was relatively easy. My tool kit for potions class allowed Ivy to grind the jade and Alicia to squeeze the required pulp from the mandrake. We mixed them with the star iron and wyvern's blood, carefully following the instructions in the book, and set the cauldron to heat over my fireplace. The concoction was hissing and steaming in no time, but that didn't seem terribly exciting. We raised our blades until they were nearly touching, a many-pointed star reaching for that steam.

"We each need to focus on a question," I said. "A possible outcome for each of us if we choose a certain path. 'What will happen if I' and then you fill in the blank. But you have to be very specific about how it applies to you because otherwise other people's potential timelines could interfere with our visions, and it could get confusing and overwhelming very quickly."

We waited, all nervous giggles and bated breath, but other than creating a cloud of swirling silver steam over our heads, dark grey and scented like honeyed iron, nothing happened. I focused on my question.

"What will happen if I continue doing what I've been doing to find the Changelings?" I asked the magical forces gathering over us.

Nothing. Apparently, the spell agreed with the Mother Book that I wasn't doing enough to find the Changelings.

I concentrated, ignoring the other girls shifting and giggling around me, focusing all of my energy on the words in my head. *"What will happen to me if I don't find the other Changeling children?"*

"Maybe we didn't do it right?" Ivy said just as the cloud over our heads exploded in shards of prismatic color that fell over us. I gasped, watching those shards re-assemble like a puzzle into an image of a mountain looming over me. Three absolutely identical peaks rose from the mountain range above me, outlined against a cloudy grey sky. Waterfalls tumbled from each peak and the air smelled of heather and snow. I turned and saw a crater carved into the mountain below.

Screams sliced through my head like a knife, the screams of frightened children. I whipped around to seek out the source of that awful screeching misery, and I stumbled back over the edge and tumbled into the abyss. But when I fell back, I landed on my rump on the sidewalk in front of the Guild Guardian Senate Hall on Lightbourne Hill. The other girls had disappeared, and I was alone, standing on the steps of the Senate building, watching smoke from distant fires roll over the ruined streets of the capitol, smearing a smoky haze across the sky. The silence of the once-bustling city was eerie, and I wondered if I was the only person left alive in Lightbourne.

The once-elegant buildings, monuments to orderly Guardian society, were reduced to piles of rubble. I turned to see the blackened shell of the dome over the Senate building crumbling under a purple banner emblazoned with an owl. In the distance, I could hear what sounded like a herd of sheep shambling down Ember Street. Hundreds of bent grey forms emerged from the fog of smoke, their arms hanging limp at their sides as they crept towards me in orderly rows.

Lightbourne in ruins

Not one body among them lived. Soldiers, farmers, Guardian children, ladies in fancy ballgowns — no one had been spared from this ghastly call to arms. Rotten, faded clothes hung loose from flopping limbs, as they reached forward, always forward, toward me. I scrambled back from the legion of dead, slack faces, their jaws hanging open as breathless growls hissed from their throats. Hot, acidic tears slid down my cheeks as I recognized bodies among them — little Madeline Sato; Callista's awful friend, Rosemarie; Mrs. Dalrymple, Ivy's grandmother.

Frantic, I searched the faces of the dead. Ivy was there, wearing her tattered gown of saffron yellow. Alicia shuffled beside her, blue-grey face slack and gaping as she struggled to keep up. Mrs. Winter led the charge, pointing fleshless, accusing fingers at me. She opened her mouth and let loose an awful, rasping growl.

"No," I murmured. "Please, no."

A familiar dark-gowned figure rose behind them, floating above the army like a wraith. Her mad, howling laughter streaked across the sky, and I could see —

"Cassandra!" Strong hands jerked at my shoulders, shattering the image around me like a pane of glass. The pieces fell away, and I was in my room again, surrounded by my friends. Their concerned faces circled around me like fretful planets in my little universe. I gulped in a shaky breath, as if my head had just broken through water.

"You were shrieking," Ivy said, eyeing me carefully. "We were afraid you would wake the teachers."

Alicia looked pale, though I didn't know whether that was from fear for my hysterical condition or some phantom from her own vision.

"I am sorry," I said, wiping at my wet cheeks.

"Was it really so terrible?" Joan asked. "Were you wrinkled and grey?"

"Did you see someone die?" Sofia asked, reaching out to take my hand. "Oh, my, your fingers are freezing!"

"Were *you* married to the man with the warty forehead?" Lydia asked pointedly as Ivy passed me a glass of water from the pitcher on my nightstand.

"No, it's silly," I insisted, giving them a watery smile. "I didn't get invited to a single research guild after Spring Interview. I was bent and grey and working in the school library, surrounded by a mountain of books that needed to be shelved. I know it's still a year off for me, but I'm just very worried about it."

"Well, that's impossible," Helena sniffed. "Unless you did terribly at the Spring Interview. Did you try to make a joke? They don't like jokes. And your jokes are particularly bad."

"Thank you, Helena," I muttered, clearing my throat. "What did everyone else see?"

"I saw myself in my forties, looking rather fabulous for my age, and running the Athena Guild," Jeanette said with a grin.

"I moved to America," Sofia said, "Which makes no sense, as it is even further from home."

"What about you, Ivy?" I asked.

She pursed her lips. "I was with you. And I was helping you with a special project."

"That's … non-specific," I said.

"You must have asked about the very near future," Helena mused.

Ivy's lips quirked into a gentle smile, but she didn't add anything else.

While the other girls discussed their pleasant visions of successful careers and happy families, I drifted out of the conversation. What kind of hell had I been thrown into? Would that really happen if I didn't find the other Changelings — the collapse of Guardian society and the destruction of everything I knew? How was it possible? We'd destroyed Miss Morton, yet there was an army of Revenants marching on the ruins of the capitol under a Grimstelle banner. Had she somehow escaped being magically unmade by our spell? I pictured her lurking outside the school, watching, planning to raise her army of the dead, and my stomach turned.

"We need to talk, after the other girls go to bed," Ivy murmured. I nodded.

Eventually, the other girls grew tired and drifted off to their rooms. I envied them their heads full of pretty dreams when I wasn't sure I would ever sleep again.

"What did you see?" Alicia demanded, when Sofia finally shuffled off to her own room.

"I asked the spell what would happen to me if I didn't find the other Changeling children and I saw… I saw the end of the world as we know it. Lightbourne destroyed, buildings razed, and hundreds of Revenants creeping toward me. There were people I recognized in the army of the dead."

I kept my eyes on the skirt of my nightgown. I couldn't tell Ivy and Alicia that they were among the shambling undead. I just couldn't. The idea of losing my closest friends, the only people who truly seemed to understand me and support me without question, made my stomach turn. And the thought of having to face them as enemies? Even if they were under someone else's control, I didn't know if I would be able to do that. But they didn't need to hear any of this.

Ivy sank heavily into the chair behind her. "I was afraid it was something like that."

"I think Miss Morton was there. I couldn't quite make her out in the distance, but the laugh. I'll never forget the way she laughed that night at the tower. But that should be impossible because we disintegrated her."

"What if we didn't?" Alicia asked. "Even we don't fully understand the spell we did together. It was instinctual and not at all thorough. What if some piece of her is still out there somewhere? Or she could have just faked being destroyed so she could escape and regroup."

"That's a cheerful thought," Ivy muttered, chewing on her thumbnail.

"It could have just been a dream," I suggested. "Or a nightmare, rather. The magic tapped into all this anxiety I'm feeling and showed me my worst fear."

"I don't think so," Ivy said. "I saw us traveling to the mountains. We were standing near a cliff in the middle of a terrible storm. And you were frightened, so frightened. I just didn't know how to make you feel better. Then Owen Winter was there, throwing flowers in my face, which I do not understand… and then nothing."

"It's funny that you mention mountains. At the beginning of the vision, I saw three mountains, each with waterfalls, and they matched almost exactly. I didn't know mountains could do that. And then I fell off of a cliff, and the scene changed to what was left of Lightbourne."

"That sounds like the Weeping Sisters," Ivy said. "It's a range near the north of Scotland with three perfectly matched peaks near the Loch of Amethysts. The waterfalls are supposed to be the coldest water in the world. The Benisses use it to break love spells."

"My family has a house on the Loch of Amethysts in Coventry, which is the closest town to the Weeping Sisters," Alicia said. "I told you. We're supposed to travel there this summer for the dreaded holiday."

I chewed on my lip, considering. "Mrs. Winter said there's supposed to be a sort of training facility for Changeling children in a range called the Weeping Sisters. The rumor is they're training the children as expendable magical soldiers, like a pack of guard dogs. She dismissed it as nonsense because it would be too difficult to build and maintain."

"The Weeping Sisters are very difficult to climb, what with the deep crags and high peaks. If I was going to build an evil secret facility, that's where I would build it," Alicia said. "It sounds like the visions are telling you that you should go to the Weeping Sisters."

"I think that the vision is telling me that waiting around for Mrs. Winter isn't helping. I think trying to take a careful approach is making the Mother Book angry."

"Why would you think that?" Alicia asked.

"A few days ago, I found another girl in my room, working some sort of magic with the book," I said.

Ivy shook her head, her dark curls springing loose around her face. "That's impossible. The book only chooses one Translator at a time."

"Was it another student?" Alicia demanded, as if she was going to track this girl down and snatch her bald. "Who was it?"

"It was my maid, Jenny," I sighed. "I wasn't going to tell you because I didn't want to betray her privacy, but everything is just building up so quickly, and I cannot handle it all on my own."

"No one said you have to," Alicia said gently, squeezing my hand.

"This shouldn't be possible," Ivy insisted. "I thought the Book only chose one Translator at a time."

"Well, a lot of things we were told were impossible seem quite possible. At this point, I suppose we shouldn't be surprised. Maybe the reason the Book never chose a Snipe was because a Snipe never got close enough to touch the book before," I said. "I was just the first Snipe who passed by within touching distance. There wasn't anything special about me beyond proximity."

"I think you're underestimating yourself," Ivy told me.

"This conversation has become quite depressing," Alicia said. "Can we move on to a brighter subject?"

"I'm sorry the subject of magical oppression and the possibility

I was never supposed to be the Translator is so boring," I sighed. "How in the world am I supposed to get to Scotland? Mrs. Winter won't let me go to an afternoon tea alone."

"I didn't say boring. I said depressing," Alicia replied. "But I still think a change of subject is in order. I suppose I'm just going to have to beg my mother to invite you two along for our summer holiday so that I will have some company. She should be thrilled. For years, she's said that I needed to expand my social circle. And while she thinks we're sipping chocolate at the Leaping Trout and shopping for new hat ribbons, we'll just have to traverse some very dangerous mountains to find a hidden magical school for stolen children."

"It's still more fun than what my mother has planned for my summer," Ivy said. "So I would be delighted."

"I doubt even Mrs. Winter would turn down an invitation to spend the summer with the McCray family," I said, squeezing Alicia's hand. "Thank you. So what about you, Alicia? You haven't said anything about your vision. Please tell me it was you sitting in a field of flowers, frolicking with a puppy, or something similar."

Alicia's pinched expression returned. "Well, I'm sorry to disappoint you. But I asked the spell to show me what my life would be life after I graduated school."

She paused to glance down at her lap.

Ivy jostled her arm slightly. "So, what did you see?"

Alicia jerked her small shoulders. "I saw nothing at all."

7

AN INVITATION AND A SUMMONS

I sat at my desk in my suite staring glumly into the pages of the Mother Book as I waited for afternoon tea to begin. Anxiety over Alicia's rather shocking announcement that she had no future had kept my appetite at bay.

"Why aren't you telling me anything?" I muttered to the book. "I could really use some help here."

I'd been staring at the delicate, blank vellum pages for hours, silently begging for some way around the Alicia's prediction. Alicia had been relatively quiet about her rather shocking announcement that she had no future. Ivy and I demanded details of her vision, but she simply shrugged and told us that while I dreamt of annihilation and the other girls dreamt of husbands and careers, Alicia simply saw a fog. She heard nothing. She saw only swirling, pearl-white mists.

We tried to imagine what that meant. Ivy suggested perhaps her future depended on something Ivy or I did in the mountains we saw in our visions. I proposed that Alicia asked the wrong question and the spell simply refused to answer her. But Alicia patted both of our heads, as if we were very simple, and said in a maddeningly calm tone, "You two seem to forget that until recently I assumed I wouldn't live to see adulthood. Reverb patients rarely live as long as I have. Having ridiculous amounts of money helps, of course, but I could only cheat the Fates for so long. Yes, I have been feeling better lately, and my magic is under control for the first time in my life. But I don't know that's a permanent change. The prospect of not having a future? It's something I've lived with for a long time. It doesn't scare me. It's possible that I asked the wrong question. It's possible I won't be alive next year. I cannot let fear of that distract me from what we need to do. Now, I'm going to go to my room and pen a heartfelt letter to my mother in which I assure her that I just don't think I will be able to enjoy the trip to Coventry without my dearest friends — on that hideous stationery she gave me for my birthday — because she considers properly written paper letters to be the only appropriate form of communication."

She rose to her feet and laid the back of her hand over her forehead in a dramatic fashion. "And who knows how many summers I have left?"

"That's not funny," I told her.

"I disagree. I happen to think stationery covered in cabbage roses and repeating patterns of little A's is very funny." And then she swept out of my room, leaving me and Ivy to just stare at each other. Even now, days later, we seemed far more distressed by Alicia's possible imminent demise than she did. It was quite annoying, actually, how lightly she was taking the whole situation. Yes, I was making new friends, but Alicia and Ivy were the dearest among them. They'd befriended me before anyone else. They'd helped me when no one else would. The idea of losing Alicia now was simply...

"Unacceptable," I muttered, shutting the book with a dull *slap*. "And you're no help."

What was I going to do? Where else could I look for information? I'd been careful to avoid the library since the situation with Miss Morton. Headmistress Lockwood promised the students that she'd personally cleared Miss Morton's workplace of any hexes and spells she'd left behind. Still, I couldn't bear to spend time there, to remember how completely I'd been fooled by Miss Morton's "benevolent, doddering old maid" act. I did most of my schoolwork in Mr. Winter's expansive book collection. But for Alicia, I would go directly to the school's selection of books on portents of doom and study how to prevent them from coming to pass.

"Right, good plan."

A light knock sounded at my door, and I stood and called, "Come in."

Rebecca, my new lady's maid, curtsied at the doorway. "Headmistress asked you to come downstairs, Miss. You have a visitor. She said you might like to change into a nicer dress."

"Is it Ga — Mr. McCray?" I asked, smiling for the first time all day.

Rebecca shrugged her rounded shoulders. "I wouldn't know, Miss."

That flare of giddy excitement in my belly died at the thought of seeing Gavin's face so soon after our last visit and how I couldn't avoid telling him about his sister's vision. How could I get through a conversation with Gavin without telling him? Maybe I should just have Rebecca tell Headmistress I was indisposed. Or walk into the room and kiss him right away. Miss Turnwoody would throw me in the detention wing faster than you could say "incorrigible youth."

Perhaps it was selfish of me, but I used all the speed at my disposal to slip into one of my nicer Castwell green day dresses. Rebecca skillfully pinned any flyaway curls away in the chignon she'd arranged just that morning. I didn't have leave to use cosmetics, so all I could do was pinch my cheeks to put a bit of color in them.

"Thank you, Rebecca," I said, as I moved to lock the Mother Book in its cabinet.

"Headmistress asked that you bring the book, Miss."

I frowned. That seemed unusual. There would be no reason to involve the book in a visit from Gavin. A sinking feeling chased away the last tendrils of excitement as I negotiated the stairs.

I glanced down to the foyer to see Mr. Winter's bald head shining in the crayfire light. What in the world?

Mr. Winter was a tall, thin man with sharp features and Owen's grey eyes. The pair of us shared a strangely cordial, though distant, relationship in the years I'd worked in his home. He generally left Mrs. Winter to manage the household staff, but he was never cruel to us as some Guardian men were known to be. He never punished us for a mistake or tried to take advantage of us or even spoke harshly in our direction.

I'd been borrowing books from Mr. Winter's library for years, sneaking them home to read and always careful to return them exactly where I found them in good condition. Somehow, I thought maybe he knew I'd been doing it, but he never said anything. In fact, there had been a few times where I suspect he left books I might like out on the fireside table to be re-shelved. But even after I'd become Cassandra, he'd left me mostly to Mrs. Winter's guidance. He'd never sought me out for conversation and he'd certainly never visited me at school.

"Mr. — Uncle?" I said, skeptically as I reached the bottom step.

Mr. Winter gave me a paper-thin smile. "Cassandra, I have received permission from Headmistress Lockwood to take you into town."

"Do I have an appointment that Auntie Aneira didn't tell me about?"

Mr. Winter held out a pelisse and bonnet, which looked strangely out-of-place in his hands. "Please just come with me, dear."

The underlying message was clear. Stop asking questions and get in the carriage. Where could we be going? Was I in trouble of some sort? Had I been found out? Was this some measure to remove me from school and Lightbourne before the authorities arrived to take me in? Mr. Winter observed all the niceties, holding my hand as I descended the steps to the school in my bulky school gown. But even I could sense the tension in his arm.

"Where are we going?" I asked softly.

"The Senate building. The Committee has requested a meeting with you."

"With so little notice?" I whispered.

He nodded. "It would seem so."

"Is Mrs. Winter coming with us?" I asked him. It was unusual for him to be alone with me at all, but Mrs. Winter would not stand to be left out of such a meeting — not when there was power to be brokered and political muscle to be displayed.

"She's in Southhampshire, visiting one of her family's farms. Something that almost everyone in her circle knows. I believe the reason the Committee scheduled the meeting at the last minute was to exclude Mrs. Winter from the proceedings," he muttered, handing me into the carriage and following me inside.

"Should I be worried?" I asked Mr. Winter after the footman shut the carriage door.

"It is disconcerting that they insisted on seeing you on such short notice, but honestly, there's only so much they can do to you as the Translator. That is, as long as they haven't discovered your origins. I haven't received any information indicating that they have, but I suppose they wouldn't let that slip to me," he sighed, drumming his fingers against his legs.

"So we could be walking into an ambush that could result in me being executed and you losing your fortune?"

He pursed his lips and then his lips quirked upwards. "Potentially, yes."

Mr. Winter's expression was oddly animated, as if this was the most exciting thing to happen to him in years. I remembered Owen mentioning how disenchanted his father was with working for the Senate. Was he entertained by the idea of self-destruction? Or was he simply so bored with a political life that any bit of intrigue was welcome?

"Just answer their questions honestly," he told me. "Be polite and charming. Shows of defiance are discouraged, but don't let them bully you. Under no circumstances should you let them think you are anything but a gently born young lady who has practiced magic all of her life."

We rumbled along the cobblestone streets of Lightbourne, the sharp ozone of the crayfire engine drifting through the window. I watched Guardian women flitting from one shop to the next in their bright silk gowns like socially aggressive butterflies. For the first time, I truly envied them. I would have loved to be anywhere in the world besides this carriage — even if it meant scrubbing chamber pots.

The Senate building loomed over us as we rolled to a stop on Lightbourne Hill. It was an imposing crescent-shaped, dark grey granite structure topped with dome and filled with tiny windows. As we ascended the ninety-nine steps it took to reach the entrance, Mr. Winter informed me that only the lowest of the low, Senators from families who had lost their power in all but name, received the tiny garret offices in the dome. Thanks to the combined power of the Winter name and the machinations of his wife, Mr. Winter enjoyed one of the larger office suites, closest to the meeting chambers.

A Senate page, a recent graduate of Palmers, met us at the door and led us down several airy arched hallways with white and gold-veined marble. The walls were lined with marble busts of great Guild Guardian leaders from over the decades. But as we took more turns and stairways, the corridors became darker and more cramped. It felt as if I was being led away from safety, away from light.

Mr. Winter took my arm as he led me into a small dim room, chiefly occupied by a raised dais and seven men in cushioned chairs. I spotted a Drummond, a Brandywine, a Cavill, and a Benisse in the mix, along with Mr. Crenshaw of course. I didn't recognize the other two sigils on the members' suit jackets. The lack of windows and the dark grey walls made the room feel claustrophobic. Incense smoke rolled thick out of censures in the corners, clary sage for truth and rosemary for fidelity. I coughed lightly at the cloying herbal scent while Mr. Winter gave me a sympathetic look.

"Cassandra, dear, as you know, this esteemed panel is the Committee for Antiquities and Artifacts. Gentlemen, you remember my beloved niece, Cassandra Reed, the Translator of the Mother Book."

With his hand at the small of my back and the warmth of his introduction, I could almost believe that I was a cherished member of Mr. Winter's family. He seemed concerned for me and that didn't exactly make me feel more secure in my situation.

In the middle of this panel of men sat Mr. Crenshaw, an older jowly man with salt-and-pepper mutton-chop sideburns. He smirked, his face pale as moon cheese, as I curtsied. I assumed it was because I had to look up at him, even at my full height, in order to speak to him. I recognized some of the other men on the panel from the impromptu meeting held at the Winter masquerade. There were all finely dressed and self-satisfied as Mr. Crenshaw annd ranged from looking bored to casting jealous glances one man's shiny gold pocket watch to … well, the one person besides Mr. Crenshaw that was paying attention to me was a lean, grey-haired Benisse who appeared to be staring at the neckline of my gown. That was certainly off-putting.

They were men, just like other men. They were no better or smarter than anyone else I'd met. Frankly, none of them looked particularly bright. They seemed lazy and greedy — and in one case, a bit of a deviant — not exactly the pillars of Guardian society they were supposed to be. I set my jaw and made direct, aggressive eye contact with Mr. Crenshaw. I was the Translator, and he was just a disappointed old man who was pouting because I had access to magic that he didn't. These men were not the masters of my fate, and I was rather tired of behaving as if they were.

I held my shoulders straighter and lifted my chin. Mr. Crenshaw drummed his fingers against his heavy wooden chair arm. "Miss Reed, it can't be a mystery to you why you were invited here today."

"Was this an invitation?" I asked airily, trying for a passable imitation of Mrs. Winter. "It seemed uncomfortably like a summons to which I had no alternative but to comply."

Given the way that Mr. Winter startled at my side, I assumed that I had achieved his wife's trademark aloofness.

"We expect results from the Translator, Miss Reed. And your results have not been forthcoming."

I cocked my head, smiling pleasantly. "And what exactly do you expect me to do about that. Mr. Crenshaw? The Mother Book reveals itself to the Translator in its own time."

"Did you not even think to bring the Book with you to this meeting?"

I hadn't even known I was coming to this meeting, which honestly was probably wise on Mr. Winter's part. And I probably wouldn't have brought the Book if I *had* known that I was meeting with the committee. These men had no right to the Mother Book, and more to the point, they didn't deserve access to it. I didn't trust them with the information in the Mother Book. I didn't trust them with access to a book of fairy tales.

"No, I did not."

Mr. Crenshaw sneered when I didn't elaborate. "We want progress, Miss Reed, and we want it quickly. The Translator answers to this committee. And if you cannot do that, perhaps a better candidate can be found for the position, someone more deserving."

I couldn't help but smirk myself at this nonsense. These men didn't select the Translator. The book chose the right witch to unlock her secrets. It wasn't as if Mr. Crenshaw could walk into Miss Castwell's and simply point out a girl he thought would be more manageable. But what if he'd somehow found out about Jenny and *her* interactions with the Book? Was that even possible?

Keeping that false expression of sweetness, I replied, "I've read the histories of other Translators kept in the library at Miss Castwell's. As those biographers see it, it's the other way around. This group answers to the Translator and has from the very beginning. You are supposed to weigh and measure the information and disperse it to Guardian society for the greater good."

The panel shifted in their chairs, their collective expression rebellious. They certainly didn't like a teenage girl informing them that she had authority over them.

"It is not your place to question the wisdom of this committee!" A gaunt, elderly man on the far right thundered suddenly. He was wearing a tie pin shaped like a salmon with a little star in its mouth.

Between the ridiculous house sigil and his petulant voice, like a toddler pitching a tantrum, it was all I could do not to laugh outright. Instead, I lifted my brow and gave him a bland smile. "I'm sorry. We haven't been introduced. What is your name, sir?"

"William Delbert!" he huffed. "Of the proud and ancient House Delbert."

"I've never heard of it," I told him flatly. Because I hadn't. Of all the houses and their histories Mrs. Winter had drilled into my before starting school, House Delbert had never come up. And I certainly would have remembered the salmon sigil. How could someone from such an insignificant family end up on such an important committee? He must have married very well a long time ago.

At my side, Mr. Winter coughed into his hand to hide a chuckle.

"I am not questioning the wisdom of this committee," I told Mr. Delbert. "I am simply seeking to reach an arrangement that gives us all what we wish for."

I turned back to Mr. Crenshaw and said, "I cannot force information out of the book any more than you can force blood from a stone. The book reveals to me as it sees fit. And I can only reveal that information to you when that happens."

Mr. Crenshaw tented his fingers over his belly. "Perhaps you should spend your school holidays considering your priorities. If it is too difficult for you to prioritize your work, we can help you remove the distractions from your life. It is not necessary for the Translator to attend Miss Castwell's. It is not necessary for the Translator to live with her family. In fact, as your parents are deceased, the Senate could very easily assume guardianship of you until you come of age. We could remove you from society entirely to a secluded spot known only to this Committee, so you might focus more fully on your good work."

While my eyes may have narrowed, my expression didn't falter. Guardianship — there was that word I'd come to hate. Such a nice word for control of my life, for taking all of my decisions away from me. I'd been a servant for nearly all of my life, without choices, without options, and now they were threatening to do that to me all over again. They were honestly threatening me with imprisonment if I didn't do what they wanted me to. What did they think would be the result they were pressuring me for? What was to stop me from simply fabricating the sort of spells I thought they were hoping for? And why did the Commission seem so desperate for this information now-now-*now*? It had been more than a century since the last Translator and almost that long since the previous Translator.

I studied Mr. Crenshaw's face more closely. The warmer season didn't seem to be agreeing with him at all. He wasn't just pale. He was wearing a thin layer of powder over his plump face, and some of that powder had been smeared away by sweat. There was a thin moustache of perspiration beads quivering over his lip. Had he been ill? Was he hoping that I would find some sort of miracle cure-all magic in the Book? Was that why he was pushing me so hard?

"You go too far, Sebastian," Mr. Winter barked. "You know very well those regulations are in place only in cases of a Translator who is completely uncooperative. That has certainly not been the case for Cassandra. She has submitted every piece of information revealed to her by the Mother Book."

"And it's simply not enough," Mr. Crenshaw shot back. "I expect new information from Miss Reed within the month. And the next time we meet with her, I expect her to bring the Book!"

"And do you think that applying that sort of pressure will be conducive to producing the results you want?" I asked crisply.

Mr. Crenshaw and Mr. Delbert pointedly ignored my question. Mr. Delbert merely smirked at Mr. Winter. "Oh, do calm down, Thomas. WSe only seek to *ease* the pressure from Miss Reed's life. By simplifying it, by removing the distractions of a proper young lady's social and educational obligations."

I stared. Words bubbled behind my lips, angry retorts, accusations, pure profanity. None of which Mrs. Winter would have used. My hands practically vibrated as the dragonfly seethed on my palms. So instead, I turned that false smile up a level and said, "If you think that is necessary, there's very little I can do to stop you. If I were in your shoes, I certainly wouldn't attempt to spend my social currency in such a manner — effectively kidnapping a young woman from a fine Guardian family, a young woman who is well-known to people at large for being chosen as the voice of the Mother Book, a young woman who has already suffered so much tragedy in her short life, when all she has ever done is strived to please the committee by submitting regular reports, even as she earned good marks in a heavy course load at Miss Castwell's... Well, I am sure you and your families can with withstand the public's perception of such a gesture."

From the corner of my eye, I could see Mr. Winter watching me carefully, and he seemed to have a small smile on his lips. Mr. Crenshaw was also staring at me, but he and the other members of the committee looked far less pleased. As things stood now, they knew I was right. I wasn't exactly a celebrated member of Guardian society, but it was well-known that I was the Translator and that I had Mrs. Winter's support. Few families would support the abduction and seclusion of a Guardian girl. It would mean the same could happen to their own precious daughters. Fewer families would want to be known to support a committee that conflicted with Mrs. Winter's agenda. For now, I was safe, and they knew it. I just needed to give them a way to exit this situation gracefully.

"Now, surely, gentlemen, a more desirable solution is to graciously allow me to return to school to complete my year. Then I will certainly spend my free time over the summer intensely studying the Mother Book. I will be the soul of cooperation in a very public manner. Your committee will get the credit for fostering a productive relationship with the Translator, and I won't have the distress of watching your families put through the social gauntlet after making such an unnecessarily aggressive decision."

Mr. Crenshaw's jaw clenched under his whiskers. "Yes, I suppose that will do."

"Excellent," I chirped. "May I consider this meeting closed?"

"You may," Mr. Crenshaw grumbled.

"Thank you, gentlemen, you've been ever so helpful," I said, curtsying and turning my back on them — a rather serious breach of protocol, considering their positions. I swept from the room, my skirts slapping against the doorway as I negotiated the narrow exit. Mr. Winter nearly had to jog to keep up with me as I followed what little light there was out of the maze of corridors. While I was careful to keep my rage off of my face, it was enough to fuel my marching out of the building and down the steps to the Winter carriage. No one stopped me, probably because my hands were glowing with the force of a highly agitated magical mark.

The footman handed me into the carriage, and Mr. Winter climbed in after me. As I sank into the cushioned seat, all the righteous anger drained out of me, and I was struck by the full force of the words I'd tossed so carelessly at men who could conceivably ruin my life if they decided to make a hobby of it. I'd behaved as if I had nothing to lose. I'd behaved as if I didn't have any secrets. I'd behaved as if I forgot I was ever a Snipe.

A wave of nausea overtook me, and I fanned my face with my hands. Mr. Winter shot his cuffs as he settled into the seat across from me. "Well, that could have gone better, but overall, I believe that you handled yourself with aplomb."

"I let my temper get the best of me," I wheezed. I attempted to lean forward to get a better breath only to realize my gown prevented anything but the straightest posture.

"Oh, do take a breath, dear. You look like you could vomit at any moment."

"I *could* vomit at any moment," I told him as the carriage rolled down Lightbourne Hill. "I shouldn't have sassed them like that. I shouldn't have challenged them. I should have just taken their criticism with a smile and promised to do better. Mrs. Winter is going to be so upset with me."

"And if you'd simpered and smiled and shown no spine, what do you think they would have done? You can't show those men weakness, and with them, even politeness can be considered a weakness. They would have assumed that they could have threatened you with much worse the next time. Mrs. Winter would have been quite disappointed if you'd shown none of her family's spine."

"Could the committee really do what they threatened to do *this* time?" I asked. "Could they really take me into custody and seclude me somewhere, keep me a prisoner chained to the Mother Book?"

"I think you would be a fool to dismiss it *entirely*," he said. "But as I said, those measures are only permissible in cases where the Translator is particularly combative with the Committee. And even with that display, you can't be considered combative. You have been, as you said, the soul of cooperation."

I nodded, frowning. "Why are they pressing this issue so emphatically, Mr. Winter?"

Mr. Winter shook his head. "I honestly don't know. The Committee seems… increasingly distressed lately, especially Mr. Crenshaw. But that is not for you to worry about. You have the backing of Winter house. We are fully invested in you, Sarah. We have as much to lose as you do — more in fact, if the Committee decides to turn on you. We will not simply let them take you."

"Thank you, Mr. Winter."

"I know that I generally let Mrs. Winter attend to you, but I must tell you that I have been very impressed with how you have handled this transition in the last year. I do not know why you were given the gifts you have been given, and I do not know why you were chosen as the Translator. I only know that not many girls your age could handle the pressure that been applied to you, and fewer could do so with the sort of grace that you have. And to think you're the same little Sarah who used to scuttle around my house, hiding behind your mother's skirts, bashing my son in the face with books when he deserved it."

I blushed. I'd forgotten that Mr. Winter knew about the book incident. "I am proud of you, dear girl. I just want to know that."

"Thank you, sir."

"Of course, I will be even prouder if you continue to put that grotesque, constipated expression on my awful cousin's face."

"That's disgusting," I told him.

"So is my cousin."

AND SO THAT NIGHT, I found myself in the exact same position at my vanity with my forehead balanced against my hand, brooding. I was no closer to helping Alicia. I was no closer to getting to Jenny. Now the Senate was threatening to take away my free will.

I would have asked myself how things were going to get worse, but the magical universe had a way of answering that sort of self-pitying question quickly and in a dramatic fashion.

I glanced up at the mirror and startled when a bright blue C formed over the reflection of my nose. *"Cousin,"* the light scrolled across my looking glass. I rolled my eyes as the sight of Owen's lazy looping scrawl stretching across the mirror.

Owen was sending me a scrying message. Fancy pressed paper was necessary for formal invitations and correspondence, but for quick notes to close friends and family, witches wrote on mirrors with the tips of their blades. The words appeared instantaneously on the mirror nearest the intended recipient, no matter where they were. And my cousin was apparently, sitting in his room at Palmer's, sending me a scrying message on a no-doubt an over-sized mirror that put the vain in vanity.

Oh, happy, happy day.

"How are you?" Owen inquired feebly. *"Father said that you had a rather difficult afternoon."*

Frowning, I picked up the blade and scratched, *"I'm just lovely, Owen. Nothing at all to report to your mother"* into the glass.

"I'm hurt, cousin. Really, I am. I'm no snitching salamander. I simply wanted to inquire as to how you are feeling. I haven't heard a word from you since I escorted you to school. When we ran into that friend of yours in the yellow dress, Posey or Blossom or something or other."

"Ivy," I wrote back. *"You know very well her name is Ivy."*

"She's —" The glass shimmered with the fading letters, and he finally added, *"Interesting. As you know, tomorrow is Sweetheart's Day. The traditional spring celebration of love, where the estimable gentlemen of Palmer's send the young ladies of Castwell's tokens of their affections. I thought it might be nice to send Miss Cowell a token on Sweetheart's Day, and I was wondering if she likes chocolates or if she would like something prettier, like a piece of jewelry or something for her room."*

I amazed even myself at the amount I was able to write so emphatically without scratching the glass. *"She's more than interesting. Samples of fairy fingernail clippings are interesting. A glamour that makes me look like your father would be interesting. Ivy is an amazing, kind, smart, talented person, and anyone would be lucky to have her friendship. If you or your awful friends at Palmer's are planning some sort of prank on her, I will release the full wrath of the Mother Book on you. You will not have a single place on your body left uncovered from the boils I give you. And your friends. And their other friends."*

There was a very long pause on the other end of the mirror connection.

"It's not any sort of joke, Sarah. I promise. I want to send her something that will make her happy, and I am unsure of what she likes. You know her best."

My jaw dropped open. I'd never known Owen to admit that he liked any girl. He'd expressed approval for certain girls, usually willowy young ladies with light hair. As absolutely lovely as she was, Ivy didn't fit that mold.

"This isn't a joke?" I wrote back.

"No, it's not a joke!"

I could almost hear the huffy indignation in his voice, and it made me laugh for the first time in days. There were rare moments like this when I was reminded of the Owen I knew when I was a child, before our circumstances in life separated us, when I went to work and when he became the little lord of the manor. Also, I happened to remember that Owen had been the one to harass Gavin into giving me the perfect gift for Sweethearts' Day.

I sighed and wrote back, *"Well, Ivy happens to like plants. You might ask your mother what she would like. A blushing orchid, perhaps. Or forever freesia. As long as they are properly watered, they never die or lose their scent. That's a rather thoughtful way to convey your message. And write something NICE and PARTICULAR about Ivy. Don't make her think that she is one of a dozen girls to whom you're sending flowers."*

"I will take that under advisement."

I snorted. Apparently, Owen was back to being lord of the manor.

"Owen, I'm being very serious. You would be lucky to receive her attentions. I love her very dearly. If you hurt her, I will be beyond disappointed in you."

For a moment, all was silent, and then my mirror framed the word, *"Understood."*

I leaned back in my chair. In all the tumult involving the Senate, I'd forgotten that the next day was Sweetheart's Day. In one of our healing classes, Nurse Waxwing told us that Sweetheart's Day was marked by taut nerves and full-scale temper tantrums. She often hovered in the foyer with smelling salts and knock-out drops to prevent major episodes. The whole school would be in a dither, and the staff would be distracted and —

The book fluttered open to a blank page, and I felt the familiar hum along my hands as golden light shimmered across the paper, leaving words in its wake and an illustration of a man walking through a stone wall, his leg and shoulder not yet absorbed into the stone. The top of the page read, "Thieves' Bliss."

"Thieves Bliss is transitive spell used by ne'er do wells for their own nefarious purposes. It is colloquially known as a "walk through," a spell that allows the user to, simply put, walk through walls or door or any solid barrier, no matter how well-locked or warded it is because the user's body is broken down into pieces so tiny they slide through the substance of the wall."

The book was no longer ignoring me! It was such a relief to have some communication with it... Suddenly, I was very glad that no one could read the Mother Book but the Translator because this definitely the sort of spell I wouldn't want Sebastian Crenshaw to have in his awful, clammy hands. I did not want him to be able to walk through walls and doors that probably had every reason to be locked.

Walking through those walls seemed dangerous. What if you ended up stuck between rooms because you solidified before you were all the way through the barrier? Would that kill you — being bisected by a door? It seemed like it would.

But the book had chosen this moment to show me this particular spell for a reason. Why? I was thinking about how distracted the staff would be on Sweetheart's Day, and the book showed me a way to walk through walls. Could the book be encouraging me to sneak into the servants' quarters to find Jenny?

On the adjacent page, another illustration showed the thief sweeping a pile of treasure into a huge sack.

I was going to take that as the book's tacit agreement.

I settled down to learn the wand movements and potion ingredients involved in *Thieves' Bliss*. I patted the book's spine. "You are a very poor influence, and I am ever so grateful."

8

SMELLING SALTS AND SLIPPING THROUGH WALLS

As predicted, Miss Castwell's was a hive of neuroses and distraction by noon the next day. Girls were hovering in the periphery of the front door, pretending they weren't keeping watch out the front windows like gargoyles. The girls practically twitched every time the bell rang, hoping that the next messenger that came to the door would be carrying something for them. And when the lush bouquets of singing anemones or the packages of bonbons in their garish pink wrappings turned out to be for some other girl, they would either hiss like angry cats or sweep up the stairs in torrents of sobs that echoed off of the black-and-white-tiled floor.

Adding to this symphony of confusion were explosions of purple glitter that spelled out Priscilla Bellick's name and the occasional burst of song from the silver hand-mirror gifted to Rosalie Archer, enchanted to sing compliments when Rosalie's face appeared in the glass. Nurse Waxwing had several older girls confined to cots assembled in the visitors' parlor. The air was heavy with golden flower pollen and the sharp, invasive scent of ammonia-based smelling salts. And the glitter was getting *everywhere.*

In the chaos, I was able to slip quietly down the hallway towards the servants' quarters. In fact, I passed Mrs. Reynolds and the head chambermaid, Maryann, bustling towards the foyer with a rolling tea service. A cloud of bitter valerian-scented steam followed in their wake. Over the rattling of the tea cups, I could only barely hear Mrs. Reynolds mutter, "They ought to do away with this awful holiday and ban the boys from sending anything all together. Turns the whole school on its ear, it does, and makes extra work for all of us when we should be running the house. Turns the girls against each other, tearing them apart with jealousy and broken hearts. It's horrible!"

I chuckled quietly as I opened the kitchen door. My mother would have said the exact same thing if she could have witnessed the scene in the foyer. Sweeping up the confetti alone would have driven her mad.

I passed the kitchen door without a second glance. I would never have been able to sneak through the kitchen, past dozens of maids and cooks already on edge from Sweetheart's Day, to access the servants' quarters from the main servants' staircase in the back of the massive cooking hall, but according to Ivy's chambermaid, Lillian, the rear staircase to the servants' quarters was on the opposite side of the wall nearest the hospital wing, behind the portrait of the first school nurse, Agathina Goode. I just had to walk through the portrait and the wall, and I could enter the servants' quarters without being seen.

I glanced around for potential witnesses and was about to pull Wit from my wrist holster, when I heard Nurse Waxwing call, "Miss Reed?!"

I froze, turning towards the nurse as she swept down the hall, her dark hair frazzling out from under it tight knot at the back of her head. She looked like she'd been wrestling with a wolverine. "Miss Reed, what are you doing in this particular hallway? Our healing class is tomorrow. Unless you're here to volunteer for bedpan duty, I suggest you move along in your business."

"Oh, no, ma'am, I'm simply admiring this lovely portrait of Nurse Goode," I said gesturing.

Nurse Waxwing lifted a greying brow and looked pointedly at the painting of Nurse Goode, who had a lazy eye, a long crooked nose with a large wart on the bridge, and a hump.

I cleared my throat. "It's a… stunning likeness."

"Move along, Miss Reed," Nurse Waxwing told me.

She ducked into the medical wing's entrance, presumably to fetch more warlock-level sedatives. Taking a deep breath to center myself, I pulled out the vial of dry potion ingredients, including ground malachite and Saharan sand, and sprinkled it over my head. Then I drew the symbol for *Thieves' Bliss* over the wall with Wit, careful not to leave a mark.

"I hope this works," I sighed, walking into the wall. While I was prepared to smack into the wall face-first, I slipped through it as if it wasn't even there. It was a strange sensation, as if I was walking through a curtain of bubbles that tickled my nose and prickled against my skin. Suddenly, I was standing on the landing of a narrow staircase lit by cloudy, spotted windows. The grubby walls looked like they hadn't been painted in decades. The color looked a little bit like moldy celery.

I mounted the steep, rickety stairs, which was no mean feat even in the simple day dress I'd chosen. I poked my head into the servants' hall, but the chaos of Sweethearts' Day demanded the staff's full attention. No one was wandering the long, badly lit corridor. The hallway smelled of coal smoke, something that wasn't used to heat the student dorms. We simply couldn't have soot staining the young ladies' immaculate green dresses or breathing in noxious fumes. But obviously no one cared what Snipes wore or breathed. Even in my own head, my thoughts sounded decidedly bitter.

I crept past the open rooms with my quiet Snipe gait. Mary and I had always prided ourselves on our ability to navigate around Raven's Rest on silent feet. A good servant entered rooms unnoticed, did their work and walked away without being heard. The servants' rooms were certainly sparer than the students' quarters. The maids shared rooms with two iron frame beds in each, a washstand, and a wardrobe. The walls were whitewashed with the exception of the smoke stains over the small fireplaces. In the distance, I could hear humming. I followed the sound to the end of the corridor to a sort of common room with a long table for late night dinners and a few threadbare chairs near the enormous blackened stone hearth.

Jenny was humming quietly to herself as she sewed by the fire. There was no elegant scent of beeswax and fresh flowers here, only the sour smell of tallow candles and old smoke. I inhaled deeply, appreciating the combination. It meant home to me.

Jenny's dark brown curls were bent over a fine silk stocking, which she was darning with tiny, even stitches. I crept quietly into the room, but I still startled her enough to make her drop the stocking. She sprang up from the lavender brocade chair, a cast-off from a set I recognized from the visitor's parlor. "Miss Reed, what are you doing in here? Students aren't supposed to come up here."

"Jenny, I'd like to talk about what happened in my bedroom," I said quietly, glancing around for Mrs. Reynolds.

Jenny's dark brows drew together. "I'm afraid I don't know what you mean, miss."

"We both know what I saw," I said. "Did you feel the Mother

Book reach out to you? Or did the magic just start spontaneously?"

"I don't know what you're talking about, miss," she said, firmly. "I was just dancing. I don't know what you saw. Maybe it was something leftover after your classes, but it wasn't me."

My eyes narrowed at her. Was she really trying to tell me I was crazy? Or lying?

"Would you just leave me alone?" Jenny demanded. "I don't know what you're doing or why you keep insisting that I'm using magic when I'm not, but I don't want any trouble. I wasn't doing magic on purpose. It just happened, and I just want to do my job and live my life."

She stood, clapping a hand over her mouth as if she couldn't believe the words that had just escaped her. Her hand had been hardened and scarred by a lifetime of work, much like mine had been before I arrived her. I sighed. I'd never meant to frighten Jenny. More than anything, I wanted to speak to someone who was going through the same thing I'd experienced. It was so lonely, knowing that you were different and alone. Alicia and Ivy were wonderful friends, but they hadn't lived through this. I believed that Jenny had.

I pulled Wit out of my sleeve and raised the blade, making Jenny flinch. I drew the blue symbol for silence. No one would hear what we were saying outside of the dome.

"You would agree that I have a great secret about you, yes, and that if I shared something of the same weight, we would both stand to lose a great deal, yes?"

She lifted her brows. "I suppose so, Miss."

I rolled up my sleeve and showed Jenny a few faint, silvery burn scars between my wrists and elbows. I'd never quite mastered the art of holding on to heavy, hot objects out of the oven while having no measurable upper body strength. The appearance of the dragonfly mark had burned away the callouses and scars on my palms, but that baby newness had not reached my forearms. They were barely noticeable, unless one was looking, but a Guardian would simply assume they'd been left behind by a spell gone awry or potions work. Jenny's mouth dropped, and she reached out a finger to touch the faint lines on my skin.

"No matter how careful you are, it's hard to work in the kitchen without getting burned every once in a while. The weight of a pot shifts or your arms aren't quite strong enough, and the metal curves right against your skin, singeing like hellfire."

Jenny shook her head and backed away from me. "No."

"I was born Sarah Smith in the Warren on Brown Street. Up until a year ago, I was a maid of all work, helping my sister collect the sheets every morning and cleaning the parlor knickknacks of dust."

Jenny blinked at me through a narrowed gaze of disbelief.

"I could show you how I can fold sheets with razor precision. I could tell you the exact recipe for lye soap. Or show you how good I am at cleaning windows with vinegar."

"I think I should like to see that," Jenny said.

"I'll not have you use this as an excuse to get me to do your chores," I told her, laughing a bit.

"I'm listening," she said, indicating I should sit in her worn chair while she perched on a nearby stool. I took the stool, which seemed to surprise her.

"I was a kitchen maid for most of my childhood and then a maid of all work," I said. "I was a perfectly normal Snipe girl, with the exception of being rather small and sickly. But then last year, I levitated a vase. I was dusting it in my mistress's parlor, and I've always been clumsy. Mrs. Winter startled me, and it slipped through my fingers, and all I could think was 'Please don't let it fall.' I waited for the crash, but it never came. I opened my eyes, and Mrs. Winter was standing there staring at me as if I'd grown a second head."

"She probably would have preferred the second head," she said.

I laughed. "That is probably true."

"How did you get come to be here?"

"Mrs. Winter thought it would be safer to pass me off as a long-lost cousin than tell the Senate she'd been harboring a Snipe who could practice magic. How did you get here?"

Jenny hesitated and then glanced at my scars again. She said, "I've been trying to get a position here for years. My aunt Lizzie works in the kitchens and finally secured a place for me when Susan left. I thought maybe what magic I did could be explained as accidents from one of the other girls. I couldn't tell my parents. It felt so dangerous to make them a part of it. If they suspected anything, they certainly didn't say so. Things would happen when I was little. My doll would fly across the room when I was fussy, or the fire would practically spew out of the hearth if my brother took my potatoes. But my parents shrugged it off as a freak wind gust or a draft in the chimney. I only realized something was wrong with me when I was six years old. A much older boy from school took the biscuits from my lunch pail, and I wished with all of my heart that he would hurt as much as he hurt me. His nose started bleeding, and he swooned in front of his all of his friends. I felt terrible about it."

"Well, you didn't know that would happen, and losing consciousness isn't that bad."

"He also wet his pants…. in front of all his friends."

"All right, but he probably deserved it, picking on a little girl like that." I said, my lips pinched together. "My parents knew right away that I was different. They gave me suppressors for my magic from the time I was toddler."

"What's a suppressor?"

"It's a pill. As I said, I'd always been sickly and undersized, and my mum told me that they were medicine to help me grow strong. But it turned out it was the suppressors that were making me so sick in the first place, cutting me off from my magic, throwing my body out of balance."

She smiled. "Do you think you could find more?"

"Suppressors?" I said. "I don't know. My mum had some sort of arrangement with Mr. Fallow, an apothecary in the Warren. I don't know if I could get them from him myself. Why?"

She swallowed heavily.

"Do you want to take them yourself?" I asked. "Why?"

"Because I don't know how to control my magic. I've tried. I snuck books from the library. I've eavesdropped on classes, but I just cannot seem to control it. I've made windows explode. I made a book fall on my schoolmaster's head from the shelf when he gave me a poor mark. Every moment of every day, I am on guard, and it's exhausting. If I took the suppressors, I would be able to sleep at night."

"It's not a long-term solution. You cannot just cut your body off from part of itself. That's why I was so sick."

"You don't look sick now!" she insisted, tears rising to her eyes.

"Because I stopped taking them. I've gained nearly a stone since then, and I'm a head taller. Suppressors may take away the magical problems, but it's like cutting your body off from the sun or food or air, the things you need to stay healthy. It's a poison."

"But could you just try to get some for me?"

I shook my head. "I don't think that's the right thing to do. What if I helped you try to control your magic? I could work with you somewhere no one else could see."

"Why would I do that when I could just avoid it all together?"

"Because it's a gift, being able to do what we do. We can do such beautiful things with magic."

"You wouldn't say if you'd lost everything in your life because of it."

"You make a good point," I conceded. "What if I talked to Mrs. Winter and she found a way to help you live in Guardian society? Maybe she could do for you what she did for me?"

"I don't want to live in Guardian society. I've seen how unhappy some of these girls are. The girls in the classrooms cry far more often than any servant here. You're the ones strapped into uncomfortable dresses, learning dangerous magic that they have to remember or fall short of their parents' expectations, and being pushed in the direction of men they don't like so they can connect their house to others by marriage. I may be wearing the apron, but you're just as trapped as I am, no matter how pretty your cage is. I just want to go home and live with my family without all this pressure to hide things from them."

"So, has the Book reached out to you before? Or was this the first time?"

She shook her head. "I'm not sure. I was just cleaning your room, and suddenly I was surrounded by that gold dust. It was just so pretty. I couldn't help myself. I wasn't afraid of the magic for the first time, and it made me want to dance. But I don't know how that happened, and I don't think I could do it again. I don't think I would want to."

I struggled to keep my face neutral. I wondered if I would be the Translator at all if the Mother Book had encountered Jenny first. What if the Book abandoned me now that there was another magical Snipe at school? Should I send her away from the school? Ask Mrs. Winter to find a way to place her at some faraway manor? She didn't seem to want the Book or her magic. Perhaps it would be safer for her.

No, that was a rationalization. I wanted Jenny further away because I didn't like the idea of losing the book to someone else.

I'd become accustomed to learning new magic and sharing my bond with the book. Losing it would hurt like losing Ivy or Alicia. But it would be wrong to send Jenny out into the world knowing she struggled with her magic and her identity. It was kinder, wiser, to keep her close.

"Have you ever talked to anyone else about this? About your earlier magic or about dancing with the Book?"

"No, I don't want to be carted off by the Coven Guild's goon brigade, thank you very much," she sniffed.

I nodded. She was a smart girl, but that certainly didn't explain Mr. Crenshaw's comments at the Committee summons. If Mr. Crenshaw didn't know about Jenny, who was he referring to when he implied that there might be a better candidate for Translator? Was he simply trying to intimidate me?

"If you took advantage of your gifts, perhaps you could gain better control over it. Would you permit me to tell Mrs. Winter about you?" I asked.

"Do you trust her?" Jenny demanded.

"Not entirely, but she hasn't done anything to hurt me since she found out about my magic."

"Because it was in her interest not to harm you."

"That's another good point." I conceded.

"Can I think about this?" she asked.

"Yes, please. I only want to help you. I don't want to make you unhappy."

"I want to believe you, but it seems too good to be true. I've felt so alone, here and everywhere else," she said, wiping at her cheeks.

"There are more of us," I told her. "More Changeling children. Don't ask me how I know, but I've been told that one or two of us are born every few years. The Guild keeps it a secret to prevent widespread panic among the Guardians. They want society in general to continue believing in the magical elite."

"What? How is this happening?"

"My father has a theory that magic is a living thing, not just some energy force that the Guardians can tap into. And it's grown tired of how the Guardians have used it, so it's giving itself to Snipes," I said.

"I don't understand how anyone could get used to this," she said, raising her hand to her eye level and summoning a small yellow ball of energy. "The fear that you feel, knowing that you could be exposed at any moment, knowing there's something special in you but being too afraid to use it."

"I am well-acquainted with the feeling, yes," I told her. "And while I'm not pressuring you for a decision, would you at least come back to work for me? It would be nice to have a maid I didn't have to hide anything from."

"I'll consider it."

"Thank you," I said, looking around and trying to guess which of the walls would get me closest to a student floor. "I will just be sneaking back to my room now."

"Wait." She stepped closer as I backed away. "Can I ask you — why are you telling me any of this? You don't know me. I could turn around and tell people about you, expose your secret. You're taking a risk in trusting me."

"Well, not to put an ugly point on it, but who would believe you? I'm a proper young Guardian lady with the support of a powerful house. You're a servant, and no one has any reason to believe you. I'm sorry. I know it's not right, but it's the way the world works right now."

She nodded her head. "That is also a good point."

Using the *Thieves' Bliss* spell, I slipped through the wall to the second story dormitories and back to my own room. I found Ivy there, marching back and forth between my desk and my fireplace, and she did not look happy. Alicia was perched on my bed watching Ivy's pacing circuits with great interest while her familiar, a tabby cat named Rudolpho, batted at one of my hair ribbons at her feet.

"What's going on here?" I asked. Ivy whirled on me.

"I received a token," Ivy said, pointing to a potted forever freesia she'd placed on my vanity. She was holding a small white box with a bow that matched the freesia's blue-purple petals.

"But that's wonderful," I said, pleased that Owen had obviously listened to me about the freesia, but had gone above and beyond my recommendations to get Ivy an additional gift.

"No, because I've never received a token on Sweethearts' Day token before, much less two. And it seems suspicious that I'm suddenly receiving such attentions this year."

"She hasn't even opened the card, so she doesn't know who they're from. She nearly fell over when Headmistress Lockwood called her name. And considering that Callista only got one token when Ivy got two!" Alicia cackled. "Callista was furious."

"What did Callista get?" I asked.

"A box of bonbons from Murdoch's," Alicia said, smirking as she added, "I suspect it's from her mother

"Someone has to be behind this, and we need to start a list," Ivy insisted. "It could be a trap. Or poisoned. Or Miss Morton could have sent it from beyond the grave to poison and trap me."

"You don't think that's an overreaction?" I asked. "Have you checked it for hexes or curses?"

"Of course. It was the first thing I did!" Ivy exclaimed, as if I was very stupid indeed.

"Then you should open it," Alicia told her.

"What if it explodes?" Ivy asked.

"Oh, for goodness sake," Alicia muttered, twirling her blade,

Resolute, in Ivy's direction. The blue bow unwound, and the box fell apart, revealing a small brooch shaped like a rose made of ivory enamel with blush brushed at the tips of the petals. Even from across the room, it smelled delicately of roses. When Ivy touched her fingertip to the petals, the bloom closed and revealed a spray of enameled ivy.

Ivy's face positively glowed with pleasure. "Oh, that's beautiful."

"Who's it from?" Alicia asked, nodding towards the card.

Ivy opened it, and the pleased light faded from her face. "Owen Winter?"

She narrowed her eyes at me. "Tell your cousin that I don't appreciate being mocked."

"Oh, Ivy!" Alicia sighed, flopping down on the bed.

"Ugh, I was afraid this would happen as a result of years of Owen's … Owen-ness. Ivy, it's not a joke. He asked me about sending you a gift, at length. He agonized over making the right choices in order to send you something that would make you happy."

"Agonized?" she asked, frowning at me.

"He was very concerned about picking the right gift. And I threatened him with grievous harm, both physical and magical, if he played you false… and some of his friends… and their parents."

"Thank you. You're a very good friend," she sighed. "I have a very hard time believing any of this or to take Owen seriously. I've never received attentions from any boy, much less a boy like Owen."

"Well, that's very normal. No one takes Owen seriously, but I can assure you that for all intents and purposes, he does appear to like you to the point of spouting gibberish when you're near — which is a good sign, I think," I assured her. "I've known him for a long time, and beneath that haughty and highly annoying exterior, he can be very thoughtful and kind on occasion. And you have to admit that the haughty exterior isn't entirely unfortunate-looking."

Ivy blushed and buried her face in her hands. "No, it's not! And that's the problem! I happen to like the haughty exterior very much. It's quite a nice-looking handsome exterior, and the fact that I have noticed makes me just as shallow and vapid as Callista and her hellhound friends. I have seen how kind Owen is to you. He's very solicitous and protective of you, though he obviously knows —" she paused to glance around as if there might be spies lurking outside in the hall. "— everything about you. There has to be some good in him. I'm just too nervous to spend enough time around him to find it for myself. What am I going to do with this?"

She held up the brooch as if it had the potential to emit a cloud of acid.

"Send a nice thank you note?" Alicia suggested. "One that doesn't include the phrase, 'There has to be some good in you?' That's difficult to follow up, I think, in terms of courtship."

"You're of no help whatsoever," Ivy told her. She turned to me. "How was your foray into the servants' quarters?"

"Enlightening," I said, sitting next to Alicia on the bed.

"I still think you should have let us accompany you," Alicia told me as Rodolpho shoved his head into my hand for petting.

"It's a lot more difficult for three people to sneak through walls than one," I told her. "Besides, Jenny barely trusts me. I don't think she would have talked in front of you two."

"What did she have to say?" Ivy said.

"If she's telling me the truth, she's definitely a Changeling. She came here hoping that she could pass her magic off as the errant work of students."

"Smart," Ivy said, nodding with approval.

"Did she know anything about the comments Mr. Crenshaw made at your summons? About the 'more deserving candidate?'" Alicia asked.

"She didn't seem to," I said. "She swore that she'd never told anyone about her magic, much less about the Book, and she's agreed to come back to my service."

"Good. You'll be able to keep an eye on her," Alicia said.

"And I'll be able to help her, since she's going through the same things I went through," I added pointedly.

"Oh, sure, altruism, selflessness, and all that," Alicia said, waving her hand dismissively.

"I'm very happy you have resolved your troublesome situation," Ivy told me. "Though I might note that I am still very much mired in my own anxiety about *my* troublesome situation."

"I know. I haven't forgotten," I promised her.

Alicia patted her hand. "Would you feel better if I told you that my mother has agreed that you may both accompany my family to Coventry for a month of our visit? So you will miss out on the Lightbourne summer season and are not likely to see young Mr. Winter at any time soon."

"Yes, actually, that does make me feel much better," Ivy said. "Because that means I will be far away from Owen Winter."

I snorted. "And of course, it means we can search for innocent children who need to be rescued from a desperate and dangerous captive situation?"

Ivy nodded without lifting her head. "That, too."

I gave Alicia a long, speculative look. "My third eye is telling me there's a 'but' in our near future."

Alicia shrugged. "Gavin's plans to join my family for the summer have been mysteriously canceled. He will spend the whole summer working with Uncle in the office. Mother is not exactly subtle."

I sighed. While Alicia was fully aware of her mother's machinations, Gavin seemed blithely ignorant. I shuddered to imagine what she would say to me if she knew that a lowly Snipe girl was trying to romance her darling boy.

I shook my head. "No, she is not."

"She'll come around," Ivy assured me.

"I doubt it," I laughed.

Ivy looked to Alicia, who shook her head. "No, she's right. It's highly doubtful my mother will suddenly decide that she's interested in sharing Gavin's time and attention."

"I'm doomed." Ivy flopped next to Alicia on my bed, dislodging Rudolpho from his cozy perch. He gave an annoyed meow.

"How does Mrs. McCray loathing me entirely mean that *you* are doomed?" I asked.

"Because if Mrs. McCray loathes the idea of her son being attached to you, the daughter of a prestigious family — for all they know — and the Translator, how is Mrs. Winter going to feel about her son being interested in the daughter of a second-tier house with nothing much to recommend her?"

"You have much to recommend you, and I will curse whoever tries to say otherwise with antlers and moles and a lot of bad things," Alicia informed her.

"And I will cover whatever spots are left uncursed by her curse," I promised.

"I really do adore you both."

9

"I don't like this," Mrs. Winter informed me as Jenny snapped the last valise shut and carried it out of my suite. "You'll be far away, and I won't be there to guide you if you run into trouble."

"I will simply endeavor not to get into trouble," I told her, shrugging into a violet pelisse that matched my traveling gown.

Mrs. Winter lifted an eyebrow and settled in my fireside chair. I pursed my lips and added, "I will try my best."

The school term was coming to an end. My marks had been acceptable, with the exception of ritual dance where Madame Rousseau had stated that I needed improvement. Apparently, Madame was still holding a grudge about the hollowhorn incident. Spring Interviews had taken place, and the invitations to research guilds had been arriving every day. In some cases, they weren't, which made the agitated nerves of Sweetheart's Day look like a Sunday picnic. We spent our entire healing classes that week helping Nurse Waxwing mix soothing teas.

Jenny and I had established a more comfortable routine now that she'd agreed to return to my service. Unfortunately, that routine depended on mutual silence. I didn't mention her magic, and she didn't mention mine. The Mother Book didn't respond to her any further, at least not while I was around, but it wasn't ignoring me any longer, so I was pleased.

Like most parents, Mrs. Winter had arrived on our final day of the term to help me pack. But I wasn't packing to return home for the summer. Mrs. McCray's begrudging invitation began immediately after school started, so Ivy and I would be taken to the McCray's right away to begin our trek to Scotland. And while Mrs. Winter had given her permission for me to travel with the McCrays almost immediately, she seemed to regret that decision more the closer we came to our departure.

"I'm very proud of your efforts in the last year, Sarah, but it's difficult to trust that you understand what's at stake if you make an error. You could reveal your secret with the slightest slip of the tongue, the tiniest breach of etiquette. Adelaide McCray is looking for a reason to dislike you."

"I've become adept at hiding my origins over the past year. No one at school believes I'm anything but what I say I am, even after Mary's outburst at the masquerade. If I think Mrs. McCray suspects something, I will pretend to be unwell and scry message you, so you can advise me."

"I suppose that will do," she said, frowning. "Is there a reason that you have insisted on my hiring your chamber maid away from Headmistress Lockwood, so you might take her along on this venture?"

"I trust Jenny, something that isn't easy given my situation, and it makes more sense to take a trusted servant with me than to be followed by one of Mrs. McCray's servants at my every step," I said.

"That is sensible, I suppose," Mrs. Winter admitted. "Though I simply do not understand why Mrs. McCray is insisting that you leave straight away from school. It's not fashionable to arrive at Coventry before early June."

"I am getting the impression that Mrs. McCray would like to meet the obligations of her invitations as quickly as possible and ship me right back to you."

"All the more reason for you not to accompany the family in the first place," Mrs. Winter sniffed.

"It would be unseemly for me to refuse an invitation from one of society's most prominent families," I reminded her. "People would wonder why I might reject such a gesture of friendship from the family of the young man with whom I am nearing courtship."

"You are correct," she sighed. "I suppose that underneath this current of concern is the fact that I will … miss you while you're gone. I'd quite looked forward to having you home for the summer. The house is ever so much livelier when you and Owen are home."

"You can always visit your home at the loch, and I could join you there when my invitation at the McCrays concludes," I said, with enough cheek that I hoped it covered my anxiety that I wouldn't find the Changeling children before my holiday with the McCrays expired. Because Ivy, Alicia, and I had been so very secretive about our motivations to visit Scotland, it was difficult sometimes, even for me, to remember that this wasn't a pleasure trip.

We were traveling with a mission, one I wasn't sure whether we would ever accomplish, but I had to try. I couldn't sit in my room, pampered and sheltered, anymore. I'd come to appreciate her support, but it was time to break away from *some* of the safety of Mrs. Winter's protection.

As much as I hated keeping secrets from Mrs. Winter, I simply couldn't tell her what we were planning, and I certainly couldn't tell her about Jenny's magic. I couldn't trust her to twist either of those things to her own agenda. I'd considered asking Mrs. Winter about suppressors for Jenny because she wanted them so badly, but I just couldn't and not just because I opposed taking them at a fundamental level. Asking Mrs. Winter to give me a substance I shouldn't have been taking in the first place would have resulted in a wheelbarrow full of pointed questions. Venturing to the Warren to visit the apothecary that had provided my own suppressors for years would have raised even more questions. It was better to smile prettily and lie through my teeth, even if it meant deceiving one of the most dangerous matrons in Guardian society

Mrs. Winter smiled, and it was almost fond. "I suppose you are correct in that, too."

I took the Mother Book from its locked cabinet and placed it inside the special willow wood box filled with salt to protect it. I whistled to Phillip, who flew from the nightstand to my shoulder and nuzzled against my cheek.

"I still don't see why you couldn't have chosen a more fashionable familiar," Mrs. Winter sighed. "You know, tortoises are quite the thing this year."

"I don't think I'm a tortoise sort of lady," I said, shaking my head.

Jenny came bustling through my doorway, holding my bonnet and gloves. "The McCray maids told me the carriage is ready to leave, Miss."

"Thank you, Jenny. Why don't you join the household staff in their carriage?"

She curtsied and backed out of the room without making eye contact with Mrs. Winter. She was a very smart girl. Mrs. Winter sniffed and stood, straightening her cornflower blue day dress.

"Well, it's time to put on a performance. Be sure to act as if you will miss me desperately."

I snickered as she slipped her arm through mine. "And you be sure to act as if your heart is breaking to send me away."

"Don't be ridiculous. As far as any of these families know, I don't have a heart."

I was giggling as we descended the staircase to find a flurry of activity in the foyer. Maids were running back and forth from the dorms to hand off bags and trunks to footmen. Parents were fussing over their daughters, whether it was to kiss their cheeks and declare how much they'd been missed or scold them for marks that were not up to par. Familiars of all breeds scampered unchecked in the chaos, except for the palomino pony, Gilded Lily, who wasn't allowed in the school building and had to wait outside with his mistresses' carriage. It was a noisy, frenzied mess, and it made me feel oddly sad that I might not see it again. I didn't know what would happen if or when I found the other Changelings. There was a very good chance I would not be welcomed back in Mrs. Winter's household or Miss Castwell's or any place in polite Guardian society.

I glanced around the foyer, as if I could memorize it all, the strange green glaze on the walls, the girls' voices bouncing off the black-and-white tiles, the smell of rosemary and spring flowers.

"Are you all right, my dear?" Mrs. Winter asked softly. "If I didn't know better, I might think you were truly sad."

"I am just taking it all in, Auntie. I've truly enjoyed my time here at school."

"Of course, you have." Mrs. Winter squeezed my arm lightly. "Ah, and there is dear Ivy, the shining example of girlhood who finally motivated Owen to observe Sweethearts' Day."

"She's a very sweet girl, smart and loyal — one of the few people I can trust with *everything* in my life," I murmured pointedly. "I might remind you that she is one of my fiercest friends and stood with me against certain parties, last year. If she's not good enough for your son, I don't know who would be. Frankly, I believe Owen should endeavor to deserve her."

"Oh, don't be so defensive, dear. While I certainly might prefer a girl from one of the major Mother Houses, Miss Cowell has grown into a lovely young lady, particularly now that she's shrugged off her mother's unfortunate tastes in clothing. And she keeps Owen on his toes, unsteady — which I believe is good for his character. Men become so tiresome when they believe they can do no wrong."

"Please, just be nice to her," I said. "She's very nervous about the possibility that you won't like her."

"Don't be ridiculous," she chided me. "I'm always nice."

I burst out laughing, making Alicia, Ivy, and Mrs. McCray glance up at me. I gave a much more lady-like laugh, like the tinkling of a bell. "Oh, Aunt Aneira, you have such a droll sense of humor."

"Indeed," Mrs. Winter muttered as we reached the bottom of the stairs.

Ivy, Alicia, Mrs. McCray, and Mrs. Cowell had formed a small cluster in the middle of the hubbub. Mrs. Cowell was a tall, fine-boned woman who had proudly trimmed her lime green gown with the prune and tan of her beloved husband's house. She noisily sniffed into her handkerchief while clutching an embarrassed Ivy's arm.

Alicia had described her mother as a bit of a gossip, so I'd pictured her as a bright, somewhat silly character similar to Mrs. Cowell. But Adelaide McCray was a tall woman whose thin frame made her no less imposing. Her dark hair was liberally threaded with silver, and her generous mouth was bracketed by deep frown lines. She had Gavin's blue eyes, though hers were colder and more calculating than I'd ever dreamed Gavin's could be. She wore her high-collared mourning gown like a queen, as if it was a fashionable choice she was making instead of a social custom.

"I just don't know what I'm going to *do* with you gone all summer," Mrs. Cowell sniffed. "It's bad enough that you're gone all year at school. I was so looking forward to our spending time together."

"I'll only be gone for a month, Mother," Ivy assured her.

"Adelaide," Mrs. Winter trilled in her most pleasant tones. "It's so good to see you out and about. How are you, my dear?"

"As well as one could expect, Aneira," she said, as the women exchanged air kisses on their cheeks. "I see that Mr. Winter's seat seems secure for now."

Mrs. Winter's voice went ice cold. "Oh, Adelaide, I've always left the crystallography to your family because it's your area of expertise. You should leave the politics to mine."

"Well, you've always been more comfortable wallowing in the atmosphere of the Capitol more than I have," she sniffed, turning her attentions on me. "Miss Reed, how nice to see you. I'm so glad you could join us on our little family holiday."

Given Mrs. McCray's tone, I doubted that very much.

"Thank you, Mrs. McCray. I truly appreciate the invitation."

"I'm sure you do," Mrs. McCray said in a tone that made Mrs. Winter's spine go stiffer.

"Ivy, dear, how lovely you look in that gown," Mrs. Winter said in the sweetest voice I'd ever heard her use. "And it matches that brooch perfectly."

Ivy held her head high, but her voice trembled slightly. "Thank you, ma'am."

Mrs. McCray was much warmer towards Ivy, presumably because Ivy wasn't planning to steal her son away. "Yes, Miss

Cowell, what delightful piece of jewelry to highlight the lovely frock you've chosen for our travels."

"My son has excellent taste," Mrs. Winter said. I could only imagine the smirk she was giving related to Mrs. McCray's accidental compliment to Owen's gift.

I raised my brows towards Alicia, who rolled her eyes a bit. "I believe the carriage is ready. Don't you, Mother? We need to move along if we want to keep to your itinerary."

"Of course, of course. Girls, please say goodbye to your mothers. Ladies, I believe you have our address in Coventry for correspondence, and of course, your daughters will have mirrors in their rooms should you need to scry them," Adelaide McCray cleared her throat and reached out to both women to take their hands. "I swear on my magic that I will do all that I can to protect these girls and provide them safe passage until they are under your care again."

Mrs. Winter and Mrs. Cowell bowed her head, a gesture Mrs. McCray returned.

"That's important," Ivy murmured out of the side of her mouth as Mrs. McCray led our party out of the main entrance. "Mrs. McCray swore on her magic, so if she fails to do everything she can to protect us, she can lose that magic, maybe permanently depending on how intentionally she let us get hurt."

I nodded. "I actually find that very comforting, thank you."

Headmistress Lockwood was standing outside on the steps with Mrs. Reynolds directing the various maids in loading trunks onto carriages. The McCray carriage, with its vibrant silver lamps emblazoned on the midnight blue doors, was not only more elaborate than all of the other crayfire vehicles; it was also twice as large with an enormous crayfire engine glowing at the back of the frame. It looked like it could seat a dozen people inside.

"Ah, the intrepid travelers," Headmistress said pleasantly.

"Miss Reed. Please take care of the Mother Book while you are away. It would be very upsetting if thousands of years of magical legacy were lost because you chose to leave it out on the beach."

"Yes, ma'am," I said, curtseying.

"Miss Cowell, Miss McCray, I trust you, along with Miss Reed, to represent Miss Castwell's with the prudence and poise we expect of you."

I wondered if Headmistress Lockwood would ask Ivy and Alicia to swear on their magic to behave. I certainly hoped not. It would ruin a lot of our plans for the summer. But before Headmistress could make such demands on the girls' loyalty, Mrs. McCray ushered us toward the enormous carriage. "Yes, yes, well, we must keep to our schedule. Come along now, girls. Say your goodbyes."

"I'll write soon, Aunt Aneira," I said as Mrs. Winter air-kissed my cheek.

"See that you do," she said, eying a weeping Mrs. Cowell with a certain amount of exasperation.

I stepped into the carriage with the help of a footman. It was like walking into a small room lined with cushioned benches. As I suspected, it would easily seat a dozen ladies, no matter how imposing their gowns.

"This is impressive," I whispered to Alicia.

"This is nothing," she assured me, grinning broadly. "This is just our transport to the launch platform."

"Launching what, exactly?" Ivy asked.

"It's a surprise!" Alicia said, waggling her eyebrows.

"Why am I suddenly more worried than I was before?" I asked Ivy.

"Because you are a reasonable person," she said, her face tight and uncomfortable. "Mrs. Winter spoke to me. Directly."

"Yes, she's not a monster. She is capable of speaking politely in public settings," I assured her.

"I thought perhaps she was going to chastise me for writing Owen a thank you note. It's unseemly for a young woman to be corresponding with a young man unprompted."

"But he did prompt you, by sending you a gift — strike that — two gifts," Alicia said.

"I don't know how to be courted," Ivy insisted. "I just don't want to make any mistakes."

"Ladies, if you will settle yourselves, please," Mrs. McCray called, making us clamp our lips shut and sit statue still in our seats.

Mrs. McCray was no warmer to me on the ride out of the city proper. She sat on her heavily padded bench seat, her back ramrod straight as she stared out of the windows at the passing cityscape. Alicia kept up a steady stream of chatter, listing all of the wonders of Coventry we would see during our stay.

The lake known as the Loch of Amethysts was once called Loch Cairngorm for the Scottish smoky quartz the water resembled, but when the Guardians established Coventry, a luxury holiday destination meant to take advantage of the Loch's supposedly curative waters, they gave it a more elegant name. Couples would stroll through private pump rooms to drink the waters in carefully vetted crowds. Some pump rooms were more difficult to access than the best gentlemen's clubs. Ladies donned neck-to-ankle swimming costumes to bob in thermal baths carved into the mountainside. The Loch's waters were pumped into these carefully-styled stone chambers and heated to an agreeable temperature with great furnaces and pipes. The ladies might want the restorative powers of the water, but they certainly didn't want to be *cold* while they did it.

Only the *richest* of the rich families built homes in Coventry, usually spread out on the loch's shores so they could enjoy the status of owning property there without having to share the same space. Families from the lower circles could rent rather lovely townhomes near the merchant district, but it didn't come with the same cache. Once when I'd helped Mum serve tea for Mrs. Winter and Mrs. Adlund, I'd overheard Mrs. Winter say, "Oh, you *rent* a holiday home on the loch? That must be so difficult."

Alicia assured us that we would not only take advantage of the baths and theatres and music rooms in Coventry but also the amazing vendors in the merchant district for books and sweets and magical ingredients and perfumes and bonnets, and I was afraid that she would run out of breath if she continued on this way. But soon, the carriage rolled to a stop and we stepped out onto a wide-open pasture, on a hill overlooking the cityscape of Lightbourne. The carriage stopped in front of a staircase leading to a large wooden platform, and behind it —

"What is that?" I asked, my mouth hanging agape

It looked a bit like three train cars joined together by flexible metal panels, sitting on top of an enormous silk pillow. The metal exterior was painted a brilliant royal blue with silver trim and silver McCray lamps emblazoned on the sides. It was floating six feet over the ground, tethered to the platform by long ropes that had been painted silver. Despite its considerable size, the ship moved easily with just the slightest touch from the workmen adjusting the silk cushion. At the very rear of the cars, I spotted an observation deck the size of Mrs. Winter's private balcony. On what could be considered the bow, some clever craftsman had painted *"The Aventurine"* in silver paint. A veritable army of servants was working to prepare the ship for launch, adjusting the cushion's fabric and loading supplies at the front of the compartments.

The Aventurine

And in the middle of them, stood Gavin, dressed in his shirt-sleeves, and tinkering with a mechanism under the metal compartment. He grinned when he saw us, waving some sort of metal tool and calling, "Ahoy, the carriage!"

"Ahoy, the *Aventurine*!" Alicia called back. "Is she air-worthy?"

"Absolutely!" Gavin said. "Just making some last-minute adjustments for a smooth journey."

"Oh Alicia, darling, don't bellow like a fishwife! Gavin, sweet-heart, look at your shirt!" Mrs. McCray swept past us, casting side-long glances at me, while she approached her son. She threw her arms around him like she hadn't seen him in months as opposed to that morning at the breakfast table. She tutted over the grime on his cheeks and the wrinkled sleeves he'd rolled up to his elbows. Something about his disheveled appearance made my belly go all warm and fluttery. I resisted the urge to fan my flaming cheeks.

"*The Aventurine* is the latest in McCray and Company's travel innovations," Alicia announced proudly as the footmen loaded trunks from the carriage to the rear of the ship. "We named it so because aventurine was one of my father's favorite stones, and it's one of the luckiest."

"But what *is* it?" Ivy asked.

Gavin attempted to walk towards us, but Mrs. McCray stopped him by grabbing on to his arm and dragging him to a different section of the ship to ask a question. Alicia said, "We haven't quite figured out what to call it yet, but for now, Gavin is calling it a hovership because it hovers over the ground and it's built very much like a ship. There are large crystals embedded in the bottom of the it — don't ask me what kind, because Gavin told me it's 'proprietary knowledge' and refused to tell me — and the crystals interact with the magnetic fields underground, which cause some sort of repulsion. Then there are stabilizing spells involved. Gavin started describing them, but I got rather bored and started wondering what was for dessert... and I don't remember much after that."

"This is why we don't trust your class notes in subjects that don't interest you," I told her.

"What does the puffy cushion do?" Ivy asked.

Gavin had apparently shrugged off his mother, who looked none too happy about it, and told Ivy, "Well, it stops people from seeing what crystals we're using for one thing, and on the small chance that the ship drops and hits the ground, it provides protection."

"Drops?" I asked just as Ivy squeaked, "Hits the *ground?*"

"Like the kiss of a feather against the grass, ladies, I promise. You wouldn't feel a thing if it happened. I wouldn't trust the safety of people I loved to some half-baked contraption."

His blue eyes lingered on me when he said that, and my cheeks flushed all over again.

"The Coven Guild seems truly perturbed by the whole concept of floating transportation, so the regulations are extraordinary. We have to record every single trip with a special Guild office. We cannot take off without the proper papers. We cannot land without the proper papers. Gavin says we have to put up with it, or the Guild might start examining McCray and Company more closely and look into *real* developments." Gavin glanced around and whispered, "High-altitude hoverships."

"You mean there are ships that go higher than that?" Ivy asked, looking more than a little nauseated.

"You would swear you could touch a cloud," Alicia told her, grinning.

"No, thank you," Ivy said, shaking her head. "I'd like to stay right here on solid ground."

"We will make the trip in half the time," Alicia brightly.

Ivy wrinkled her nose. "Still, it doesn't seem worth it."

Mrs. McCray approached us, eying my dubious expression. "Surely, you didn't think we were going to take a horse-drawn carriage all the way across the country?"

"Of course not, ma'am. I just never thought to fly," I said politely, as she threaded her arm through Gavin's.

She frowned slightly. "Well, some people define their lives with their lack of imagination."

Gavin's head snapped towards his mother, his expression annoyed. Before I could reply, a long gangplank smacked against the platform near us. Mrs. McCray watched as two Snipe technicians secured the walkway to our level. "Ladies, please make your way onto the ship. Gavin, you should go home immediately and take a bath. You're filthy. I would hate for anyone to see you like this."

"I will after I say goodbye to Alicia and her friends."

"You bid your goodbyes to Alicia this morning. There's really no reason for you to be here in the first place. Now, run along." Gavin's mother was using a voice I'd only hear Mrs. Winter use with Owen when he was a small child, dismissing him to his nursery. Gavin's expression went from annoyed to mutinous.

"I had every reason to be here, Mother, as the chief engineer on *Aventurine* project," he told her. "If you have a problem with how I am over-seeing the project, I would of course be happy to meet with you and discuss that at the offices of McCray and Company with Uncle Edmund and the other members of the board."

Mrs. McCray pressed her lips together and shot a glare in my direction before calling out to one of the footman. "You there! That trunk should be loaded in the *guest* compartment, not the utility compartment!"

"We are going to pay for that, later," Alicia told him as Mrs. McCray squared her shoulders like an admiral boarding her queen ship.

Gavin sighed. "Mother is having some difficulty making the adjustment to my working at the company full-time. She still sees me as the little boy bringing her pencil sketches of pirate ships."

"Oh, I'm sure it's your job that's the problem," Ivy muttered.

"Why don't we leave you two to a moment of privacy," Alicia said, hugging her brother and kissing him on his dirty cheek. "I love you. Be a good boy while we're gone."

"That's not funny," he told her.

"It's very funny!" she shot back as she walked toward the gangplank.

"Miss Cowell," Gavin said, bowing to her.

She curtsied back with a knowing grin. "Mr. McCray."

Ivy sauntered after Alicia. "I would move quickly before Mrs. McCray returns her attention to the platform."

Gavin turned to me, his smile warm. "You have the most interesting friends, Miss Reed."

"I've actually never met those girls. I believe I got into the wrong carriage at school."

He laughed. "Well, that is a shame because I did not really need to come here today to see you off." He leaned close so I could smell the scent of leather and light, clean sweat. "I only came here so I could wish you farewell."

He kissed my lips lightly, moving away quickly before anyone could see. "I will write you often."

"And I will answer," I told him as he bowed over my hand. I curtsied, looking down so he wouldn't see the embarrassed glee on my face.

"Safe travels, Cassandra."

"Wash your face, Gavin." I laughed as I walked away.

Phillip landed on my shoulder, chirping excitedly as if this was a much-anticipated holiday for him. Rudolpho trotted at Alicia's heels, looking far more accustomed to this sort of venture.

"Your mother definitely doesn't like me..." I whispered to Alicia as we negotiated the swaying bridge.

"Lately, she doesn't like anyone, so don't take it personally," Alicia whispered back. A footman wearing a nautical uniform trimmed in blue and silver opened the steel door to the interior.

As my eyes adjusted to the lower lights, I tried to contain my gasp. Comparing this ship to a train was an insult. It was a mansion in the air. I thought I was accustomed to luxury, serving at Raven's Rest for most of my life, but this vehicle took it to entirely new levels. Mahogany floors, velvet drapes, chandeliers dripping with tiny crayfire crystals, all done in the silver and blue of House McCray.

Mrs. McCray greeted a thin, humorless-looking man who was dressed as a butler. "Crawford, I trust everything is in order for our journey?"

"Yes, ma'am, the baggage is loaded, and the servants assigned their quarters. The pilot says we are ready to make way."

"Excellent as usual, Crawford. Please show the young ladies to their rooms and prepare a tea to be served in an hour. That should give us enough time to freshen up. I'm afraid our guests have been left somewhat wilted by the carriage journey."

I glanced down at my gown, which was just as crisp and smooth as it had been when I put it on earlier that afternoon. I certainly didn't feel wilted. Mrs. McCray pretended to be a gossip, a society matron who thrived on chatter and the next invitation, but she was far sharper than that. She was what Mrs. Winter called a mosquito, a small biting insect that nipped at you while you weren't expecting it, and you often didn't realize that you'd been struck until long after the encounter — but the itching aggravation left by the bite lasted for days.

I was going to have to figure out how to anticipate her bites. I doubted very much I would be able to return the comments, but I certainly didn't want her to think she could just insult me with impunity. I actually missed Mrs. Winter, which I certainly did not expect. She would have been full of advice on how to handle the situation in a swift, decisive fashion. Perhaps I would be able to send her a scrying message.

My guest room was located at the end of a short, windowless corridor in the middle compartment of the ship. While it was less than half the size of my suite at school, it was sumptuously appointed with a large feather bed covered in a fluffy blue duvet and a writing desk situated by a small porthole. Behind a screen depicting blue flames, in the corner of the room, I could see a small copper tub for bathing.

"What, no marble fireplace?" I murmured as Phillip flew in behind me and landed on the perch Jenny had set on my tiny bedside table. I placed the Mother Book's case inside one of my trunks, ordered especially for this trip in green and emblazoned with white Brandywine apple blossoms.

I sat down on the narrow bed and glanced around the room. In the last few hours, I'd come to understand that while the Winters were comfortably wealthy and quite powerful, the McCrays had a staggering amount of money. Only an indecent fortune would allow this sort of indulgence in what was essentially an enormous toy. Alicia had never let on how well off she was, which it made me love her all the more.

I suddenly understood why Callista fought so hard for Gavin's attention and why Mrs. Winter had pushed so hard for me to enter a courtship with him. A connection with the McCray family, even through a false niece would be a boon to any family, and Mrs. Winter liked to collect connections.

Even thinking about Gavin made my insides do this strange little electric dance. I pulled the charm bracelet he'd given me from under my sleeve — I hadn't dared wear it in front of Mrs. McCray — and stroked the chain. I enjoyed looking at the tiny colorful book covers and running my fingers over the spines. It had been such a thoughtful gift, and I adored that he'd known how much I would enjoy it.

Outside, I heard voices raised as men shouted orders. The bed beneath me lurched as the ship began to rise ever so slightly. The motion made my stomach tumble a bit as my inner ears adjusted to the not-inconsiderable swings back and forth. I breathed deeply and focused on rubbing my fingers over the links of Gavin's charm bracelet.

In my old life, I'd never thought I'd be in the position have a beau or a husband I could love. With my health being so delicate, I had my doubts of whether I would make it to adulthood. If I did live long enough to marry, I had no doubt Mr. Winter would have arranged my marriage to some other Snipe that they thought might tolerate a sickly wife who couldn't handle a servant's full workload. Love would have very little to do with the union.

Of course, love had little to do with many Guardian unions, either, as Ivy said. I was simply fortunate that I was developing feelings for Gavin as Mrs. Winter nudged me towards him.

But could I love Gavin? Very easily because he was easy to love — kind and intelligent and generous — but I didn't know if I had it in me to be a good partner to anyone. I'd lived in the shadows for so long, not even considering those parts of myself that would want to love someone. And now? I was a liar. I spent my days treading on a carefully constructed web of lies. It felt wrong to be starting any sort of relationship without Gavin knowing the truth about me, which was probably why I remained so reserved around him. I wanted so badly to just give myself over to these feelings I was having, but I couldn't. Not as long as I was lying to him.

I tapped my finger twice on the miniscule copy of *Shakespeare's Comedies* because I needed a laugh very badly right now. The book exploded to its full size, red linen cover chafing lightly against my fingertips. Phillip hopped onto the bed, nesting in my lap as I turned to the first page of *The Taming of the Shrew*.

Katherine reminded me a little bit of Mrs. Winter. Who could tell why? It was a mystery, really.

10

UNCERTAIN SKIES

I'd expected stale biscuits and lukewarm oolong for afternoon tea on some cramped little banquette, but we were led to dining area where a small, polished mahogany table was spread with tiered silver trays of warm goat cheese tartlets, tiny watercress sandwiches, and frosted cakes.

While Ivy ate with gusto and chatted animatedly, eyes bright with excitement, it so happened that air travel didn't agree with Alicia. She sank back into her chair, her face a pale, cheesy green, swallowing thickly any time a plate was passed in front of her. While I was concerned for Alicia's discomfort, I couldn't help but think this was a bit of payback from the Fates, as Ivy had been so frightened by the hovership.

Mrs. McCray's manner did not warm as she daintily ate from a bone white china plate painted with silver McCray lamps. If anything, she seemed wearier and more put out the longer we were in the air. Ivy attempted to draw her into a conversation about school multiple times, but Mrs. McCray only smiled thinly and applied herself to her teacup, which smelled of brandy if I wasn't mistaken. Crawford knew his mistress's tea habits quite well. I wondered if she would be more talkative if I wasn't at the table. But as throwing myself from the ship wasn't an option, she was simply going to have to suffer through my silent presence at her table.

I excused myself as quickly as it was polite and made my way to the very rear of the ship to the observation deck. The sun was setting magenta and gold over tall peaks on either side of us, and the grass beneath us was a dizzying streak of dark green. The late spring breeze was brisk on my cheeks and smelled of clover.While I had no basis of travel comparison, it felt like we were moving swiftly over the landscape of northern England, through the peaks district. Still, it was a bizarre concept that we would wake up in another country the next day. I wondered if the air would smell different or if it would just *feel* like I was in some faraway place. While we were obviously traveling with an underlying mission, I was starting to feel the simple joy of seeing something new. I would take it and be grateful for it.

Jenny was there, sitting on the deck with her feet hanging through the railing, munching on golden, buttery sugar biscuits. She seemed perfectly relaxed as she watched the scenery roll underneath her from twenty feet in the air. I wondered when she last got any sort of break or holiday.

"How do you find the servants' quarters? Are you comfortable?" I asked her.

"How do I find them?" she asked, imitating my airy tone and pressing a hand to her collarbone. "They really did fix you up to be a fancy lady, didn't they?"

When I sat down in a puffy circle of skirts instead of answering, she added, "I found them by following that stuck-up Mr. Crawford. You need to watch that one. He was asking all sorts of questions about you. He tried to dress it up like he was just trying to make sure you had all of the things you like, but it felt like he was trying to sniff out your secrets. Devoted to his lady, he is, and eager to give her the gossip she wants."

"So the servants know she's not exactly thrilled by Alicia's invitation to me?" I asked quietly, even though the rushing wind drowned out any noise we made.

"If it makes you feel any better, I don't think it's you she doesn't like. She wouldn't be pleased with the queen of Avalon. The other staff say the missus clings to her son like a climbing vine ever since his father passed. Doesn't like the idea of him growing up and having a life of his own away from dear old Mummy. She wants him right back where he belongs, in his nursery, wearing short pants."

I shuddered at the image of Gavin in a high chair, wearing leading strings. "And they said all of this in front of you?"

"It's more like they talked around it. They said it without saying it. You know how servants are. We hear and see everything, even when they don't think we're listening. I'll keep my ear out for anything else."

"Well, don't be too obvious about it. I don't want you to get in any trouble."

"Any servant worth her wage is sneakier than that," she scoffed.

I laughed. "True enough. So do you have to share quarters with any of the McCray servants? Do you need anything to make you more comfortable?"

"Nah, I have everything I need. I'm sharing with three other girls, which isn't too bad," Jenny said. "The room is so small they have us in bunk beds attached to the wall to save space. But there's a window, which is nice, and the other maids say that I'll have my own room at Moonstone Manse. It's the 'privilege I'm afforded as the servant of an honored guest.' Miss Ivy's maid, Abigail, gets her own room too. She's never had her own room, so she's very excited. Your room on this contraption looks very nice, smaller than I expected, but I guess they don't have room for suites on this thing."

I nodded. "It's comfortable, but …"

"A bit too much of too much?" she quipped.

"Exactly," I laughed. "Certainly not what I'm used to. I'm pleased that you've agreed to come along, Jenny."

"So am I, Miss," she said, staring into the distance.

"Will this be your first time in Scotland?"

She shrugged. "It's my first time anywhere."

"Mine, too."

She frowned at me. "Really?"

"I grew up in the Warren. I went to work at Raven's Rest and back home and that was it. That was my world, and then when I was found out, I went to school and that was my world. I never thought about it as small. And then, here we are. I never realized that England was this big, even after years of studying the atlas in Mr. Winter's library."

"Is it strange to have people waiting on you after all those years of serving?"

"Very. I still struggle not to get up and help every time a meal is served. Nothing about my life is remotely the same since I discovered I had magic."

"I don't remember a time when I didn't have it," she said, her brow furrowing. "So, do you think you'll be able to find some solution to my problem?"

"Meaning finding a way to take your magic from you? No, I don't think so. I could no sooner take a limb or an organ from you. You can't just take someone's magic away and expect them to be a healthy, functioning person."

"But I don't want it to be part of me," she insisted. "I want it gone! I want to go back to my family! I want my life back!"

And in her snap of temper, the window glass of the door behind us cracked just the tiniest bit. I grimaced, wondering how I would explain that to Mrs. McCray. A flying rock? A self-destructive bird?

"I know how you feel, Jenny, better than almost any person could. I still think that if you concentrated on what you can *do* with magic, you would adjust a little easier," I said, standing and pressing my palm against the jagged fracture in the glass. Because I didn't happen to know any glass repair spells, I did what Headmistress Lockwood told us to do, to think of magic as science. I pictured all of the tiny sand molecules that formed the glass moving in their nearly frozen state and blending together again, becoming a smooth sheet. When I lifted my hand, the pane was whole again. The corner of Jenny's mouth lifted, but I could tell that I hadn't changed her mind. "And I haven't found another supplier for suppressants, either. I'm trying, Jenny, I promise."

"You saved them a sheet of glass they can easily afford," Jenny muttered. "Hardly seems like magic worth doing."

"Well, they can't all be evil unicorn slaying spells," I told her.

"Beg pardon?"

"It's a long story," I sighed.

"We have a very lengthy hovership ride," she noted.

As the last fingers of sunset drifted over the horizon, I began my epic tale of dance class humiliation and hubris. "So, what you need to know is that neither Alicia, Ivy, or myself can dance very well…"

11

A COLD RECEPTION IN A RAINBOW OF SHADES

oventry was just as crowded and sprawling as Lightbourne but aggressively quainter. The hovership skirted the outlying areas near the shore, and I could see the carefully arranged restaurants and shops that took advantage of the picturesque view. The cobblestone streets were kept impeccably clean as there were no horse-drawn carriages or wagons — only those powered by crayfire engines — to avoid the earthy animal leavings. The architecture was a mix of early Georgian and Palladian, resembling a Pre-Restoration resort town called Bath. Not one building spoiled the aesthetic with modernity or opposing building materials. Every inch of visible cityscape was sparkling clean and whispered, "Spend your money here."

I'd never seen the ocean, but I couldn't imagine that it was bigger than this loch that seemed to go on forever. As I was pretending to be a pampered and worldly daughter of a Guardian family, I kept that thought to myself.

Like most well-to-do families, the McCrays built their holiday home miles from other residences. Moonstone Manse was built into a rocky cliffside overlooking the water, the Georgian stonework the same imposing grey as the cliff-face itself. A black slate roof capped a three-story façade of neatly spaced, white-framed windows. Each window had its own solid steel shutter that was not merely decorative. This seemed like an odd touch for a leisure cottage. I supposed this read on my expression because Mrs. McCray sniffed and informed me.

Moonstone Manse

"It's nothing like our home, Quartz Hill, of course, but Moonstone Manse was built as much as a defensive stronghold as it was a retreat. When you're people of means, you can't be too careful."

I nodded because I couldn't imagine any other reasonable response. Outside, I heard the hovership slide to a stop and the shouts of servants tying it into place. Ivy and Alicia busied themselves with tying on bonnets and shrugging into their pelisses. Mrs. McCray moved between us so I couldn't join them.

"I wouldn't get too comfortable here, Miss Reed," Mrs.

McCray said. "After this invitation, I would imagine you won't receive another. You may visit many homes in the future but never mine."

I lifted a brow. I knew I was new to Guardian social experiences, but this seemed like a strange way to welcome a guest into one's home. I said the only thing that came to mind, "Thank you for your hospitality, ma'am."

"Cassandra, dear! Come on! I can't wait to show you the house!" Alicia said, giving her mother a pointed look as she took my hand.

"What did my mother say?" Alicia asked quietly out of the side of her mouth.

"She indicated very strongly that this will be my only invitation to Moonstone Manse or any other home she controls," I said as the port door opened and the brisk Scottish wind slapped at our cheeks. Even in the summer, the breeze over the water was cool enough to make you grateful for long sleeves.

We traversed the gangplank carefully or as carefully as I could while goggling at the house. It looked like some sort of magic trick, a fortress built into a cliff. What would it be like to sleep underground? I'd never dreamed of such a place, but Alicia assured me that the Cavills built most of their homes in such a fashion.

"They do so to hide their mining operations and treasures like dwarves. We did it for the added security, as Mother mentioned, and to hide some of our more advanced laboratories — which no one would think to look for in a holiday home anyway, but I digress. There are other houses across the lake," Alicia said. "But our ancestors intentionally built far enough apart from each other so every family would feel like they had privacy."

"Our ancestors knew the value of seclusion to keep out the lesser elements," Mrs. McCray interjected as we approached the carefully aligned servants in McCray livery. "All of the best magical families have homes on the west side of the Loch. Sebastian Crenshaw owns that newer home on the ridge over there. A strange little man but he holds an interesting position on the Senate Inquiry Commission, so we tolerate him."

Mrs. McCray pointed across the Loch, miles into the distance, where I could barely see the outline of a large white stone house.

"Oh, wonderful," I muttered.

"Coventry was a safeguard for women and children during the Restoration. Our ancestors feared that if the Snipes responded to our efforts with violence, the men wanted their families to be safely hidden away. And of course, we needed the support of a village nearby. After our resounding victory over the Snipes, it became more of a resort area like Bath or Blackpool but much more exclusive."

If the hovership was an indulgence, the interior of Moonstone Manse was an exercise in obscene extravagance. We stepped through the large door into a surprisingly light and airy foyer. Portraits of McCray ancestors, each more intellectual-looking and stern than the last, hung in silver frames of all sizes on the three stories worth of silver plaster walls on either side. Everything else was made of carefully cultivated marble, even the tables and the stands where the brightly burning crayfire lamps rested. On the right, a large parlor with uncomfortable-looking silk furniture sat situated around a fireplace large enough to roast an ox and every ox relative — and then some. On the left, through pocket doors, I could see an enormous dining room with a dark walnut table large enough to fit twenty-five people to sit in velvet-upholstered chairs. Mrs. Winter would be furious enough to know that Mrs. McCray had a larger dining table at Quartz Hill but to know that Mrs. McCray could entertain more people in her holiday home? Mrs. Winter could never know.

"All is in readiness, Madame," Crawford assured her as she handed him her gloves and hat. "The kitchens are stocked and prepared for your requested menus. The ladies' maids have been sent ahead to prepare their rooms. Your suite is, as ever, just as you expect it. Luncheon will be served in an hour."

"Thank you, Crawford. It's good to be reassured that a change of location does not dim your efficiency," Mrs. McCray said with a tone so patronizing I was surprised she didn't pat Mr. Crawford on the head. "Ladies, your rooms are in the guest wing: the Lapis Room for Miss Cowell and the Malachite Room for Miss Reed. The rooms are clearly labeled. I'm sure you will find them to be very comfortable. Alicia, dear, you are in your usual room close to mine."

Alicia said, "I'm three hallways and a staircase away from my friends? Why can't I just stay in the guest wing near them?"

"Because that's not appropriate, dear," Mrs. McCray said, pointing towards the sweeping marble staircase to the second and third floors. "Family stays in the family rooms. Guests stay in the guest rooms. Surely, they instructed you girls in this sort of domestic detail at Miss Castwell's."

"Mother, the point of my friends traveling with us was that I would have young people to spend time with, as you saw fit for Gavin to spend the summer in Lightbourne working. If I'm not going to be able to spend that time with them, it would only make sense for Gavin to come to Coventry as well."

She gave me a pointed look. Mrs. McCray's face looked like she was sucking on a lemon. She gritted her teeth and turned to Mr. Crawford. "Could you please move Miss Alicia's things into the Carnelian Room?"

"The Carnelian Room?" Alicia said, wincing. "But everything is so... orange."

"I believe you've always found the color scheme in your room in the family wing to be agreeable," Mrs. McCray said with an arched brow.

Alicia straightened. "The Carnelian Room is perfect. Thank you, Mother."

Alicia grabbed our hands and dragged us up the marble staircase at a speed that could only be considered hazardous in the shoes we were wearing.

"I don't appreciate your using your mother's dislike of me against her so blatantly," I told her as we climbed to the third floor.

"Well, one needs every weapon at one's disposal when at war with Mother," Alicia said, leading us to a long corridor lit exclusively by crayfire lamps surrounded by glass prisms. I imagined this was to keep the guest rooms on the exterior side of the house with natural light so the guests didn't feel like moles.

Ivy frowned as we passed several closed grey doors marked with silver plaques reading, the Tourmaline Room and the Jasper Room. "I don't understand your dynamic with your mother. She spoils you, and yet you seem very angry with her."

"Mother was more comfortable in the days when I was an invalid because she knew where I was and what I was doing at any minute of the day. At the same time, she feels terribly guilty for my condition and tries to make up for it by spoiling me. It's very frustrating being treated like an incompetent child all of the time and even more so now that both of us realize I am far healthier and more capable than I was before. And sometimes I relieve some of that frustration by deviling her a little bit."

"Ivy's right. That is confusing and unhealthy."

"I make my own fun," Alicia said, sweeping a hand over a silver plaque that read the Lapis Room. "Here you are, Ivy."

Alicia opened the door and revealed a perfectly lovely guest room with a squashy sofa by a large fireplace, a thickly cushioned window seat, and a fluffy duvet on an enormous bed, all in varying shades of deep blue. The cushion on the chair of the writing desk, situated under the wide window, also blue. Even the floral carpet on the floor featured blue flowers.

"All of the rooms in the guest wing are named for semi-precious stones. All of the rooms on the family floor are named for precious stones," Alicia told us. "My room, the Sapphire Room, actually looks quite a lot like this only, well, with finer fabrics and newer furnishings. Please don't take it personally. My mother stays in the Diamond Suite, and it's very boring, everything is silver and white. She can't even enjoy a cup of tea in there without worrying about worrying about stains."

"So in the Malachite Room everything is green, I'm assuming?" I asked.

"Yes, you'll feel like you're still back at school, really," Alicia said, throwing open the door to the Malachite Room which, indeed, looked exactly like my room back at school, right down to Phillip's perch on the nightstand and the box for the Mother Book on my desk. At least I would be comfortable here.

"And what about your room?" I asked.

The delight in Alicia's eyes died as she opened the door to the Carnelian Room. My jaw dropped as I took in the sheer orange-ness of the interior of the room. Every single surface was covered in some shade of bright citrus — tangerine cushions, persimmon-colored upholstery, a pumpkin duvet, pillows the color of squash, and the carpet featured an orange tree. The whole room looked quite edible but at the same time ruined one's appetite.

"You won't develop scurvy while sleeping here," I offered.

"The Sapphire Room is done in very restful shades of blue," Alicia said. "Just so you know what I'm giving up, staying here in this ginger-colored hellscape to be with you."

"We appreciate the sacrifice," Ivy assured her, her lips twitching.

"I'm going to be haunted by nightmares of carrots chasing me through the halls," Alicia said with a shudder.

Ivy laughed and flopped onto the giant pumpkin-colored bed. Alicia followed suit and I perched on the end of the bed as Rodolpho the cat sauntered into the room and made himself comfortable in a sunbeam on the window seat.

"How is Jenny?" Alicia said. "Has she told you anything else about her interactions with the Book?"

"She doesn't seem to want anything to do with the book," I said, untying my bonnet from my chin. "She doesn't want her magic. If anything, she desperately wants it removed. She's a little unhappy with my progress in removing her magic to be honest."

"I don't trust her," Ivy muttered.

"Why not?" I asked, turning to her.

"Who wouldn't want magic?" Ivy said. "It's sad and sort of ridiculous to want it removed like an unsightly mole. I know that I haven't lived through what she's lived through or what you've lived through, Sarah, but I have difficulty trusting anyone who could do that. And you haven't told her why we're really here, so deep down, you don't really trust her either."

"I compared removing her magic to removing an organ, but I concede your point," I said, resting my back against the bed post. "But it's difficult to know what you would do given the situation. I don't even know what I would do given the situation. I was lucky enough that Mrs. Winter found a safe way for me to practice magic. I don't know that I wouldn't feel the same way if I was still trying to hide it."

Alicia patted my hand. "And you haven't told her about finding the other Changelings because…?"

"Because the fewer people who know about this, the safer we'll all be," I suggested.

"Because you don't trust her," Ivy added.

"Because I don't want to make her vulnerable to being manipulated or interrogated by Alicia's mother," I insisted.

Ivy's dark eyes quickly cut toward Alicia, who shook her head. "Oh, no, she's right. My mother would turn the thumbscrews on poor Jenny, or at least, she would have Crawford do it in my mother's stead. You've seen how she decorates rooms for guests she's not fond of."

"That's what this room is for?" I said, wincing.

IT TURNED out that travel was more tiring than I had believed, and within hours, I was asleep in my green-tinged room, not to be seen again until the next morning. Jenny claimed to have tried to wake me with a dinner tray like the other ladies' maids had done, but I'd slept soundly and would not be roused. So she ate the dinner tray by my fire while Phillip pecked little crumbs from my dinner roll from her fingers.

The little feathery traitor.

The next morning, Alicia insisted on showing us the town, something Mrs. McCray trusted us to do only under the supervision of an extremely burly footman named Wallace. He was built like tall mountain range, all lumpy shoulders and biceps. His bald head was shaped like a boulder with a heavy, craggy brow and misshapen nose, but his gray eyes were kind when he bowed to Alicia and gave her a crooked smile. I had no doubt we would be safe with him against any obsequious social climbers that tried to attack us while we were window-shopping. In fact, I had no doubt we would be safe from a squadron of dragons with Wallace looking over us.

Mrs. McCray spent breakfast reminding us of several key points of our expected public decorum — no speaking to young men we didn't know, no boisterous or attention-seeking behavior, no boisterous or attention-seeking magic, and Alicia was only allowed to visit the sweet shop once in an afternoon, otherwise the increased sugar intake made her unmanageable. Given the mutinous look Alicia gave her mother, it seemed the mere mention of Alicia's sugar intake made her unmanageable.

It was going to be a very long summer.

Still, she let us leave the house with only Wallace as a chaperone, which seemed to speak to an attempt of lenient indulgence from Mrs. McCray. We rolled down the main thoroughfare in the crayfire coach, past tea shops and ribbon shops and book shops and the multitude of sweet shops all done in the same insistently charming style as the rest of the town.

"We're stopping at the sweet shop first," Alicia insisted.

"Which one? There are a dozen sweet shops just on this street," Ivy said, pointing to three in the same block, all of which seemed to specialize in taffy. "Is this the taffy district?"

"How do they stay in business selling the same thing so close together? Why would you need one sweet shop per person in this town?" I asked.

"It's just the way it is here in Coventry," Alicia said. "Everyone has their favorite sweet shop where they insist the taffy is the best, and generations of their family purchase exclusively from that shop as a show of loyalty."

"Where is your mother's favorite shop?" Ivy asked.

"Snowberry's," Alicia said, indicating the shop with the lurid green awning that promised the most luscious lemon taffy in the world.

I gave her a pointed look. "And we're stopping at?"

"Pinkstone's," she said, nodding to another shop with an

awning so pink it reminded me of the monochromatic horrors of the Carnelian Room.

"Of course," Ivy said, nodding as the carriage rolled to a stop.

Pinkstone's boasted of the world's best peppermint taffy. Every shop had their own specialty flavor and insisted theirs was the best in the world, which seemed both optimistic and geographically unlikely.

Wallace was kind enough to hand us out of the carriage.

"Thank you, Wallace," Alicia chirped ever so sweetly. "Feel free to go down the street to the pub to enjoy a pint."

"Nice try, little lady." Wallace's voice was low and gravelly as he followed us like a hulking shadow to the garish window displays of stacked jellies and twisted clear candy sticks in every shade of pink.

"I had to brave an attempt," she snickered, looping her arms through ours.

"It will be our usual bargain, little lady," he grumbled. "I give you enough breathing room to have a little fun. You don't do anything to cost me my job."

"Yes but our definitions of fun are very different, Wallace."

He laughed but covered it with a thunderous cough. "That is true, but now that you have two friends to help you make even more trouble, I will have to change those definitions all over again."

"Very well, Wallace, no candied limes for you. You've pushed me too far," Alicia said airily, thought she was smiling as he opened the door for us.

Though being surrounded by that amount of pink might have burned my eyes a bit, the shop smelled heavenly — sweet like chocolate and peppermint and citrus and every delicious thing. I was a bit disoriented being surrounded by shelves full of prettily wrapped tins of humbugs and taffy, all with bows in — yes —

pink, but it was a pleasant sort of dizziness in wanting to take in all of the details at once.

While I was particularly tempted by the rosewater jellies, I was seized with the urge to send something to Mum and Papa. They loved sweets but rarely indulged because we couldn't afford them, and Mum was so worried about Papa's health. I paused, wondering if sending them the largest tin I could buy was a nice gesture or something they would see as rubbing my travels in their face? No, it would be Mary who would respond that way. Oh, she would certainly eat every candy in the tin before Mum and Papa could enjoy one, but she would pout and complain about how cruel I was to remind her that she would never see the Loch of Amethysts.

No, no. I would not let Mary's responses control me anymore. Papa would love raspberry jellies, and Mum, she would go crazy for sherbet lemons. I chose two of the most attractive packages and then helped myself to a pink pulled taffy from the sample bowl floating near my head. It tasted of cherries and summer and —

"You know, if Mother was here, she would say something awful like telling you that all of that sugar will rot your teeth or make your skin break out in spots," a cultured voice said behind me, nearly making me choke on taffy. "But I've always wanted to be the more attractive cousin, so help yourself to two."

I turned to find Owen smiling at me in that superior way of his. He looked dapper in his navy blue summer suit with his father's pin securing a tie of blue and white striped silk. I rolled my eyes dramatically, chewing the taffy quickly so I could snip at him. "You know, I was actually trying to choose something to send you because I felt bad for you being stuck in Lightbourne for the summer."

Owen grinned. "Really? That's rather darling of you."

"No," I said, shaking my head as he kissed my hand with cousinly familiarity. I nudged him behind a table featuring a massive rainbow-colored tree of twisted clear sugar sticks to keep him out of Ivy's sight. "What are you doing here?"

"Jarrod Enswick, another Palmer's lad, invited me to his home on the north end of the Loch. I couldn't just let you waltz off and do whatever it is you have planned here. And please spare me any feeble protests that you don't have anything planned because you always have something planned, and honestly, it's much easier if you keep me in the loop."

"Really? That is rather darling of *you*," I said.

"And of course, I would like to try to get to know Ivy better," he said, nodding towards the rear of the store where my afore-mentioned friend was inspecting a pyramid of boxed candied orange slices. "I thought she might be more relaxed away from school."

"I would be careful there. She thinks you're mocking her."

"But she sent such a sweet thank you note!" Owen said, looking genuinely horrified. "I would never do that! Why would she think that?"

"You've spent most of your life cultivating an attitude of not caring about anyone or anything," I suggested quietly.

"But I do care for her," he insisted. "I mean, I think I do. She's a strange girl but interesting and intelligent, and obviously, she is very brave if she has remained friends with you."

"Thank you," I deadpanned. So far Ivy hadn't noticed that he was standing there with me. She was so engrossed in keeping Alicia from buying a box of pear comfits that approximated her body weight.

"I think about her in a manner and frequency with which I've never thought of any other girl. It's almost disturbing."

"I probably wouldn't include that part in your first love letter to her," I told him.

"You think I should send her love letters?" he whispered, peering around the prismatic sugar tree to catch a glimpse of her even as I pushed him back.

"I think you should ask permission from your parents and hers first, but yes."

"Is there a problem, Miss?" Wallace asked, giving Owen an evil eye so thorough that it made me want to giggle. "Is this young man giving you trouble?"

It occurred to me that I was violating the first of Mrs. McCray's points of expected decorum — no speaking to boys.

"No, thank you, Wallace," I said, smiling. "This is my cousin, Owen Winter of Winter House. His parents are my legal guardians, and I live with them at their residence in Lightbourne. I'm afraid I'm accustomed to his poor manners."

"I'll just be watching, from over there," Wallace growled, still giving Owen that warning look as he jerked his meaty thumb towards the shop door. It was rather sweet, really, how this huge man that Alicia obviously adored pretended to be an ogre to protect his charges. I resolved to buy Wallace a package of candied limes if I could find one that wasn't so relentlessly pink.

"Owen, Ivy's not ready to see you. We just got here. She's barely settled into what is a very tense atmosphere at the McCrays' house, *and* she thinks you're playing with her feelings. Also, there are some complications with her thinking that your mother doesn't like her. It's an Italian opera come to life."

"But you think love letters would help?" Owen asked again, his brows drawn together in a determined expression completely out of place on him.

"Any letters would help because, as far as she was concerned, you didn't know her name up until the moment she received the brooch. Explain to her why you find her interesting and attractive without making it sound like a mystery even you don't understand. Give her information and give her time to process it. Prove to her that you are worthy of her attentions. For that matter, prove to me that you're worthy of her attentions because I think she can do better."

"This is the thanks I get for pointing your own suitor in the right direction?" he asked, nodding toward Gavin's charm bracelet on my wrist.

"Yes, it is," I told him. "Now, leave quietly before she notices you."

"Fine," he sighed, slipping a card out of his vest pocket. "This is the address where you can reach me in town. If you need anything or if you decide you're about to do something very foolish, please contact me first."

"I promise that I will inform you of all my foolish decisions," I said, shooing him towards the door. "Please do me the same kindness."

Owen slunk toward the door, pulling his hat low over his face as Wallace pointed his enormous hand towards his eyes and then towards Owen.

"Family," I said, shrugging. "What can you do?"

Wallace harrumphed. "Cousin he may be, Miss, but I don't like the looks of him."

"You're a good judge of character, Wallace," I said, making him chuckle.

After we talked Alicia out of buying a carriage full of candy just to spite her mother, we visited the book shop and the milliners, all while the ever-patient Wallace trailed behind us carrying our parcels. I'd never been shopping just for the pleasure of it. My encounters with Mrs. Winter's *modiste*, Madame DuPont, had been rushed, goal-oriented affairs intended to outfit me as a believable Guardian young lady. I didn't have time to debate the color or texture of hat trimmings the way Alicia and Ivy did. I believe Ivy was simply happy to be away from her mother's sense of fashion while holding spending money.

Beyond the sweets for my parents, I spent very little of the pocket allowance Mrs. Winter had given me. I didn't know what challenges could lay ahead for us, but I was sure every extra penny could help. It was rather fun just to look at the available purchases and imagine. I supposed I could see why Mrs. Winter and her friends spent so much time at it.

Still, I used my time wandering the town wisely. I watched for people who seemed to be acting secretively, magical children wandering around alone, or grocery wagons labelled, *"To feed children being held in a secret facility in the mountains."*

I didn't see any of those things. Coventry was a picture-perfect town where every person seemed to have a smile on their face, Guardians and Snipes alike, but there was a strangely brittle quality to that holiday cheer, like it was a thin candy shell that could crack any moment and reveal the discontent and frustration of their everyday lives.

It was also possible I just had candy on the brain, thanks to Alicia's heretofore unknown obsession with sweets.

By the time we arrived at a shop that specialized in lace shawls, I was rather exhausted, and my feet ached. I was eager to get back to Moonstone Manse even if it meant afternoon tea with Mrs. McCray.

"Just one more," Alicia promised. "I know I've pushed you terribly today, but I've never been shopping without Mother before. I'm having so much fun."

"Oh, it's fine. This way we get all of your shopping urges out of the way on the first visit, and we never have to do it again," Ivy said.

Alicia looked to me for some sort of promise that Ivy was only joking, but all she got from me was the addition of, "Ever."

"You two have no sense of adventure," she grumbled.

"I object to that on multiple grounds that I cannot discuss here on an open thoroughfare," I said, glancing over my shoulder as we entered the shop. I wasn't paying attention to where I was walking and promptly bumped into another woman.

"Oh, my goodness, I'm so sorry," I apologized immediately before my eyes could focus on the face of the person I'd jostled.

That person happened to be my sister.

Mary was wearing a silk dress in a lurid shade of yellow that clashed with her blond hair, cut low at the neck and tight at the waist. While the fabric was high-quality, I'd spent enough time in Madame DuPont's gowns to know that, but the style was incredibly overdone. It was as if she'd run through the modiste's shop covered in glue, and every bead, bauble, and bit of lace in the store stuck to her. The overall effect came across as trying too hard to make the wrong impression, and Mrs. Winter and her circle would have verbally decimated anyone who dared wear it to a social gathering.

That old familiar feeling of being embarrassed for Mary rose like stomach acid, and I spit out, "Mary? What are you doing here?"

The most disorienting part of this experience was that my sister didn't seem at all surprised to see me. She didn't seem to want to escape or hide, despite the fact that she was breaking several regulations for Snipe behavior right out in the open in front of Guardian society's elite. She simply stood there with her usual expression of annoyance, like she couldn't believe I was interrupting her lovely afternoon with my presence. She was brazening through any internal alarms she might have felt, so really, nothing had changed.

"I'm doing the same as you, *Miss Reed*," she said breezily. "Shopping."

And then I realized that I was standing in front of one of Mrs. McCray's servants, and if I had an altercation with my sister in front of Wallace, he would likely report everything that was said to Alicia's mother the moment we returned. Alicia also seemed to pick up on this and turned to Wallace.

"We'll just step in the shop to give Miss Reed and her acquaintance some privacy," Alicia told Wallace in a tone that was more authoritative than I'd ever heard her use. Wallace appeared to be uncertain, but when I nodded and smiled, he opened the door and let Ivy and Alicia into the shop.

"I'll be just inside, Miss Reed," Wallace said, giving Mary a scathing look, which she dismissed with a flirtatious fluttering of her eyelashes. Some things never changed.

I pulled Mary into an alcove in front of a closed linen shop, I pulled Wit from my reticule and cast the blue sigil for silence. To passersby, we simply looked like two ladies having a conversation they couldn't quite pick up. "You know what I mean, Mary. What are you doing here in Coventry? Have you talked to Mum and Papa? Sent them a letter? They're so worried about you. They think the worst."

Mary inspected the lace edging her violet gloves. "No, I'm beyond them now. No one needs to know where I came from, now that I've established a life in the better Guardian circles. Just like you."

I lifted my brow and wondered exactly how tenuous my sister's grip on reality could be.

Mary smirked at me. "You've managed to separate yourself from that life, Sarah. Why shouldn't I?"

"And now what? Have we come to the point of the conversation where you threaten to expose me unless I introduce you to people here in Coventry?" I asked.

"Oh, for goodness sake, not everything is about you, Sarah. You're not the only one who can get the support of a rich man," she sniffed.

"What are you talking about? Who is this patron?"

"Like I would tell you," Mary laughed. "And no, I won't tell you where I'm staying. I think I like having this mystery about me. I like knowing that it will drive you mad *not* knowing. He's promised to arrange a grand match for me, maybe even to a member of the Winter family. And all I have to do is the same that you've done, pretend to be Miss High and Mighty Guardian. It's not really that difficult."

"Are you mad? Do you honestly think he can give you anything he's promising? Do you honestly think you can get away with this? You don't have magic, Mary!"

Mary's lip curled into a cruel line. "Well, that's not how it looks to other people. My patron helps me with little tricks, here and there, the same thing that I asked you to do for me. But you just didn't care enough to because you were too scared."

"Scared?"

"Yes! Scared that I would outshine you in Guardian society, just as I outshone you for all these years. I'm just as smart as you, just as pretty — prettier! I've always been prettier, and you've always been jealous. You've always wanted what I've had, and now, I'm going to take what you have," Mary seethed, stepping out of the cone that protected our conversation. I followed her out of the alcove. "Just stay out of my way. I'm going to have everything I want, and nothing's going to stop me, even if I have to run you down to do it."

With that, she disappeared into a passing crowd of giggling girls. I couldn't follow without running down the street after her, which would violate point two of Mrs. McCray's decorum rules regarding boisterous behavior.

I watched her violently yellow dress disappear into the crowds of Coventry and muttered to myself, "I've got to talk to Mrs. Winter."

Wait, no, I couldn't tell Mrs. Winter. She would come up to Coventry, and I wouldn't be free to look for the Changeling children. She would fill my schedule with irritating social engagements and *not* trying to overthrow a government organization intent on misusing magical children.

At the very least, I was going to have to warn Owen that it was no longer safe for him to walk the streets alone.

12

TRUSTED BY NO ONE…WHICH IS PROBABLY APPROPRIATE

We were very closely supervised in our first few days at Moonstone, so sneaking away to look for the training facility was impossible. We hoped that our (mostly) incident free venture into town would convince Mrs. McCray that we could be trusted, but Wallace remained at our sides any time we thought about leaving the house — walking along the shore of the loch, exploring the McCray gardens, the one time we considered venturing out onto the loch on the family's boat, *The Agate.* He was always right there, the hulking shadow, though a slightly more cheerful hulking shadow, snacking on candied limes.

As long as we stayed inside, Wallace stuck to his usual duties, lifting heavy objects and reaching high shelves none of the other servants could access, so we spent a lot of time in the library, studying maps of the local mountain terrain, practicing spells that would aid in stealth or sneaking. Of course, I had no idea how we were going to get up to that terrain, and when I mentioned that, Alicia, whose cheeks were full of blackberry humbugs, simply shrugged and smirked at me. It was at once infuriating and adorable — she looked like a mischievous chipmunk fueled by sugar mania.

Both Ivy and Alicia were concerned by Mary's presence in Coventry, but without alerting Mrs. Winter about the situation, there wasn't much we could do about it. Alicia made some discreet inquiries to her own maid, Essie, a sweet and hard-working girl who also happened to be a well-known gossip, about any new companions any of the local gentlemen might have brought with them this season — something that always caused quite a stir among the local servants. But Essie only shrugged and asked Alicia what *she'd* heard. All we could do was wait and ask Essie to listen for any details of gentleman putting some new young lady forward as his ingenue.

So we established a routine at the house. In the morning, I would wake early and complete correspondence, then take break-fast in my room with Ivy and Alicia, as any meal taken with Mrs. McCray resulted in me being in insulted in decreasingly subtle ways over thick, bland porridge. In our rooms, we could plan and relax and eat bacon.

Jenny would occasionally join us for breakfast, but she clearly didn't feel comfortable blurring the social boundaries between us. She didn't laugh or share anything about herself. She certainly didn't ask Alicia and Ivy questions about themselves. And when asked about her magic, Jenny simply pretended she hadn't heard and ignored the question.

After breakfast, we would attempt to elude Wallace and go outside unchaperoned to search for the Changeling children. We would fail, because Wallace was exceedingly clever and very quiet on his feet for a man of his size. He was also surprisingly immune to distractions or silencing spells that we tried. Then Mrs. McCray would pull us into visiting the library or a museum or some such outing. We would return to the house and dress in uncomfortable gowns for dinner. I would be insulted over a delicious meal that didn't quite make up for it — usually involving jellied eels because I'd shown a particular distaste for them in our first week there and Mrs. McCray knew I was too polite to turn them away. Afterwards, we were expected to sit in the parlor and play the piano or sing — neither of which I did well — or we would go to bed to start all over again the next day.

I believed that Ivy was receiving letters from Owen, as I'd suggested. The servant in charge of the post, a kind older footman named Robert, certainly seemed to be carrying that little silver mail tray to her room often enough, but she never said anything about letters. She just stared off in the distance, smiling sort of dreamily and occasionally blushing so hard I feared for her blood supply.

For my part, I received no letters from Gavin. Considering that Mrs. McCray paid Robert's salary, I didn't think this was a coincidence. So instead of reading his letters I hoped for, I spent my evenings consulting the Mother Book, searching for a location spell or some other magic that would help us find the Changelings. Instead, the Book offered up a spell called "The Silent Shadow," which seemed to make the caster invisible and undetectable to those around them and could prove very handy.

I wrote the instructions down for Alicia and Ivy and shared it with them immediately so they could begin practicing. Another spell translated to "Deep Division," which I didn't quite understand. It seemed to involve dispelling a dangerous infection, but it described the infection as "like a parasite" and didn't really describe what type of parasite it might be, nor did it describe the part of the body that would be affected by the spell. Everything I'd been taught in healing class thus far had stated that the types of parasites (insect or worm or amoeba) had be treated with different herbs and stones, and you certainly didn't treat a parasitic eye infection the same way you would treat an intestinal infection. The spell didn't even state how that infection would be removed, only the wand movements.

The Silent Shadow seemed like something I shouldn't share with the Antiquities committee. I did not want Mr. Crenshaw to be able to sneak up on me without warning. But I wrote Mrs. Winter a very formal letter describing Deep Division, as this revelation seemed largely useless. While I did include the information about the hollowhorn powder, I did not inform Mrs. Winter that I happened to have a personal supply of that powder. I was still saving that as a sort of nest egg — though it did feel ghoulish to keep it in my room here at Moonstone in my box of keepsakes like a war trophy gone terribly wrong.

I delivered the letter to Robert in front of Mrs. McCray to announce that this was Translator business and a high-priority commission — just to drive it home to my hostess that I was not some feckless girl she could push around. I was the Translator, and I was someone to be reckoned with. But she only looked vaguely annoyed and served me more jellied eel at dinner.

For Mrs. McCray's part, she took us to Sanderson's Vault, the most exclusive pump room in Coventry. We sampled the famous waters of the Loch. It tasted... like water — flat, rather bitter water that smelled a little of fish. I really didn't see the point, other than prancing around an overly ostentatious marble room in one's best clothes to see and be seen. Unfortunately, I happened to be seen by Sebastian Crenshaw.

I'd been preparing for it since the moment Alicia mentioned Mr. Crenshaw had a house in Coventry. I had no doubt the committee would eventually find out my location and Mr. Crenshaw wouldn't be able to follow me to an isolated location to continue to bully me about the Mother Book.

Fortunately for me, it seemed that Mrs. McCray liked her

neighbor as much as she liked me, and he wasn't inclined to approach her. I was sure at some point he would approach me, but for the moment, he just glared at me from across the room.

Given the distance and the time to observe Mr. Crenshaw without being required to speak to him, I could see there was something very wrong with Mr. Crenshaw's face. It seemed slack, like his skin wasn't connected to his skull. Sometimes you saw that when an aging matron asked a lesser Benisse cousin to perform anti-aging glamours on them. Sure, their wrinkles were pulled smooth, but their faces didn't shift properly as they spoke or expressed emotion, like they were wearing an ill-fitting mask. But Mr. Crenshaw didn't look refreshed or younger. He looked distinctly unhealthy, his skin was pale and dry, and seemed to be covered in a layer of fine white powder. And his eyes were different, shinier and a little pink from tiny broken blood vessels.

Had Mr. Crenshaw been ill? Was that why he was here taking the waters? I was horrified by the vicious hope that thrilled through my belly. It wasn't that I wished pain and grief on Mr. Crenshaw — well, not a *wealth* of pain and grief — but if he was distracted by an illness, perhaps he wouldn't have the time to pressure me about the Mother Book or threaten my free will. If he were dead, that would solve a lot of problems for me.

Maybe Jenny was right about magic. It didn't seem to be making me a better person.

ABOUT TWO WEEKS after our arrival in Moonstone Manse, I woke up to an earthquake, which was unusual for Scotland.

"Happy birthday!" Ivy and Alicia shrieked as they hopped on my bed, dressed only in their nightgowns and robes. My mattress being firm as it was, their weight bounced me off the side, and I found myself hovering inches above the floor. My nose barely brushed against the unforgiving floor boards. I turned, still floating mid-air, to find Ivy drawing the symbol for "halt" with her blade, Prudence.

"Sorry about that," she muttered, waving her blade in a pattern that would draw me upwards like a rag doll and throw me back onto the bed. Phillip chirped indignantly, insulted by both the rude awakening and the launching of his mistress onto the floor.

"Thank you," I said, my eyes finally focusing enough to recognize that Ivy and Alicia were holding gifts wrapped in pretty paper. Silver trays with domed covers, the same kind that we received our meals on in the dining room, hovered nearby.

I'd completely forgotten about my birthday. Birthdays felt like something Sarah Smith had, not Cassandra Reed. She didn't have a birthday. After all, she'd never been born. Mrs. Winter had only listed my own on school records because she couldn't think of a more advantageous date. Did that mean I was becoming more Cassandra than Sarah? I'd been so focused on searching for the Changelings, on not being found out by the McCray household, on not letting the Committee take over my life, I hadn't even thought about turning fifteen. I felt so much older than that, like an elderly woman sometimes, which was probably the result of the responsibilities on my shoulders and the secrets I was keeping.

It could have also been the result of having friends who woke me from a sound sleep and threw me out of bed face-first.

"How did you know?" I asked.

"The school newsletter lists all the students' birthdays," Alicia said. "And the last issue of the year included the summer birthdays."

"I knew I should have read that thing," I muttered.

Finally settled on the bed without a damaged face, I sat up and slipped into my robe. We gathered around the fireplace, sitting on the carpet to distribute the pastries and sausages on the trays.

Jenny came rushing into the room, her cap off-set on her dark curls and her dress buttoned wrong. Her apron was hanging off of one arm, not fully wrapped around her waist, which is what she was trying to do as she ran through the door.

"I'm so sorry, Miss! I didn't mean to oversleep!"

I jumped and caught her before she tripped over one of the gifts Alicia had set on the carpet. "You didn't oversleep, Jenny. Alicia and Ivy just surprised me for my birthday. How did you even know we were awake?"

"My room in the servants' quarters are just over this room so I can be nearby if you need me. I heard the ruckus," she said, adding several small logs to the small blaze my fireplace. With summer warming the mountains, we wouldn't need the fire in a matter of weeks, but it gave the room a cheerful glow.

"Would you like some breakfast?" I asked, removing the lid from one of the floating domes. "Toast? Bacon?"

"Oh no, I couldn't," she said, shaking her head.

"What else would you be doing, if you weren't here?"

"Sleeping," she deadpanned.

"Did you have to wake any of the kitchen staff to get breakfast this early?" I asked, turning to Ivy and Alicia.

"Oh, no, Mrs. Duncan is always up before dawn to get the kitchens going. It's why she goes to bed directly after dinner," Alicia said. "And when she found out it was your birthday, she promised to make that lemon-rosemary cake you liked for dessert tonight."

"That's very sweet of her," I said, pouring Jenny a cup of tea. "Here, Jenny, make yourself comfortable. I doubt you'd get back to sleep anyway, after a jolt like that."

Jenny sighed, eyeing the tea as if she didn't want to take it. "It's not right, you serving me."

"Pouring you a cup of tea at my own birthday breakfast is

hardly serving you. It's basic courtesy. Now have a seat and have some bacon. Mrs. Duncan always makes it extra crispy."

"I know," she said, gingerly sitting in the fat green-upholstered chair by the fire. Alicia handed her a plate with toast, scrambled eggs, and bacon.

"Would you like some jam?" Ivy asked. "I think we have marmalade."

Jenny nodded. "Thank you."

I helped myself to some toast spread thick with raspberry preserves. "I think you two might have gone a bit overboard with the gifts."

Ivy turned to the pile of gifts behind her. "Oh, those aren't all from us. They've been arriving all week. We just saved them to surprise you with this morning,"

Munching on my breakfast, I examined the packages and found labels from several girls from our study circle. I noted that my parents hadn't sent anything, but I supposed that they couldn't without awkward explanations.

"Sophia Cortina, Joan Montbatten, Madeline Sato, Jeanette Drummond, and many more" Alicia said. "I have to admit I was a little surprised to see them arrive. Of course, our plans for this summer were well-known at school, but I didn't know those girls even knew my address here."

"Well, I've been keeping up correspondence with all of them since school let out," I said. "They just used the return address from my letters."

"You've been writing to all of them?" Ivy exclaimed. "How often?"

"Every day I write to someone different, sometimes more often if I have a question about spellwork or there's something interesting going on in their lives. Poor Madeline feels very lonely staying with her family, whom I'm disliking more and more with every letter. They sound simply awful. Sofia has some very interesting opinions on botanical compounds for healing spells. Joan is having quite the romance, but she's being very cagey as to who with. And poor Jeanette somehow managed to get another exotic rash — hedgehog pox. I'd never even heard of hedgehog pox, but I looked it up, and it is in fact a disease one catches if she touches the pustules of an infected hedgehog. Jeanette insists that she has not touched any hedgehogs. She suspects Callista did something to tamper with her laundry before she left school, but she's not able to prove anything. And then I write to a few other girls but not as often."

"You're going to give yourself joint failure at this rate!" Ivy exclaimed.

"I miss our study circles, back at school," I said, shrugging. "I feel like we were building something important there, and I didn't want to lose that."

"Are we not friends enough for you?" Alicia asked archly.

"Oh, do shut up," I muttered into my tea, making Jenny choke on a bite of bacon. I wasn't sure if it was because she'd never seen proper Guardian ladies tell one another to shut up or because she knew my origins and expected some sort of retribution from my high-born friends. When none came, she cleared her throat and took a sip of her tea.

"You miss them?" Ivy said, smiling gently. "That's sweet."

"I do, I think. I've never had a wide circle of friends before. And as much as I adore the two of you, if our endeavors go the way we expect them to, we're going to need support beyond just the three of us," I said, glancing at Jenny, who did not need to know the exact details of said ventures. "It never hurts to cultivate friendships with those who can help you."

"How very Winterish of you," Alicia mused.

"Is it?" I said, wincing. "I don't mean it that way."

"Well, it can't be all bad if you got presents out of it," Alicia said, grinning. "You open them, and I'll take the names and gifts down so you can write proper thank you notes."

"Thank you." I opened the first.

My first very brief thank you note went to Alicia, who gave me a new leather wrist holster for Wit. The leather was embossed with what looked like a slain hollowhorn. Ivy gave me perfume enchanted to give off whatever smell matched your mood. Joan sent a set of paste-gem earrings that would whisper compliments in your ear when you were feeling low. Jeanette sent a book on medicinal spells from the Americas. Madeline sent a pair of dancing slippers that would never allow the wearer's feet to get sore. Sofia sent exotic Spanish chocolates. I was overwhelmed with baubles and books and little trinkets from all of the girls in our circle.

Birthdays at home in the Warren had been quiet affairs. We never had much money to devote to gifts or special treats, and Mary always turned moody when she felt ignored. Normally, Mum made our favorite meal, and maybe, I would get a home-made scarf or something my father had whittled. I had opened more gifts that morning than I had ever received in my life.

Guilt tugged at my chest because I knew it was better here not to feel the tension between my parents, not to mute my happiness because I didn't want to hurt Mary's feelings. Yes, things between my parents were better now, but being able to enjoy myself with my friends without worrying about how it affected other people? There was a dizzying freedom to it. I felt loved. I felt appreciated. I had expanded my circle of friends beyond Alicia and Ivy.

"Gavin tried to make it here for a visit, but Mother found a reason for him to stay in Lightbourne for a very important project at McCray and Company," Alicia told me. "It appears that Mother has found several very important projects to keep my brother in

Lightbourne, coincidentally timed for every attempt he has made to leave to visit us. Mother is not very subtle."

"No, she is not."

"But he did say he would like to give you your present in person 'following what has become a tradition of giving you gifts early or late,'" she said, handing me an envelope with "Cassandra" written in Gavin's messy scrawl. "And he would like to do it very soon. For the meantime, he sent you this letter inside a letter he sent to me. I think he's finally figured out that Mother is not giving you his correspondence. I happen to know my mother isn't sending him the letters you're writing. I think you both need to take up scry messaging, even if it isn't strictly proper. What choice is she leaving you?"

"I'm sorry. I know that has to be very awkward for you, Alicia."

"My mother is wrong to demand so much of him, to expect him to serve so many roles in her life. I happen to think you're good for my brother. You keep him young."

"Even though I'm lying to him," I said.

Alicia glanced toward Jenny and shrugged. "You'll find a way to tell him the truth. I just hope it's soon."

"Are you going to read the letter?" Ivy asked, giving the grey linen envelope a pointed look.

I smiled. "In private."

"Spoilsport," she sighed.

"Would you like to take out the letters you've been receiving from Owen Winter?" I asked, making Alicia gasp.

Ivy's mouth dropped open. "How did you — did you tell him to write me?"

"I suggested it as a means to get to know you better and build trust. And before you ask, no, I never told him what to write. I've never even read them."

"I can't believe you kept that from me!" Alicia cried.

"I didn't know what to say about them," Ivy said, her hands covering her warming cheeks. "I don't even know what to think. He's so different in his letters, not at all the aloof Owen Winter we see at school socials. He's sweet and funny and thoughtful… and far more intelligent than I expected. It's been nice, seeing that side of him. I wasn't ready to share it yet."

"How many letters has he sent you?" Alicia asked.

"Seven," Ivy said.

"We've only been here two weeks!" Alicia exclaimed.

"Change of subject. I'm going to go get dressed and ready for the day. You be sure to dress warmly. Alicia and I have a plan for how we might finally leave the house unchaperoned today. We will finally," she glanced at Jenny and added suddenly, "taste a bit of freedom. Get some fresh, unsupervised air."

I nodded, a little disappointed that Ivy still didn't trust Jenny though I saw the wisdom in it. Ivy tied the belt of her robe around her waist and kissed my cheek. "Happy birthday, sweetheart."

"Thank you. I love you both, very much."

"I'm only here for the cake." Alicia threw her arms around me before leaping to her feet and following Ivy out of my room.

Birthday Cake

"You're a terrible person!" I called after her, only to be answered by her echoing cackle.

I glanced around at the chaotic mess of torn wrapping paper and immediately felt guilty for leaving my room in such a state. I concentrated on the paper and held out my hands, waiting for the familiar *zing* of energy to travel along the metal lines of my dragonfly mark. I pictured the air in the room stirring, creating a funnel of wind and pulling all of the paper into a pile and pushing into it into the fireplace. The flames leapt in a violent flash of color. I probably should have thought of the chemicals involved in creating brightly colored paper before I tossed it into an open flame, but it was a nice break from the uncompromising green of the Malachite Room.

Jenny watched this process thoughtfully, her eyes going wide at the leaping prismatic flames. "Is it always like that?"

"Magic?" I shrugged. "It can be. Magic is a tool. It's a wonderful, marvelous tool, but it's a tool. It's all in the intention. It can be useful and mundane, or it can be spectacular and dramatic and make you feel like you've just conquered the world when you've mastered a spell. And it can be awful, frightening, like watching a death."

"Have you ever felt like that? Like you were watching a death?"

I thought back to watching Miss Morton disintegrating from a hateful wraith to dirty grey-green smoke. "Yes. And it leaves a mark on you. But it's worth it, I think. I'm willing to make that trade."

Jenny made a face, as if she didn't think I was playing with all my marbles. "And your friends, are they always like that?"

"Cheeky and borderline inappropriate?" I asked.

She smiled and nodded. "No — well, yes, I suppose. They don't treat me like most Guardians do. And they treat you… they know where you come from, and they treat you like you're one of them. They seem to consider you an equal. I never expected that, and it confuses me."

"Well, they didn't know who I was at first. I didn't tell them until well after we'd become friends. I thought that would be the end of it when they found out where I came from, but here we are. People are sometimes far more decent than we give them credit for."

"But are they always so silly and funny?" she asked.

"Ivy and Alicia? As a rule, yes."

"And the other girls at your school? Is it normal for them to do such sweet things for each other and send each other letters and presents? I've been working for Guardian families for a long time. I've never seen that."

"No," I said shaking my head. "That part, I believe, is a rarity among the Miss Castwell's set. You've met some of the other girls at school, and they're awful. I was just lucky to find a group that found more value in being kind to each other."

Jenny looked thoughtful for a moment. "Can you clear away the dishes the same way you did the paper?" she asked, jerking her head towards the fireplace.

I threw my head back and laughed. "Not without making Mrs. Duncan — and Mrs. McCray — very angry with me."

As INSTRUCTED, I bundled up in a thick grey wool jacket and my best walking boots before meeting Alicia and Ivy in one of the studies on the far east end of the house, nearest the exit towards the stables. The McCrays hadn't kept horses there in ages, Alicia told us, as all of their vehicles were powered by crayfire. But we needed something from that stable in order to start our search. Alicia was carrying a heavy canvas sack that she only referred to as supplies.

The McCray's study was just as impressive as you'd expect in a highly scientific family's library to be: rows and rows of book-shelves, floor to ceiling, with a small alcove built overheard to accommodate even more titles, lit by hundreds of cray-fire lamps. Several large desks were arranged in front of the triptych window, the top arches featuring stained glass scenes depicting the discovery of crayfire. Alicia pressed her finger to her lips as she tiptoed across the blue and grey carpet. She pulled an unlit sconce on the wall in a rare space between two bookshelves.

"What are you doing?" Ivy asked.

"Shh!" Alicia hissed, as the wall slid behind the bookshelf to the left as if on casters, revealing a corridor dimly lit by soft blue crayfire light. "This passageway leads to a secret entrance to the stables."

"Why would you need a secret entrance to the stables?" I asked.

"Moonstone was built as a stronghold, remember? What better way to help your family and servants escape safely but to keep them concealed as they run for transportation?"

"My family doesn't have anything like this," Ivy mused. "My grandmother has a few important family athames sewn into the lining of an old mink cloak, but nothing like this."

"Well, the Dalrymples and the Cowells have always been fairly easygoing families. You haven't made the enemies that the McCrays have."

Ivy nodded, peering down the long dark hallway that smelled faintly of old brick dust and damp. "True enough."

"Is it safe?" I asked. "We're not going to get stuck inside your walls, are we?"

"Of course it's safe. Mother has it inspected for damage every few months. Always prepared, the McCrays," she said, nudging us toward the opening.

"If I die in the course of this adventure, I'm going to haunt you both," Ivy warned us as we stepped into the corridor.

"Young ladies, please don't tell me you're about to leave the house without an escort."

All three of us jumped as Wallace's voice boomed behind us. How *did* that man move so silently? He was standing just a few feet behind me, his enormously muscled arms crossed across his barrel chest, and he looked very disappointed in us all, which affected me more than I expected. Wallace had been very good to us since I'd arrived, and we were being quite cavalier with his employment, sneaking around like this.

Alicia actually unleashed a pouty face, which I had never witnessed her employ in person. Her trembling lower lip and wide green eyes were devastating in their vulnerability and adorableness. "Wallace, please, we just want to take a walk in the hills and get some fresh air by ourselves. We want to be able to talk without being overheard. We just want a few hours of freedom. It's Cassandra's birthday. It's humiliating for us to have babysitter —"

Wallace actually gasped in indignation, so she added hastily, "No, matter how appreciated and beloved that babysitter may be — at the age of fifteen."

Wallace sighed, his arms dropping to his sides. The poor man was powerless in Alicia's wake. "Miss McCray, your mother would be furious with me if I let you go out unattended. And if you got hurt? The *best* thing that would happen to me would be losing my job."

"We're not going to get hurt on a walk," she insisted. "We'll stay away from heights, water, and any surface that could result in a sprained ankle."

"You promise me that you will be careful? That you'll use good judgement?"

"As much judgement as we possess," she swore.

"That doesn't make me feel better," he told her, making Ivy snort. He gave her a stern look, and she pinched her lips together.

He sighed. "I never saw you here. And that is what I will swear on a stack of crayfire crystals if anyone asks. I couldn't possibly have stopped you."

"How could you stop us if you never saw us?" Alicia asked, her expression innocent.

"Exactly, Miss," he said, inclining his head to me. "Happy birthday, Miss Reed."

"Thank you, Wallace," I said, waving as Alicia slid the wall back in place.

Once you looked past the general menace of walking in a tight, enclosed space where we would not be found if we were trapped, the secret passageway was a perfectly nice way to get around. The stone floor was a bit dusty, but it was free of obstructions and vermin. I stood less chance of tripping here than I did in the cavernous parlor.

Alicia walked us to what used to be the family stable, another space carved into the mountainside with openings overseeing the loch, where several crayfire carriages sat unoccupied. In the very back of the stable closest to the secret passage, hung several oversized canoes made of blue-finished wood. They were tethered to the ceiling by way of eight long silver chains each. I glanced up and saw that there were large blue crayfire crystals attached to the chains.

The deck of each boat was open save for a traditional ship's wheel near the rear that controlled a large fan-shaped sail. I supposed it functioned like a rudder, guiding the ship as the crystals forced it upwards.

"What is that?" I asked and Alicia guided one of the larger canoes along tracks on the ceilings toward a large open area in the center of the stable. She turned a crank that gently lowered the closest canoe to the floor.

Alicia swept her arm over the contraption with an air of pride. "The latest in personal conveyance, an air gondola, powered by crayfire and very specific levitation charms — designed by my genius brother, I might add. The stones are charmed to pull the chains, the chains pull the gondola up to high altitudes."

"That seems like a very dangerous and silly way to travel when you have perfectly safe carriages that stay on the ground," Ivy told her. "Need I remind you of your vision of having no future? Maybe this is how that happens!"

"It's actually safer than carriage travel, and it's definitely safer when someone, say, wants to travel into the mountains where there are no roads."

"How high can it go?" I asked.

"We're not sure yet, but some of the racing models at Gavin's labs topped out at four thousand feet."

"No," Ivy said, shaking her head as she marched right back to the secret passage. Alicia caught her arm and dragged her back to the gondola. "No, Alicia, I mean it. I humored you with the hover-ship because it was only a few feet off of the ground. This is not a matter of cowardice. It's a matter of common sense. Falling from a great distance causes injury."

"Do you honestly think I would let you get hurt, Ivy?" Alicia asked.

"No?" Ivy said, not sounding completely sure.

"I wouldn't put you in this gondola unless it was safe," Alicia promised. "For the most part."

Ivy groaned and pinched the bridge of her nose.

"If this is such a convenient and safe method of travel, why don't we see these all over Lightbourne?" I asked.

"Well, we're still in the testing phases, as I said. Also, Light-bourne has too many tall buildings. The skies are a bit more open here in Coventry, smaller populations and all that. Gavin thought this would be a better place to try them out. Besides, the regula-tions on the hovership were enough to want him to keep them out of Lightbourne."

"You could barely hold down your dinner on the hovership," I reminded her. "How are you going to feel, being tossed around on a much smaller vessel?"

"I have taken all of the motion illness remedies I could get my hands on, so I should be fine," Alicia said.

"Well, that doesn't sound safe, either," Ivy muttered.

"So we're going to steal an airship from your family and go on a secret mission into the mountains after we promised Wallace we would stay away from potential risks?" I asked.

Alicia nodded. "Precisely."

"What about your mother? Doesn't she expect us to go calling or some such thing? What happens when she asks what shops we visited or whether we saw Lady Something-or-Other at the pump room?"

"I left our agenda rather vague when I spoke to my mother."

"What does that mean?"

"I told her we had plans this morning, and every time she asked what those plans were, I changed the subject," she said, turning another crank that caused a series of doors to open up overhead, revealing a well-like tunnel to the open sky.

"This whole endeavor is bringing out a disturbing aspect of your personality," I told her.

Alicia secured her hair with a thin wool scarf and climbed into the boat. "Are you coming?"

"How are we going to operate this thing?" Ivy asked as we climbed in after her. The gondola was deeper than I expected, and the sides came up to our hip level, which I hoped would keep us from pitching overboard in the sky.

"It's really quite simple," Alicia assisted. "Tap your blade to the center crystal and then make this sigil." She demonstrated a twisted shape that looked like a small blue waterspout. "And shout, 'Skyward!'"

We took out our knives and followed her instructions. The ship lurched up beneath our feet, pulling us through the opening in the stone ceiling, only to jerk to a stop. All three of us toppled to our bottoms with a considerable amount of yelping. I peered over the gunnel to see two of the anchoring chains, still tethered to the ceiling, had reached the end of their lengths and were holding us in place.

"What in the world!" Ivy yelled, shoving her thick dark hair back from her face.

To my surprise, no one came running into the stable to find us thrashing around on a stolen gondola. Somehow, the Mother Book's Silent Shadow spell rose through the panic, and I quickly cast it over the ship and ourselves. It wouldn't do to escape from the stables only to be spotted and brought down before we could even begin.

"I probably should have mentioned that we needed to remove the anchor chains holding us to the ground," Alicia admitted.

We groaned collectively as Ivy and Alicia scrambled to their knees and loosened the anchor chains from the moorings. The ship rose sharply, which was a little easier to weather when one wasn't standing. I kept a close eye on the stable as we floated away, but no one came running to stop us. However, once we broke free to the open sky, Phillip flitted from the general direction of the house and landed on my shoulder.

"I suppose you can't resist a nice flight, hmm?" I asked, rubbing a gloved finger over his head. He cooed and nuzzled against my hand.

Now that we'd stolen the gondola, we had to fly it, which took some time to figure out. Phillip chirped what sounded like instructions for the silly humans who didn't know how to fly, but since none of us spoke bird, we didn't find it particularly helpful. But after some false starts and one plummet towards a rather tall peak which we all agreed we would never speak of again for the sake of our friendship, we finally got a sense for how to control the ship.

In the distance, I could see the city of Coventry. It looked like a tiny maze, with its side streets and puzzle-piece neighborhoods. Somewhere out there, Mary was helping some mysterious bene-factor plot against me. I'd spent a lot of time thinking about this over the last few days. I tried to search myself for some speck of hurt or surprise, but all I felt was resigned. Somehow, I'd known for a long time that it would come to this. Sighing, I wrapped my scarf tighter around my neck and covered my chin.

The wind was cold against our faces, even in summer, and I was happy I'd listened to Alicia about the warm clothes. The motion illness remedies seemed to have worked for her. She was able to navigate us west of town, and it was all I could do not to hang over the gunnel in awe of the country side. I'd never seen anything like the mountains, their rough grey-green peaks rising like the fists of angry giants against the sky. They seemed to go on forever into the horizon, and it almost made me dizzy when I thought about the sheer scope of what we could see from that height.

The world was much larger than I'd ever imagined. I'd only lived in one tiny corner of it, only ever saw myself living in that tiny corner. I knew that the Winters had a house in the south of France and another in Coventry — called Raven's Roost of all things. Because Mr. Winter was a bit of a recluse and didn't enjoy socializing beyond what was absolutely require of him, they rarely ventured that far. Those houses were staffed by other families. We simply worked less during the Winters' absence.

For the first time, I let my imagination reach further. What could other places be like? The Winters sometimes traveled to France on holidays, where it was sunny and warm. Mrs. Winter often spoke of America but not necessarily in glowing terms. The only positive she mentioned was an abundance of rolling farm-land. Madeline Sato had visited Japan to meet relatives and made it sound so peaceful and beautiful with snow-topped mountains and living trees twisted by wind. What if I could see those places, too? What if I could find a way to live far away from anyone who knew me as Sarah or Cassandra? And then those dangerous thoughts of handing the Book over to Jenny as the new Translator popped up again, and I shook them off in favor staring at the Weeping Sisters.

Alicia didn't have to tell me we'd reached the fabled range as I recognized them immediately from my dream. They looked exactly as they had in my vision, three tall mountains sending rivers of tears into an abyss. The mist of the waterfalls swirled out through the distance to our ship, leaving tiny silvered beads on our lashes and hair.

Alicia worked the ship out in circles, systematically skimming over the hills, trying to find any sign of people living in the mountains. But other than awe-inspiring countryside, we saw nothing. We sagged against the bow and stopped exclaiming over every little blip in the landscape, losing our enthusiasm as the hours wore on. Even Phillip lost interest and nested into the drape of my skirt for a nap.

"This is ridiculous," I sighed, slumping to the deck. "We're never going to find it. I've sent us on a potentially deadly wild goose chase for no bloody reason."

"Well if a few hours of searching doesn't reveal results on our first day, it's clearly too difficult, and we should just give up," Ivy said, blithely.

"You know, it's becoming very difficult to tell when you're joking," I told her. "I never should have taught you the malevolent magic of sarcasm."

"Good," she said, grinning. "We'll come back and try again. We have the time. We have weeks. It may just take more time than we expect."

"All right," I sighed, pushing to my feet. "We have been out for much longer than we promised Wallace. Let's head back to the house before Mrs. McCray realizes I've stolen more than just her son."

"Don't be surprised when she checks your trunks for the good silver before you leave the house," Alicia observed as she turned the wheel to shift our course. Suddenly, Phillip chirped from his refuge in my scarf. He flitted to the wheel casing and hopped up and down while chittering, as if he was quite angry about this change of direction.

"What's he trying to tell us?" Alicia asked.

"I haven't the foggiest," I said. "Most of his communications are largely unintelligible, and those that are pointed sound rather obscene."

Phillip chirped one last time and darted off of the gondola entirely, flying due east. Ivy watched him disappear into the clouds and looked to me. "Do you think he just flew away because he thinks we're about to crash?"

I frowned. "Probably not."

"Do you think he wants us to follow him?"

Before I could answer, a strange sensation spread from my chest to my hands, trembling along the metal lines of my drag-onfly mark. It was as if I was being drawn after Phillip hands-first by an enormous magnet. "Yes, turn in that direction."

Alicia spun the wheel to follow after my haughty blue blur of a familiar. We eased into a region of mountains that were separated by great valleys, making climbing them seem both inadvisable and impossible. We came close to a gentle sloping mountain covered in gorse and thin grass, and I was seized by the sudden urge to jump overboard.

"Stop!" I flung my arm up and the gondola dropped below the rockline, so it wouldn't be spotted. The gondola settled abruptly on the grass and the chained crystals dropped in neat coils around the hull. I wasn't sure how I had done that, but it seemed to have settled the ship sufficiently on the grass.

"That is not how we land the gondola, Sarah!" Alicia hissed. "There are procedures!"

"Shhh," I whispered, climbing over the side of the gondola, with my right ear tilted towards the sky.

Ivy whispered, "What?"

"Don't you feel it?" I asked.

"The wind?" Ivy asked exasperated with me. "Yes, it's cold here. Are you determined to die on your birthday? Is that what this trip was about? Some misguided attempt at ironic symmetry?"

"Magic," I said. "It's like the hair is rising on my arms. Can't you feel it?"

I crawled on my hands and knees up the ridge until I could see over its edge. Alicia crawled to my side and handed me a pair of binoculars from her canvas bag. I peered through their lenses and gasped in horror at the scene below.

13

THE CHICKENS INSIDE THE CRACKED EGG

The mountain just below our ridge was open at the top like a cracked shell standing in an egg cup. From the ground, it would look like any other mountain, but from the edge of the crater, we could see a completely level section had been carved out of the mountain and several austere biscuit box buildings there painted in shades of lifeless grey. In the center of these buildings lay a large open courtyard where a dozen or so children dressed in plain black cotton clothes stood in carefully spaced rows of three, following the movements of a witch leading them through defensive spells.

Training Facility

"That's it," Ivy whispered, her expression horrified as she took another pair of binoculars from Alicia. "Oh, I'd hoped that it was just some preposterous rumor and we would spend this summer chasing phantoms, but there it is."

Fog slipped over the edge of the cup, falling into the depression and swirling around the students' feet. It made them look like they were walking on clouds, though their surroundings were far from heavenly. We watched them work as the cold, damp wind crept down our collars like clammy fingers. The children represented a wide scope of sizes, ages, and ethnicities. The youngest looked to be around seven, a little dark-haired girl with almond-shaped eyes and steady legs as she moved through her forms. The oldest looked to be a tall boy of sixteen with reddish-brown hair and huge ham-sized hands clutching his practice blade. The one thing they had in common was that they looked remarkably healthy for children held captive. Their eyes were bright and cheeks flushed from the fresh air and wind. They looked sturdy and well-nourished. They moved with the grace of children who exercised frequently.

I supposed it made me feel a little better that they didn't seem to be starving or tortured. But still, they certainly didn't look happy. Focused, yes, but not overflowing with the natural joy of children. This could have been me. I could be standing in that foggy courtyard, far away from my parents and anything I knew. I would have lost the opportunity to know Ivy and Alicia and the other girls. I would have lost the opportunity to know Gavin. I wouldn't know what the world looked like beyond the grey drudgery of living under someone else's control. It wasn't right.

I noticed that the children weren't holding real ritual athames but wooden practice blades. I'd seen the wooden dummy blades before used with the youngest students at Miss Castwell's. Designed to allow the student to practice spell motions without cutting themselves, the wooden blades sent out a shower of silver sparks when the appropriate motions were achieved.

The Changelings appeared to be learning what Headmistress Lockwood called the "Lady's Resolve" charm. I was sure it was called something different at Palmer's or other magic schools, but the spell essentially focused one's magic to create a bubble of energy that would send all those standing nearby flying back five feet, farther if one concentrated on distance while making the tilted, yellow, vaguely S-shaped sigil required. Headmistress Lockwood said the charm was intended to help young ladies protect their virtue from overzealous suitors, but it seemed it could also come in handy if one was protecting an important government official. Of course, it would only give the Changeling time to prepare another spell for offense, but those few precious seconds of the attackers' distraction could mean the difference between life and death.

Their teacher was a short, white-haired woman, dressed in a dull grey blouse and a long matching skirt that seemed to be separated up the middle like a very loose pair of trousers. She called instructions and corrections to the children as they moved through their forms. Her voice sounded not cruel but certainly devoid of the encouragement we received at Miss Castwell's. These were not the pampered sons and daughters of Guardian society. These children were being trained like soldiers — just cold, hard instruction and high expectations.

The only person who showed any affection for the children was a plump, ginger-haired matron with rounded, freckled cheeks and a thick Scottish accent. She served them an enormous lunch of steaming soup and thick sandwiches, encouraging them to eat their fill with affectionate nicknames called so loud I could hear them even from our vantage point. She called the group at large "my little chickens," but each child seemed to have their own claim on her heart. The oldest boy, the one who ducked his head and cringed when she called him "sweetling," was her particular favorite, but all of them were give their own nicknames, "dearest" and "little bairn." In fact, that was how we differentiated each child in the notes Ivy was manically scribbling in a notebook Alicia supplied. "*Sugar lump*, boy, approximately eleven years old, brown hair, seems gifted at levitations." Or "*Wee darling*, girl, approximately nine years old, South Asian descent, particularly clever at face-cloaking." She also noted any adult we saw, their description, and what we thought their position might be.

While there were several buildings available, they seemed to spend most of their time in their practice yard. They even ate their luncheon outside on a long wooden table against the far wall. We hunkered behind the rocks, watching as forms practice turned to sparring. Bigger children were paired with much smaller partners and given real ritual blades to cast spells, meaning the smaller children were tossed bodily across the court-yard, knocked down, and generally left bruised and battered while the teachers yelled instructions. From what I could see the through the binoculars, the older children felt uneasy about this task. They seemed to be pulling their spells, trying to do as little damage as possible to their smaller classmates even as the instructors screamed for more.

"How could they do that?" Ivy whispered. "If they have real athames, why don't they just turn the spells on their teachers?"

"I would imagine the teachers have thought of that," Alicia said. "Counterspells or wards? The older children seem protective of the younger ones. Perhaps it's a threat against them? Or there's some other system in place we can't see?"

By the afternoon, we proceeded to be astonished and horrified when we realized that young children were being taught advanced level magic, advanced magic that Headmistress Lockwood was reluctant to teach the senior students because she didn't think it was safe to teach us how to change our faces to disguise ourselves. Far beyond a mere glamour, face-cloaking involved shifting the bones in one's face to achieve another person's appearance. It was nasty and intensive magic. They were teaching this technique to *children?* What possible reason could they need it?

"We should go," Ivy whispered. "We can't do anything for them today. We've found them. We've managed to do it without getting caught, which is a small miracle. I've copied down our heading so we can find the school again. And now, we go back to the house and make some sort of plan to get them out of here."

I nodded. "I hate to admit it, but you're right. I don't want to leave them here for one more minute, but what are we going to do? Drag them back to Moonstone Manse and hide them in our rooms? Hope that no one notices as we feed and house a dozen children? We need a plan — a good one. And Mrs. McCray is only going accept our absence for so long before sends Wallace out looking for us with a small army of footmen."

"Alicia, can we pilot the boat back to the house without being seen?" Ivy asked, but Alicia was still staring into the courtyard through her binoculars. "Alicia?"

"Sweetling is very handsome, don't you think?" Alicia said, her cheeks going pink as she watched the children jog in circles around the courtyard. I supposed that counted as a sort of recess.

Sweetling was, in fact, very handsome. Tall and broad with auburn hair and a raw-boned face, he would probably reach Wallace-proportions, in terms of size, when he was fully grown. He would dwarf Alicia if they stood side-by-side, something I didn't think she would mind too much given the way she was looking at him.

"He seems very kind, the way he takes care of the younger children. So many boys of his size would be prone to bullying, to push those smaller children around, in a situation where they have no power of their own. It's just nice to see someone who doesn't take advantage of his circumstances," she sighed.

Ivy smirked and seemed to open her mouth to tease Alicia, and even though Alicia thoroughly and completely deserved it considering how often she teased us both, I shook my head. This was the first time I'd ever heard Alicia express interest in a boy, much less list his virtues. Ivy pinched her mouth shut, but she didn't look thrilled to miss her opportunity for mockery.

As we were packing up any evidence that we'd camped there, the children were led into the building marked "Classrooms." I could only hope that they were being taught arithmetic and geography, but I doubted it. With the children inside, we watched for any signs of other adults or staff or guards. The courtyard remained empty and eerily silent.

I didn't want to leave. I wanted to march into that abyss, blade drawn, and demand that those wretched teachers release the Changelings right that minute. Of course, that would probably result in my capture and being turned over to the Inquiry Commission, not to mention ruining Alicia and Ivy's lives. We had to be patient and thoughtful. We had to have a plan. We had to have a much larger gondola because we could not carry all of those children in this little canoe. It wouldn't be safe.

Still, it felt wrong to leave those children behind in such a miserable place when I was going back to a soft, warm bed, rose-perfumed bathwater, and a hot dinner — that would most likely include jellied eels, but that was beside the point. I was going to a warm, safe place, where some people, at least, loved and valued me. What did these children have besides an affectionate cook?

Reluctantly, we climbed back in the gondola and pushed hard away from the crater, the damp wind slapping at our cheeks as we rose. I focused on the tasks of launching the gondola safely. Once the Weeping Sisters were out of sight, swallowed by a grey curtain of clouds, all of the tension in my body seemed to drain away. I slumped against the deck as my thoughts whirled.

I turned, propping my back against the wood of the gondola and staring at the clouds rolling so close overhead. I thought back to my meeting with Sebastian Crenshaw and his cronies and how easily they thought they could replace the Translator — a young girl mystically connected to one of the great magical artifacts of our time. Snipe children without family or connection would be considered expendable. They were magical cannon fodder.

"Are you all right?" Ivy asked gently, sitting beside me.

"No, I'm not. Not at all," I said, shaking my head. "They were just children. That's not a childhood they're getting. Even young Snipes get to go play after their work is done. Something tells me they don't get to run for fun after classes. I didn't see a swing or even a ball in that courtyard. The only affection or softness in their lives seems to come from the cook with all the funny nick-names. It's not right, Ivy. It could have been me so easily if someone else found out about my magic. It's not fair that I managed to escape that fate just because Mrs. Winter didn't know it was an option."

I reached up and surreptitiously swiped a tear from my cheek.

"We're going to find a way to help those who want to leave," Ivy said. "We'll make it right. You found it, Sarah, when no one else cared to look. That matters."

"I had help," I conceded, taking her hand and squeezing it. She laughed and laid her head on my shoulder, a welcome warm weight against the chill. "Now I just have to keep Mrs. Winter from finding out what I'm planning while fending off a Senate committee as they try to snatch the Mother Book from me. Oh, and keeping Mary from ripping apart my complicated web of lies and Mrs. McCray from snatching Gavin from my life entirely."

"That should be easy," Alicia said, guiding the sails towards her home. "We can work it out over afternoon tea."

I snickered. "And possibly some cakes."

Flying back was a bit easier since we had some idea of where we were going. It took all three of us to aim the gondola to the McCray's landing pad, but we managed to do it without damaging the ship or ourselves. We got back it back into the stables, tying it back into place without anyone noticing, which was no mean feat considering the number of servants the McCrays employed. We secured the gondola and scurried out, giggling nervously to ourselves as we traversed the bumpy stone floor. Alicia was prac-tically giddy as we walked out of the stone stable into the sunlight.

"Wait, why aren't we taking the secret passageway back into the house?" Ivy asked.

"We're going to have to act like we're coming back from a very long nature walk," I said. "We can't do that if we're sneaking back into the house through the study."

"I can't believe no one even noticed that we took it," Alicia whispered, her eyes fever-bright and her grin manic. "It feels... exhilarating, doing things we're not supposed to do and getting away with it. Let's do other bad things. Let's steal a carriage or a boat! Let's switch the crayfire crystals in the streetlamps with shiny rocks!"

"We just awoke a monster. This can only go badly from here out," Ivy told me as I stared at our friend in alarm.

"I'm just saying that the three of us clearly have a skill for this sort of thing!" Alicia exclaimed. "We could probably steal Merlin's Wand from the National Museum, and no one would know!"

Fortunately, Alicia spouting her increasingly elaborate criminal plots had me smiling by the time we reached one of the rear doors into the manor. Crawford, the most loyal of Mrs. McCray's servants, met us at the door with a disapproving expression and a silver tray stacked with damp, hot towels.

"There are visitors waiting for you in the parlor, Miss Alicia. I recommended that you change to be suitable for company, but your mother insists that you join her and your guests."

Crawford cleared his throat gave us a pointed look toward the tray. Alicia sighed and grabbed one of the steaming lavender-scented towels. She wiped her face and hands with it, dropping the used towel onto an empty tray. Ivy and I exchanged a glance and followed suit. Mrs. McCray stepped out into the hall wearing a formal slate-colored afternoon gown and spotted us. She sighed with a very put-upon expression. "Alicia, girls! What have you been doing! Look at you! All windblown hair and chapped cheeks! Have you been walking in the foothills? I told you that's too much exercise for you! Ladies, really, you mustn't encourage her to push herself past her limits! There is entertainment enough to be found in the pump rooms and museums. And if you must go outside, the beach or the park are much more ladylike, wholesome activities!"

As Crawford helped us shrug out of our jackets, I saw mischief glimmer in Alicia's eyes. Fooling her mother into thinking we'd been traversing the hills all day seemed to only add to her enjoyment of our nefarious activities. I would have to put a stop to this before she began robbing banks… or became the world's tiniest highwayman.

"We're sorry, Mrs. McCray," I said. "I've never seen anything so beautiful as the hills around the Loch, and Alicia promised she was feeling very well this morning."

"Next time, I hope you all show better judgement," Mrs. McCray said, herding us all towards the parlor. I glanced at one of the long mirrors as we passed and saw that, while Ivy's curls had arranged themselves around her face in a fetchingly casual manner, my hair was sticking out at all angles like a great helmet of frizz. Other than looking a bit squished by her scarf, Alicia looked just fine. She was the wisest of us all.

I was seized with the sudden dread that Mrs. McCray was shoving me into the parlor for some impromptu meeting with Gavin at the very moment my head looked like I had been trapped in a very specific hurricane. I smoothed my hair back from my face as best I could, knowing that comb-less hands could only do so much.

Sighing, Mrs. McCray opened the double doors to the parlor and swept inside. Instead of Gavin's tall frame folded onto the couch, I saw Owen rising smoothly to his feet. His mother was at his side wearing a lovely peridot-colored traveling gown. While Mrs. Winter was staring right through me, Owen only had eyes for Ivy, who had turned the color of a distressed beet.

"Auntie Aneira!" I exclaimed, rushing forward to curtsy before my beloved aunt. "What are you doing here!"

"I know it's a bit after the usual calling hours, dear, but we just couldn't wait to see you after making the journey north," she said, kissing my cheeks. "Happy birthday, dear."

"Mother decided to come north, cousin, as a surprise to wish you a happy birthday, with my encouragement," Owen said, giving me a light hug. "It was becoming terribly boring at Jarrod Enswick's. His family plays parlor games every night. Can you imagine? It was disgustingly domestic — made my skin crawl, to be honest. Besides, our holiday home could stand a good airing."

"That's very … honest," I said. "And I'm very surprised."

"So, my dear, what have you been doing with yourself?" Mrs. Winter asked.

"Walking," Mrs. McCray sniffed. "Apparently your niece's idea of appropriate activity for a young lady is traipsing about the countryside like a feral sheep."

"Oh, Cassandra's always been such an active person. It doesn't surprise me that she brought these healthy habits with her to the country. Surely, there's no harm in the girls getting fresh air and exercise, but if you're really so unnerved by their engaging in a simple walk, I can take Ivy and Cassandra into my household for the rest of their time here."

Mrs. McCray looked distinctly annoyed at the implication that she could not handle supervising three relatively well-behaved girls. "Oh, don't be silly, Aneira. I'm simply concerned that the girls may be over-exerting themselves. Miss Cowell and Miss Reed have been perfectly pleasant guests while they've been there. Quite tolerable."

"Thank you, ma'am," I said, without letting too much sarcasm bleed into my voice.

I glanced at Owen, who had been quiet all this time. Ivy was staring determinedly at the ceiling. He actually looked nervous, which I believed was good for him.

"Miss Cowell," Owen said, bowing over Ivy's hand. "It's lovely to see you in person again."

"Mr. Winter," she said softly, curtsying. "Thank you again, for your correspondence. It has been very enlightening."

Mrs. Winter was watching their interaction with a speculative expression but turned to Mrs. McCray and smiled sweetly. "Would you mind, Adelaide, if I took Cassandra to her room to give her a birthday present? And of course, there are a few matters of Translator business we must review."

Mrs. McCray frowned as if she didn't appreciate being reminded that I was the Translator. "Of course."

"I'll just trust you to keep an eye on the young people," she said, giving Owen an arch look.

"Of course. Children, do sit down and have some tea," Mrs. McCray commanded in the most authoritative display of hospitality I'd seen since my time in Raven's Rest.

Mrs. Winter looped her arm through mine and drew out into the hall. I led her to the guest wing and muttered out of the side of my mouth. I was well aware that Crawford was still standing near the stairs and that he had ears like a bat.

"Is everything all right?" I asked. "Are my — the Smiths, are the Smiths well?"

"They're fine, dear, hale and healthy. We'll discuss the rest when we reach your room in this — charmingly overdone mansion," she said as we climbed the stairs. "Were you really wandering around the countryside like a feral sheep?"

"I'm afraid so," I told her.

"Young people," she muttered.

We reached the Malachite Room. I could tell Mrs. Winter was perturbed because she didn't take a moment to comment on the sheer greenness of my room. She simply cast a powerful silence spell over the room, a spell that never stopped reverberating blue sparks around the room as we spoke. Mrs. Winter dropped her lithe frame into my fireside chair.

"Your parents are just fine, dear. As is Mr. Winter, thank you for asking," she noted dryly. "The committee has offered a grudging amount of gratitude for the healing spell. The reason for this surprise visit has very little to do with your birthday. I received reports from my sources that your sister has been spotted spending money like water, making quite the spectacle of herself in the local markets."

She gave me a pointed look. I sat in the chair across from her, folding my hands in my lap. "Yes, she is here. I saw her out shopping myself, but I didn't know if I could send you that information without Mrs. McCray finding out. I'm sure she reads the mail, and I don't trust her mirrors enough to send a scrying message. The whole family is deviously brilliant, and she seems to distrust me intensely."

"We'll have to discuss the advantages of subtly coded messages at some other time," Mrs. Winter said, her expression thoughtful. "Though I can appreciate your instinct for discretion, and I will admit that the mere presence of your sister wouldn't have prompted my travel to this remote area of the country. I never have understood my husband's appreciation for it, honestly. I prefer France or even Italy to all of this wildness. But when I heard that your sister's keeping was being provided by Sebastian Crenshaw, well, I simply had to travel to this tourist pit to see you myself."

If I had been drinking tea at that very moment, I would have sprayed it all over the Malachite Room. As it was, I shouted, "Sebastian Crenshaw?" so loudly that the blue sparks of Mrs. Winter's continual silence spell rippled indignantly.

"Yes, I have it on good authority that Mr. Crenshaw is keeping

Mary at that horrid little house of his across the loch. He has referred to her as his 'ward' to those who ask about her."

"How were you able to get that information?" I asked. "We employed one of the most dedicated gossips in the household and weren't able to get so much as a whisper."

Mrs. Winter tilted her head and gave me a pitying glance that was almost its own condescending pat on my head. "I've spent decades cultivating my network of informants and observers. One household maid wouldn't compare."

"Fair enough," I sighed, sitting back in the chair. "So why would Mr. Crenshaw be helping Mary? How would he even know about her? And how much damage could she do telling him what she knows about me?"

Mrs. Winter waved her hand dismissively. "Oh, darling, if Sebastian Crenshaw was going to try to damage your reputation with Mary's information, I believe he would have done it by now. My sources say they have been keeping company for months now, after she sought him out. There were rumblings about you over the Yule season after Mary's little *outburst*, but we managed to stamp that out easily enough. No, I believe he has some larger plan in mind. I believe he plans to put young Mary forward as some sort of magical debutante, much like I have put you forward. After all, if I could get away with it, so could he. I suspect he plans to present her as some sort of rival to you, one that he can control. Perhaps he'll even suggest her as this mysterious replacement for you as Translator."

"But Mary is about as magical as a piece of toast."

"It wouldn't matter if he thought he could make it *look* like she has magic," Mrs. Winter said.

"She did mention something along those lines," I muttered. "But why? What would be their goal, beyond humiliating us both?

Would he really do all this to get control of the Mother Book? He wouldn't be able to read it without the true Translator."

"I don't believe Sebastian has thought that far ahead. I believe he only sees himself being thwarted by the Winter family, and he is lashing out. And as for his using Mary in particular, who else could he control like a puppet? Who else would be as motivated to seek revenge against you?" Mrs. Winter asked.

"Callista Cavill? Millicent DeCater? A few of the teachers at school, certainly Madame Rousseau. Headmistress Lockwood, depending on the day."

Mrs. Winter laughed. "It seems you *do* take after me, dear."

"So what do we do now?" I asked. "Do I move into Raven's Roost with you and Owen and pretend like we're on some sort of family holiday while we try to prepare for whatever Mr. Crenshaw is planning?"

Honestly, I didn't want to leave the McCrays' house where I had access to my allies and floating gondolas. I didn't want to give up my efforts to help the other Changelings, but I could hardly help them if Mr. Crenshaw destroyed my life as Cassandra. Without that life, I wouldn't have the resources to help them in the first place.

Mrs. Winter sighed. "No, that would look suspicious, as if I had been called up to Coventry to get my ill-behaved niece in line. And Adelaide doesn't feel warmly enough towards you to put those rumors to rest, should they come up."

"That is certainly true."

"Just finish out your visit here while I do all that I can to mitigate the damage Sebastian is trying to do. We'll take care of this, Sarah. That little toad has been trying to drag my husband down to his level for years. He hasn't gotten the best of me yet."

"Yes, ma'am."

"Is there anything else I should know, dear?"

I thought to this morning's flight to the mountain and the discovery of the magical children training like soldiers. Oh, and my ladies' maid, who wanted her magic removed more than anything else in the world.

I shook my head and smiled blithely. "No."

14

CAUGHT RED-HANDED AND RED-CHEEKED

Knowing that our invitation to stay at Moonstone Manse was coming to an end soon, we began flying up to the facility every few days to collect information. We made a map of the buildings and determined who slept where. We kept track of the training routines. We watched for the adults who seemed to be in charge and realized there were very few of them. There were no guards overseeing the facility because it was too remote to approach. Besides the cook, there seemed to be three teachers. There was bald, bearded man who led the children through their physical exercises. We called him Egghead, which may have seemed cruel, but well, his head did rather come up to a point, looking exactly like a farm-fresh egg. He was the lone spot of color in the drab grey courtyard, always wearing work clothes that resembled my father's but in a blinding shade of orange. Alicia claimed that some cousins in the Mountfort family believed that the color orange made them invulnerable to cold and illness — refusing to believe that it was citrus fruits that created this wonder of immunity. His wardrobe choices did make him rather easy to spot, but I supposed he wasn't really hiding from anyone.

Two very severe-looking women seemed to focus more on the children's spellwork. One was very tall and broad and the other very small and short. We'd come to call them Salt and Pepper, given the stark-white hair of the small one and the mixed shades of grey for the other. Ivy speculated that the two of them must have worked together for a long time because while they spoke to the children quite firmly, they moved in almost perfect unison without speaking to each other.

Three adults didn't seem like enough people to supervise so many children and keep them from running away from, but we supposed the fewer people who knew about it, the fewer people could reveal the secret. The children never attempted to run away. They rarely glanced up to the rim of the crater. I supposed that was the result of failed attempts or some threat the faculty held over their heads.

The children had very little time to themselves throughout the day. They worked out in the open all morning, took their lunch, trained in magical combat throughout the afternoon, and then went inside for classes. We could only guess at what they were learning there. I held few hopes that it was long division.

Unfortunately, we had no idea what the children's evening routine consisted of because we had to leave long before dark in order to get the gondola back to the McCray stable without our absence being noticed. We told Mrs. McCray all sorts of lies about where we were spending the afternoon — shopping, lectures, poetry readings, and museum tours. And while she seemed suspicious, our continued lack of trouble seemed to get her to slowly reduce Wallace's supervision of us. It was a relief. I hated the idea that could get him into trouble with our sneaking, but our increasing skill piloting the gondola combined with the cloaking spell kept us from getting caught. And Ivy was finally comfortable enough to get in the gondola without complaint about the lack of logic in such a venture.

After a fairly short morning venture into the mountains, I noticed a gondola, nearly three times the size of ours, floating past our vantage point near the facility. I grabbed the binoculars and saw Sebastian Crenshaw piloting the overwrought ship with the help of two servants in his red and silver livery. He turned towards me as if he sensed he was being watched. If I hadn't been sure that the cloaking spell was in place, I would have been tempted to throwing myself to the ground. Instead, I simply winced at his increasingly grey appearance.

The miraculous waters of the Loch of Amethysts certainly weren't doing Mr. Crenshaw any good. He looked even worse than the last time I'd seen him, his skin sagging away from his face like wet crepe paper. His mouth seemed slack, like his lips couldn't quite hold the shapes they needed to make for words. It reminded me of poor Mr. Yeatts, a neighbor in the Warren who had suffered an apoplexy years before and spoke with a distinct droop to his mouth on the left side. Mr. Crenshaw looked like a man who was dying, and I wasn't sure how to feel about that.

"Alicia, why does Mr. Crenshaw have an air gondola?" I asked, handing her the binoculars.

She didn't bother looking through them. "It's all part of that regulation I mentioned. Several of the Senators, including Mr. Crenshaw, demanded that they be given access to the gondolas in order to 'assess their safety and feasibility as a means of public transportation.'"

"So they wanted air gondolas at no cost to themselves?" Ivy guessed.

Alicia nodded. "Essentially, yes."

"Why is it so much bigger than yours?" Ivy asked, frowning.

"That's a rather personal question, Ivy," I told her.

"It's bigger because Mr. Crenshaw's ego is bigger, and Gavin wanted to give him something to match. There's a galley below and a sitting area which Gavin called 'luxurious,' but it also makes the ship harder to maneuver than the smaller gondolas, so Mr. Crenshaw can't cause much trouble with it," Alicia said, smirking evilly.

"He is a genius, that brother of yours."

Alicia preened. "Of course he is."

We watched in silence as Mr. Crenshaw landed his gondola in the courtyard. Salt and Pepper came out to greet him with much fawning and simpering. Mr. Crenshaw waved them off as if this attention meant very little to him and seemed to be making demands of them given the amount of finger-pointing he was doing.

"Do you think Mr. Crenshaw is there to get a Changeling guard of his own?" Ivy whispered.

"This seems like the sort of venture he would support," I muttered. "He's probably one of their biggest patrons. I would imagine he considers himself important enough to merit protection from a student there," I grumbled.

"If he's visiting the facility, that means he has some sort of plans for them," Alicia said. "All the more reason to get those children out of the facility sooner rather than later."

After several more minutes of emphatic arm-gesturing and speechifying from Mr. Crenshaw, he was admitted in to the classroom building. The two servants in the Crenshaw gondola settled with bottled tea and cards as if they expected to be there for some time.

"Let's get back to Moonstone," I said. We packed up and climbed into the gondola. "We need to pack supplies in earnest and try to figure out transportation. It's not like we can pack twelve extra bodies in this gondola, and I don't think any of us is adept enough at piloting to take three separate ships on our own. Then of course, we need to figure out where exactly we're going to go once we have that transportation."

"I may have transportation resolved," Alicia said as we lifted off of the ground.

"Is this one of those mysterious solutions that we don't get to hear about until we're forced into unsafe and largely untested air travel?" Ivy asked.

"Yes!" Alicia chirped.

We flew back to Moonstone, and Alicia landed the gondola with little noise or fuss. Each of us seemed lost in our own thoughts, considering all of the angles of what we were planning and how those plans could affect us in the long term. I removed the cloaking spell. We climbed out, only to have Mrs. McCray come thundering out of the shadows of the stable. "What do you girls think you are doing?"

All of us froze in our tracks, like fauns caught in lamplight. Alicia managed to collect herself first, pasting on a sweet smile. "Mother, we just took the gondola for a little ride. It wasn't dangerous at all. It was lovely!"

"No danger!" her mother scoffed. "Do you honestly believe I don't recognize mountain blue trumpets when I see them?"

She pointed to the climbing vines that had snagged on the hull of the gondola at some point during our journey.

"Those could have come from anywhere, Mother," Alicia said, shrugging blithely.

"Do not compound your mistake by lying, young lady. These flowers only grow in the shadow of the The Weeping Sisters. How could you go so far into the mountains? I let you girls venture out without Wallace's supervision because I was coming to trust you, and this — *this* is how you repay that trust. Do you have any idea what could have happened? You could have crashed! You could have gotten lost! We might never have known what happened to you! What a ridiculously stupid thing for you all to do!" There was a hint of triumph in her eyes, like I'd finally done something she'd been hoping for.

"Mother, honestly, we were very careful," Alicia protested. "We've been flying for weeks without any problems. You let Gavin fly all of the time without a word. Why not me?"

Behind her, Ivy was shaking her head, as if she could get Alicia to stop talking by sheer force of will. It did not work.

Mrs. McCray turned to me, her eyes icy as the depths of the loch. "I believe it is time that you returned to your aunt's home, Miss Reed. I believe you have become a negative influence on my daughter. She never would have done anything like this before she began her ill-advised association with you."

I bit my lip. So much for staying out my invitation to protect my reputation. "Yes, ma'am."

"No, Mother, that's not right. It was my decision to take the gondola. You shouldn't punish Cassandra for my mistake."

Mrs. McCray turned on her daughter, and I couldn't blame Alicia for shrinking back. "You're right, Alicia. I'm not punishing Miss Reed. I am also punishing you and Miss Cowell, as she will be leaving as well. Ladies, I will tell your maids to pack your bags. You will depart immediately."

All of us were left, not speaking, in the stable and staring after Alicia's mother.

"What do we do now?" Ivy asked. "Where will I go? My parents don't have a home here."

"I'm sure she means you to come with me to the Winters' house," I assured her. "I'll write Mrs. Winter a scry message to let her know to expect us. I'm sure that conversation is going to be deeply unpleasant."

"Don't panic," Alicia assured us. "She's just angry now. I can talk her out of this. We might not be able to move about as freely as we were, but you're not going anywhere."

I WOULD LIKE to think that Alicia could have talked her mother out of all that anger had the following events of the afternoon not occurred. I returned to my room, horribly embarrassed and guilty because, frankly, I didn't blame Mrs. McCray for being angry with us. We'd taken something that didn't belong to us, and we'd done something unsafe involving her much cherished daughter. All that was without the added element of seeking out the Changeling children and committing what amounted to magical treason.

"Is everything all right, Miss?" Jenny asked as I entered the Malachite Room. She was already packing, bless her, gathering all of the birthday gifts and trinkets I'd been storing in my window seat with the box where I stored the Mother Book.

"No, Jenny, it's not all right," I sighed and when she looked stricken, I added. "It would seem that we will be leaving soon."

"Yes, Mr. Crawford informed me just a few minutes ago, but I thought we weren't leaving for a few more weeks," she said as I took a day dress from the pile of clothing on the bed. Jenny helped me unbutton the back of my gown and slip into the clean dress.

"It's difficult to predict the whims of the Guardian class, Jenny."

"Truer words were never spoken," Jenny conceded.

A knock at the door had Jenny hurrying with my buttons. When I was decent, I called, "Come in!"

And under-maid, a sweet-faced brunette named Olivia who worked for Alicia, came into the room and curtsied. "Miss Reed, you're being called to the family parlor."

Following Olivia down the stairs, I wondered if Mrs. McCray

had already called Mrs. Winter to the house to chastise us as a group. I wondered what Mrs. Winter's reaction would be. I couldn't imagine that she would be furious, but it would be embarrassing for her niece to be removed from Moonstone Manse. It was odd that I was being called to the family parlor, the more intimate gathering space for the McCrays when no guests were staying in the house. I could only imagine that Mrs. McCray didn't want to sully the sacrosanct parlor with my wanton disrespect for her hospitality.

But when Olivia led me into the family parlor, a small understated room done in the McCray colors, with significantly more comfortable looking furniture, I didn't find Mrs. McCray or even Mrs. Winter waiting for me. It was Gavin.

"What are you doing here?" I exclaimed.

"I thought it would be nice to surprise you with a visit because if I sent word that I was coming, complications might have prevented me from making it to Coventry."

"Oh," I sighed, throwing myself forward into his arms. "It is good to see you."

After a moment of hesitation — hardly unexpected given my breech of propriety — Gavin wrapped his arms around me and pulled me close to his warm, solid frame. I buried my face in his shirt, letting myself enjoy that sandalwood and ozone smell that was uniquely Gavin. "Are you all right? Not that I mind this unexpected embrace…"

I turned to find Olivia standing behind us as our chaperone. Her cheeks flushed pink as she hid her giggle behind her hand.

"I made your mother very angry, and she's removing me from the house," I told him.

He laughed for a moment, and when I didn't add something along the lines of "I'm only joking," his expression went grave. "Really? Why?"

"We've been using the air gondolas without permission to go exploring in the mountains."

He scoffed. "Well, that's hardly an offense worthy of ending your invitation. I've done it myself, many times."

"Your mother didn't seem to think it was a minor offense. She was incredibly upset."

"I'll talk to her," he promised as he motioned for me to sit on the sofa. "This wasn't what I hoped we could spend this precious time alone discussing. I came here unannounced because I have something to tell you. Your aunt and uncle have given their permission for me to court you. It's really a formality, I think, given the way we feel for each other. But it's an important step, and I wanted to speak to you about it before anything is announced."

"Courtship," I said as all of the air seemed to seep out of my lungs without hope of replacement.

Mrs. Winter would be so pleased. Everything she'd hoped for me, socially, was in my grasp, and I was pleased too. I adored Gavin and was well on my way to loving him. And yet, when I thought about accepting this courtship formally, about making it public and starting down that road toward a greater commitment, I couldn't breathe. All of the warmth seemed to leave my hands and I could feel tears gathering at the corners of my eyes.

I wheezed, "Courtship."

He reached out and took my hand. Would he still be interested in courting me if he knew that my father was a gardener with dirt under his fingernails? Would he consider me a suitable potential bride if he knew that I'd spent most of my life washing sheets and scrubbing windows?

"I think our parents' generation attach too much weight to the word, to be honest with you. I'm not asking for anything perma-nent. I won't want to discuss anything like marriage for a long time. We're too young to be thinking in those terms. I simply want a more formal arrangement with you, a more meaningful arrangement. I want people to know that we are together, that I'm proud to be with you, and that I hope you're proud to be with me."

He was proud to be with me. A liar. A fraud. The weight of all of the lies I'd told Gavin wound its way around my shoulders, choking me like a constricting snake. Gavin couldn't love me. He didn't really know me, and if I let him know me, he never would.

He would never know the depth of my relationship with his sister and how she'd risked her life and limb to help me with a venture that I doubted very much that he would approve. He would never know the risk I posed to his family. Alicia was already receiving death omens in the form of futureless visions. How much more danger would she be in if she continued with my schemes and plans?

I couldn't let him go through with this. I couldn't let him tie himself to my lies. If I followed through with my plans to find the Changeling children, eventually I would leave Gavin and his family in ruins by association. I couldn't have both. I couldn't do as my conscience commanded and have this comfortable life Mrs. Winter tried to create for me. I couldn't have the love I hoped for, and the one thing I could give him in return for causing this hurt was to stop the risk I posed to him and to Alicia, to sever my connection with them entirely.

"I can't," I told him, though my lips struggled to form the words. "I'm sorry."

He squeezed my hand. "I'm so happy to hear — Wait, what?"

"I'm sorry, Gavin. You're a wonderful person, but I'm not the right young lady for you. You should find someone else."

He stood, scrubbing his hand through his dark hair. "Is this because of my mother?"

"No, I — well, it doesn't help that she seems to dislike me so much, but no, it's not *only* because of your mother," I said, shaking my head.

Gavin began pacing. "I thought this is what you wanted, what we were both leaning toward. It's not as if we haven't spoken about it."

"I know, I'm sorry. I can't — You can't ask it of me."

"Ask it of you? As if it's some unpleasant and difficult task?" he demanded, his voice rising. He was always so calm, so kind, and now he was looking at me, like he didn't even know me. My heart cracked, and I wasn't sure that fissure would ever heal. This anguish must have spilled onto my face because he immediately rushed forward to drop on one knee before me.

"I'm sorry. I shouldn't have raised my voice," he said, his tone gentle. "I can't say I'm not angry because I am, but I don't want to take that out on you. That's not right. I just want to know why. Why would you wait until now to tell me? Do you not feel the same way that I do?"

For a moment, I found myself doubting my design. I could tell him. I could reveal everything and hand him my every secret. If he truly loved me, he wouldn't care. I would finally know whether he liked me for myself or the image I'd presented to him for months. But when I looked into those deep blue eyes, already so filled with pain, I couldn't do it. I couldn't take the selfish route. I couldn't hurt him more.

"It simply isn't meant to be," I told him, fiddling with the catch on the charm bracelet I was wearing. "I'm not the person you think I am. You'll see that soon enough."

"What does that mean?" he asked, shaking his head.

"I like you very much, Gavin, and I just think the world of you, but —" I cleared my throat and gave him my coldest, most level gaze. "I'm not interested in a courtship with you, Gavin. I'm not interested in any sort of future relationship with you."

I took off the charm bracelet and tried to place it in his hand. He stared at my palm as if I was offering him a dead fish.

"No," he said, stepping away from me. "I gave that to you because I wanted you to have it."

Gavin turned on his heel and walked out of the parlor, his shoulders rigid. I buried my face in my hands and for a minute, allowed myself to wallow in the misery clawing up my throat like spiny creature made of ice. He'd been so *upset*, and that was without me revealing the lies I'd told him. I could only imagine what he would think of me if I told him everything. It was better this way, to let him think I was just some cold fish who had changed her mind.

I'd done the right thing, but the cost was high.

I walked out of the parlor and saw Alicia waiting for me, her face near purple. I was setting new records for angering McCrays today.

"What did you just do?" Alicia demanded. "I only just talked Mother into letting you stay, and Gavin just walked out here, saying that you ended your understanding? He was offering you courtship! You knew how he felt about you!"

"I couldn't accept. It's not fair to him. I've been lying to him about who I am and what I am. I cannot enter into a courtship with him and let it be known all over Lightbourne that he considers me a worthy partner and then it gets out — when everything comes out? What becomes of your family? Your business? You'll be a laughingstock. I can't do that to you."

"I don't believe you're giving my brother the credit he deserves, the way he looks at you." She pushed me up the stairs, towards the Malachite Room.

Ivy stepped into the hallway. "What's going on? Are we all being thrown out?"

Alicia grabbed Ivy's arm and dragged her through the door to my room. Alicia and I cast simultaneous silence spells on the door. Jenny was nowhere to be seen, but Phillip seemed very agitated, hopping up at down on his little perch.

"Sarah broke her understanding with Gavin when he offered her courtship," Alicia said.

Ivy's jaw dropped. "What, why?"

"To protect him!" I cried. "And we happen to have more to worry about than my romantic entanglements right now, so can we please stop talking about it?"

"You just want to drop the subject as if it's nothing?" Ivy frowned. "Sarah, that's not like you. You like Gavin so much. You can't just —"

"I can, and I will," I barked at her. "There's more at stake right now than my feelings or Gavin's."

"What if I tell him?" Alicia offered.

"Do you believe that will make it easy for him to accept me? That I lied to him and let his little sister do the dirty work for me?"

"Well, that wouldn't be necessary if you would just tell him why you won't accept his courtship," Alicia insisted.

"It's not an option, Alicia. Besides, maybe it's better this way. I keep pulling you two into these awful adventures with me, risking your reputations and your safety. Maybe this is one way to avoid that vision of yours. Maybe you'll have a future if I'm nowhere near your family."

"I might see your point if we were *just* talking about your relationship with Gavin, but there's more to our friendship that just that, Sarah. Why are you acting as if we're not just as involved in helping the Changelings as you are?"

"Because it's not your duty. It's mine!" I exclaimed. "You weren't chosen by the Book. I was. You just want to vex your mother with your little rebellions and parade me into her house as a guest, when she clearly hates the sight of me. It's better if you just stay here and think of new ways to annoy her. I can't do what I need to do if I'm worried about you getting hurt!"

Her eyes narrowed at me, her expression an odd mix of cold fury and hurt. "Perhaps it is a better idea for you to go to Mrs. Winter's house for now. Mother already had a carriage waiting for you. It will not take much effort to call it back"

I swallowed thickly around the apologies already forming on my tongue. I'd wounded Alicia, and I wanted to cry for it, but if it would keep her safe, I would let her hate me. "If that's how you feel, that's what I will do. Could you please have Jenny follow me with my trunks?"

Ivy objected, her eyes desperate and shiny. "Girls, please, let's not do or say anything we'll regret."

Alicia swept out of the room without another word, her shoulders held very much like her mother's. Ivy turned to me and shook her head. "You hurt her feelings. Helping you has given us a sense of purpose, Sarah."

"I know."

"It seems cruel to take that away," she said. "Particularly to Alicia, who never thought she would live long enough to serve a purpose."

"Well, according to her vision of her future, it's still possible she won't," I replied without looking at Ivy. "So perhaps it's better that she's angry enough at me to turn away from my plans and keep herself safe. Now, if you'll excuse me, I'll finish packing."

"You both just need time to calm down," Ivy insisted. "Cooler heads will prevail."

"I don't think that's possible, Ivy. Just, please go take care of Alicia." I shut the door and sat on the bed, with Phillip chirping wildly at my side. A plan was forming in my mind, bubbling up between the waves of panic and regret.

It was not a good plan, but it was the only one I could cobble together at the moment.

I grabbed my sturdy walking boots and jacket and the box containing the Mother Book and my treasures from school, which I slipped into a large rucksack I'd been using for our mountain trips. "Come on, Phillip. We're going to do something very reckless and stupid."

15

EVERYTHING GOES AWRY

Once I'd decided what I was going to do, it was simply a matter of getting out of Moonstone Manse unnoticed with the supplies I needed and stealing an air gondola.

I wasn't proud of it, but I liked to think that Alicia would eventually forgive me.

With Phillip perched on my shoulder and the Mother Book under my arm, I slipped down the stairs and into the study. I opened the hidden passageway and navigated my way to the stable. It was considerably more difficult to get the gondola out of the stable and into the air on my own. I promised I would try to find a way to find a memory charm that would wipe away exactly how terrifying my flight up the mountain was without two other people to help pilot.

Phillip sat quietly on the other side of the gondola, silently judging me as I worked the rudder.

"Oh, do stop it," I told him.

I found the school easily enough, remembering at the last minute to cast the Silent Shadow over myself and the gondola to prevent being seen. I was pleased to see Mr. Crenshaw's oversized gondola was still anchored in the courtyard of the facility. I moored my gondola on the far side of the courtyard, wincing as I rapped the side against a wall of rock. Mr. Crenshaw's footmen were still playing cards on board their gondola and didn't notice a thing.

Egghead, however, was practicing some sort of meditative stretching near the classroom building and stopped, squinting in my general direction as I silently climbed out of the gondola. I stood there for what felt like forever, holding my breath, waiting for him to sound the alarms. But after a while, he resumed his stretches, and I managed to inhale again.

The facility was no friendlier up close: cold, grey stone with nothing to soften it. I crept toward the dorm building, where I could see candlelight flickering in the small windows. To my surprise, it wasn't locked, which said plenty about the teachers' confidence in how badly they'd intimidated the children.

The Changelings were sitting on single iron beds with gray blankets, reading and napping and, in the case of two small girls, playing with dolls made of what looked like cut up pillow-cases. There was no cheer or comfort here. No decorations or pictures or even encouraging words painted on the walls. I watched them for several minutes, waiting for some alarm to sound or for an adult to come in, but they were largely unsupervised. I took the Silent Shadow spell off and stepped out of my hiding place. "Please don't scream."

Several of the smaller children screamed anyway because I was a stranger who showed up in their bedroom without walking through a door. This seemed like a reasonable response.

The oldest boy, "Sweetling" stepped forward, pushing some of those frightened children behind him. "Who are you?"

I just realized that I hadn't considered how I would approach the Changelings, which was rather short-sighted and a little arrogant of me. I'd just assumed that I would walk into the dorm and they would see a chance for escape and take it. What if they didn't believe me? What if they thought my offer was a trap? What if they screamed for Mr. Crenshaw's guards?

I thought of Headmistress Lockwood and how easily they controlled the legions of girls at Miss Castwell's. I thought of Mrs. Winter and how she would charm people into believing in her causes. I thought of Mrs. McCray and how easily she assumed authority over the people around her. Their tactics seemed to be a mix of smooth talking and simply believing that your way was the right way and the people around you should naturally agree with you. But I didn't want to use those tactics. I didn't want to force children like me who had already spent enough time under someone else's control to do what I thought was best for them. I wanted to tell them the truth and let them make them decide for themselves. As effective as Headmistress Lockwood and Mrs. Winter were in their roles, I wanted to be better.

I cleared my throat and smiled. "Hello. My name is Sarah Smith. I was born in the Warren in Lightbourne. My mother is a housekeeper, and my father is a gardener. But I can do magic, just like you, even though I'm not born to it."

"Are you a new recruit?" Sweetling asked, his eyebrow raised.

"No, I snuck into the crater. I have the means for us to get down the mountain safely. If you want to leave this place right now, I can take you somewhere else."

"Where?" one of the younger boys asked.

"I haven't quite figured that out yet, but I would imagine it's better than this place."

"It's not that bad," a girl my age with a sweep of dark hair called "Honey" protested. "Regular meals, no housework, the promise of a good job after we graduate."

"Is this some sort of test?" Sweetling asked. "Is Mr. Feltman testing our loyalty?"

"Who's Mr. Feltman?" I asked.

"Tall gentleman, bushy beard?" he said, looking at me as if I was quite dim. "Bald?"

"Egghead?" I said, making the smaller children laugh.

"You call him 'Egghead?'" Sweetling replied.

"Well, certainly not to his face," I said, swearing that I would never tell this boy that my friends and I had dubbed him "Sweetling."

"Do we have to come with you?" One of the younger boys, Lovey, asked from the floor, where he was reading a book on poisons.

"No," I promised. "And if some of you want to stay here, I suppose that's reasonable, but why would you want to?"

"Because we don't know where you're taking us or if this is a trick or some sort of test," Sweetling insisted. "Mrs. Fernway and Ms. Bloch have a very important visitor right now, a Senator who wants to take on at least three of us as his Protectors. It's a very important night for us, and the teachers would be furious if we embarrassed them."

"True. But isn't it worth the chance that I'm not trying to trick you?"

"How would we get down the mountain?" asked one of the younger girls, "Little Bairn."

"Mr. Crenshaw's air ship," Ivy's voice sounded behind me. I turned to find Alicia and Ivy wearing dark clothes, sneaking into the dorm.

I raised my hand in a questioning gesture, but all I could manage to say was, "How?"

"Oh, please," Alicia scoffed. "You're not the only one who can work the Silent Shadow spell. Your instructions were very thorough. We used the certain sleep charm on his footmen. They're resting comfortably and stowed away behind the classroom building."

Ivy said, "We can take off right now if we hurry. The ship is big enough to carry all of us, and we would get to steal Mr. Crenshaw's air ship, which would be an added advantage — also entertaining."

"But how did you get here?" I asked.

Alicia stepped forward and took my hand. "We took one of the spare gondolas when we realized you'd disappeared and done the same. You are an idiot, coming all this way alone to do something so dangerous. You're an idiot for trying to keep us safe by leaving us behind. You're also an idiot for not trusting my brother and his feelings."

I opened my mouth to protest. "All right, fine, I'm an idiot."

She added quickly, "But I love you anyway, and I won't let you do this alone."

"I won't let you do it at all," a loud female voice sounded from the shadows. A rounded form stepped into the light. It was the cook, her red hair frazzled around a snow-white sleeping cap. She was holding a rather large cast iron frying pan, which I imagined would keep any daring kidnapper away from her beloved charges.

Sweetling sighed and pinched the bridge of his nose, "Mum."

"Mum?" Alicia said, her gaze traveling from the rather enormous teenager and the little woman who had birthed him.

The woman gave all three of us the evil eye. "It's bad enough I had to follow my Robert up this godforsaken mountain just to make sure he was safe and fed. But I'm not going to let him run off with some strange girls who tell a pretty story."

"Your name is Robert?" Alicia said.

Robert glanced down to Alicia, his cheeks in full blush, and ducked his head. "Yes, miss. And you are?"

"I'm Alicia McCray. We'd just gotten so used to calling you 'Sweetling.' It's going to be strange calling you anything else."

He closed his eyes and shook his head. "Thanks, mum, ever so much."

"You are my sweetling," his mother sniffed. "I have no regrets."

"I think we're getting off on the wrong foot," I said, holding out my hand to the red-haired mother. "Hello. My name is Sarah Smith. I was raised in the Warren in Lightbourne. I'm currently the Translator of the Mother Book."

"Well, I'm Mrs. Lucy Lumpkin, and I'm the queen of Siam," the little woman retorted.

Behind me, I heard Alicia snicker — which was not at all helpful.

"Give me one reason I shouldn't shout the house down and bring the teachers running," Mrs. Lumpkin said.

"Because it's not likely you will never get another opportunity to get your son out of this place," Ivy said. "So, unless you are content letting him be a guard dog to the very people keeping him here, we would like take these children from this place and take them somewhere they'll be safe and won't be forced to learn magic that could hurt people."

Honey protested, "Some of us aren't forced. I like learning magic. It's what makes all this worth it."

"But wouldn't you like to learn other kinds of magic? Magic that creates as well as destroys?" I asked.

"It might be nice," Honey conceded. "To learn whatever we want, but how will we eat? Where will we live?"

She made excellent points.

"To be honest, I don't know. We'll figure all that out as soon as we get off of this mountain. It will be easier to make plans when you're not being held captive by a shadow branch of government.

Just pack what you need. We need to go before anyone realizes we're here."

Honey gave me a long skeptical look while other children had already run off to begin making improvised bags out of their pillowcases. "All right then."

The children had pitifully few possessions of their own. Most just grabbed a change of clothes and a jacket. Robert and Mrs. Lumpkin made sure that one child had his spectacles and another had the cough medicine she needed twice a day. Ivy and Alicia checked for adults in the courtyard before we scurried out as a group, my rucksack slapping against my back as I ran.

The ship was waiting for us, ready to launch. Robert had almost climbed over the hull and was pulling Honey along with him when lights suddenly blazed to life around the courtyard. Mr. Crenshaw appeared from nowhere with Mary, Egghead, Salt, and Pepper in his wake.

I skidded to stop, with Ivy and Alicia careening into my back.

Apparently, I *wasn't* the only one to have mastered a cloaking spell.

"Miss Smith," Mr. Crenshaw purred, his face chalky and lifeless in the light of the crayfire spotlights. "How charming. Thank you for joining us."

"Mr. Crenshaw," I said, my voice flat.

"I told you it was a test!" Honey lamented.

The white-haired teacher, Salt, growled, "Be quiet, all of you."

"You've shamed your teachers," Pepper added. "We are disappointed in you all."

Egghead simply glowered at us.

"I would ask how you managed to find the Crenshaw School for Gifted Youth, but you're a very resourceful girl when it comes to making trouble," Mr. Crenshaw said, his dark eyes boring holes into me.

"Of course, he named it after himself," Ivy muttered.

"Mary, do you have any idea what's happening here?" I demanded.

"Mr. Crenshaw is assigning me my own personal bodyguard as I'm very important to him," preened Mary, who was wearing a dress of eye-melting violet. "I've already got my own ladies' maid, and I need to complete my — what did you call it, Uncle Bastian?"

"Entourage, dear," Mr. Crenshaw said absently, still staring at me.

"My entourage," Mary said, smiling smugly. "Though the ride up here was *very* uncomfortable. I had to stay below in the hold to protect my complexion from the wind."

"Your sister has been such a help to me, giving me all sorts of information about your unfortunate childhood," Mr. Crenshaw said, dropping his hand on her shoulder like she was an especially appreciated pet. "I knew that as long as I kept her close you would eventually come to me, and when I saw you anchored here this afternoon, I knew it was just a matter of time before you came here, meddling in my employment of these children. You're very predictable, *Sarah*."

"But I used a cloaking spell," I protested.

"Do you honestly think I'm so unskilled that I can't counter a concealment spell? Granted, yours was stronger than most, but it's not the only one in existence."

While I didn't take my eyes off of Mr. Crenshaw, I groaned inwardly. In my haste to get the children out, I'd walked right into an ambush. I'd just jumped, without a plan and without examining all the angles. Alicia was right. I *was* an idiot.

Ivy was at the end of her patience with Mr. Crenshaw's posturing. "What now? You've caught us. We are clearly doing something we're not supposed to be doing."

"Oh, my dear, you and your friends and these children have

very little to do with my plans," Mr. Crenshaw said, the skin of his cheek rippling. "Jenny, would you be a dear and come out here?"

Jenny appeared from the deck of the spare gondola, the one that Alicia and Ivy used to get up the mountain. She tossed off her own cloaking spell like an annoying swatch of fabric. In her hands, she held the Mother Book.

I gasped. How was that possible? I yanked off my rucksack and opened the box where I stored the Book. While my hollowhorn trophy and other keepsakes were intact, the Mother Book had been replaced with a copy of *A Treatise on the Use of Lace Doilies During Ritual Ceremonies,* which happened to be the same approximate size and weight.

"Jenny, how could you?" I cried. "How do you even know Mr. Crenshaw."

"All those times you let me have time to myself, I went for walks, and Mr. Crenshaw found me. He explained what you were really doing, that you were about to make life even harder for Changelings like me, and he said he could help me. You said you would help me get rid of my magic, and you never did!"

"Because I didn't want to hurt you in the process!" I exclaimed.

"He promised me!" she cried. "He promised he could take this away from me! I could go home to my parents! I wouldn't have to hide anymore! I can be normal! All I had to do was break the wards you had on the Book and find a way to sneak out and bring the Book to Mr. Crenshaw. You'd given the Silent Shadow spell to your friends, so that was easy enough to learn. Your wards aren't as strong as you think they are."

"I told you to practice," Ivy hissed.

"Not the time," I shot back.

"I stowed away while Miss Alicia was launching her infernal air boat," Jenny said, glaring at the gondola. "They were afraid that you were walking right into a trap laid by Mr. Crenshaw."

"Which should make you question why you would ally your-self with Mr. Crenhsaw!" I cried.

"Enough!" Mr. Crenshaw shouted, his mouth drooping. I watched as he rolled his neck, stretching his jaw, as if he was trying to snap his face back into position. Something was moving under his skin like a burrowing insect. His face was sagging, like it was no longer connected to his skull. He looked a lot like Tom, the poor gardener who had attacked me the previous year after he'd been turned into a Revenant by Miss Morton.

And then I realized that Mr. Crenshaw wasn't simply ill. Mr. Crenshaw was dead.

"It can't be," I whispered.

"What was that, dear?" Mr. Crenshaw asked, cocking his head toward me. It was a decidedly feminine gesture, now that exam-ined it more closely. It was something Miss Morton used to do that during our long talks in the library.

"You're dead. You're gone. We *unmade* you," I whispered. "I just can't be…"

"What can't be?" Alicia asked.

"Miss Morton?" Ivy gasped.

For a second, I could see the impulse to laugh us off in Mr. Crenshaw's dark eyes, eyes that reflected Miss Morton's manic energy. He laughed, alright, and rolled his shoulders, relaxing into a softer posture. Miss Morton's high-pitched tone mixed with Mr. Crenshaw's voice as she sighed, "The very same. Did you think I wouldn't have a plan in place in case I failed? You have only delayed the inevitable. I don't need a body to work my will. I rule the dead, child. Oh, I was a bit out of sorts for a while, but you certainly can't kill a spirit as determined as I am," she said. "Do you have any idea how tiresome it is pretending to be a man? Particularly a man as pompous and pig-headed as Sebastian Crenshaw?"

The Changeling children were frozen in shock as Mr. Crenshaw's voice faded away and was replaced by Miss Morton's voice and mannerisms. Salt and Pepper and Egghead were similarly stunned, so I supposed they had no idea Mr. Crenshaw was being used as a meat puppet. Mary had no reaction because I don't think she understood what was happening.

"What is the meaning of this!" Egghead thundered, his face going flushed and red against his orange workclothes. "We run a respectable institution here, Mr. Crenshaw."

Alicia scoffed. "Really?"

"Oh, do be quiet," Miss Morton sighed, flicking her athame at the three teachers. They slumped to the ground in a heap.

"Have you been inside of Mr. Crenshaw all this time?" I asked.

"Only for the last few weeks. He was working his own plans, trying to ruin you with your fool sister's help. I simply took over and nudged things along. He dislikes you very strongly. The silly man actually had aspirations to gain control of the Coven Guild, as if that was some lofty goal. But his shallow desires, not to mention the terminal illness he was trying so hard to cover up, made it easy to slip into his body, and slowly choke the life from him. Of course, I suppose I'm a bit shallow myself, as I was hoping to try on a vessel that would be a bit comelier. I was looking forward to being pretty for a change, but the access to Mr. Crenshaw's resources are a nice compensation."

"I never thought I would say this, but poor Mr. Crenshaw," Ivy muttered.

"Is that why you took on Mary?" I asked, backing up, so that Ivy and Alicia moved back and we herded the children towards the gondola. "Were you looking for a pretty vessel?"

Miss Morton scoffed. "Oh, don't be silly, Mary would be useless as a magical vessel. She's quite lovely, of course, but completely lacking in magical spark."

Mary had been supremely confident in her place in this situation until this moment. "But you said you would launch me in magical society, make me as well-known as Sarah!"

"I said that I would help you get revenge on Sarah for what she did to you. I never clarified how. And I'm sure that the betrayal of her sister, seeing how far you would go to ruin her life, is vengeance enough," Miss Morton said blithely, her breezy tone seeming very out of place coming from Mr. Crenshaw's face. "You distracted her from my true agenda. You've served your purpose. I do plan to launch the next Translator on society. But it won't be you. It will be Jenny."

"You can't take control of Jenny. She's not dead," I said, shooting a rather venomous look toward my former servant.

"I wasn't planning on taking control of her," she said, taking the Mother Book from Jenny.

"So why do you need her or the Mother Book?" I asked, still backing away, even as if took me further away from the Book. "You can't read it, and she doesn't want to. You proved last year it's no use to you."

"I want to make my place in Mr. Crenshaw permanent," Miss Morton said. "I believe by consuming the ashes of the book, I can bring Mr. Crenshaw's body back to a reasonable state of health and anchor myself in this vessel, limited as it is. All that power coursing through this body. I will be unstoppable."

"But that's madness," I whispered. "It's like believing that eating a lion will make you a jungle cat."

"You never have grasped the subtle fundamental sympathy of magic, dear," Miss Morton sniffed. "Jenny will be put forward as you were put forward, as a proper Guardian lady translating what the people will believe are new spells from the Mother Book. She will be my figurehead, the symbol of the changes needed in the Coven Guild, a transition from the old elite guard, and of course, I can't have you running off with my prized Changeling children. I do have plans for *them*. I need enforcers if I'm going to pursue my plans for the Coven Guild. I will unmake the government from the inside out, gathering their resources for purposes. My armies will rise, Sarah Smith, and I will make your family the first among them."

"No!" I cried as she scratched the symbol for flame in the soft leather cover of the Mother Book. It burned, the flames hot and blue as Miss Morton dropped it casually into a metal bowl being held loosely by Jenny.

I wanted to drop to my knees and cry. The Mother Book was the greatest weapon in my arsenal. It was one thing that made me special among the Guardians. It was a friend before I met Ivy and Alicia. All that knowledge, all that power, and it was burning into nothing.

Miss Morton sighed, "It's a shame really, but one must break a few eggs to overthrow a government and re-shape the world in your own image."

My head snapped up, and I was practically snarling at Miss Morton. "You're an infection. You were an infection at the school. You're an infection in Mr. Crenshaw. You're nothing but a festering, angry soul-sucking infection, and you ruin everything you touch."

I sincerely hoped Alicia and Ivy picked up on my emphasis on *infection*. Alicia's hand flexed at her side. Ivy made the smallest nod.

Miss Morton pouted. "That's hurtful, dear. I suppose I'll have to forgive you in the future, long after you're dead."

I lifted my arm to draw the sigils for the Deep Division spell with Alicia and Ivy following my movements. We threw the spell, a smoky silver near-A shape that struck Miss Morton in the chest, but nothing happened.

"Really? That silly Deep Division spell you so helpfully sent along to the committee?" she scoffed. "Largely useless with necromancy, but a nice trick if you plan a dreary career like Nurse Waxwing's."

The mention of Nurse Waxwing sparked a question at the farthest corners of my mind. What else did Nurse Waxwing recommend for infections? Garlic. Lavender. Tea tree. None of which I had in my pockets. Hollowhorn powder was useful for purging the effects of malevolent magic but that was hardly the same thing.

I was an idiot.

I reached into my rucksack and pulled out the powdered horn of the hollowhorn. Ivy and Alicia made the sigil again, as I lobbed the entire container of powder at Miss Morton. I followed as soon as my hand was free.

Miss Morton shrieked, dark smoke rising out of Mr. Crenshaw's mouth. His body flopped onto the ground, next to the still unconscious teachers, that column of smoke billowing into a cloud over his body. It was vaguely human-shaped, the dirty grey surface boiling and angry and smelling of rotten eggs. I could swear I saw Miss Morton's face swirling inside of it, screaming.

I stood there, transfixed in horror as my blood roared in my ears. The children were screaming. Mrs. Lumpkin was hollering for everyone to get back to her kitchen, and finally, one voice broke through the chaos.

"Ivy, start up the crayfire engines!" Alicia yelled as the last child boarded the ship with Mrs. Lumpkin's help. Mary scrambled over the hull, never one to miss an opportunity. Jenny stood alone, clutching the bowl of Mother Book ashes.

Egghead sat up suddenly, roaring with rage as he flung his arm up, but rather than flinging a spell, he had thrown his athame, a wicked-looking twisted silver blade with a carnelian set in the handle. I shrieked, jerking Alicia out of the way before it embedded itself in the side of the gondola. If I hadn't moved her, the blade would have struck Alicia in the neck.

We shared a look of wide-eyed disbelief before throwing a certain sleep spell at Egghead and knocking him out again.

"Jenny, are you coming?" I yelled as I climbed into the ship.

She shook her head, biting her lip as the ship rose.

"Come on!" I yelled. "It's not too late, Jenny! Please!"

But she just backed away from us, growing smaller and smaller as the gondola cleared the courtyard... a tall, vaguely human-shaped shadow hovering at her shoulder.

16

A DEBT SETTLED

*I*vy and Alicia did an admirable job of piloting the ship without me. Robert and some of the children helped while I sat on the deck, trying to absorb everything that just happened.

The Book was gone. Why had Miss Morton burned it? Was Miss Morton's spirit still viable, or had I destroyed it? How would this change my plans with the children?

I should have known Mary would make it through this situation unscathed. Mary was a survivor. "I'm so sorry, Sarah."

I shook my head, not even looking up. "Don't. Don't try to explain why this all very reasonable and understandable on your part and I should just let the past be the past and move on and help you. I'm finished with you, Mary. You have finally struck the limit of my patience. When we land, you will go your way, and I will go mine. Go back to Mum and Papa. Go find a new place in the world. Just please stay away from me."

"But, Sarah…"

I pushed to my feet and stood next to Alicia, who was steering. "Thank you for coming to my rescue," I said.

252

"Oh, you know I can't resist it when you get yourself into a hopelessly dangerous situation," Alicia said, shrugging. She smiled. "I'm very angry with you, but I still love you. You did, after all, try to protect me from myself and my vision of no future."

"I did," I admitted. "Because I love you, too, and maybe that blade that Egghead threw at you was what was keeping you from having a future."

"Perhaps," she said, cheering slightly as Ivy joined us at the wheel.

"I'm very sorry," I told them. "I acted without thinking."

"Oh, you're going to suffer enough when we land," Ivy said. "I'll just take comfort in that."

"What does that mean?" I asked.

"No, no, I writhed with discomfort for hours while we flew up that mountain," Ivy said. "I will enjoy the anticipation!"

The answer was clear when we landed the gondola in the back garden of Raven's Roost, the Winters' holiday home. Mrs. Winter and Owen were waiting for us beside a decorative pond and Mrs. Winter looked none too thrilled with me or my choices. Owen, however, did look thrilled, like Christmas and his birthday had come early.

"Land!" Little Bairn cried, tossing herself overboard as we anchored the gondola.

The Changeling children poured out of the ship.

"Hello, children, if you could just come this way and help yourselves, we should have plenty of clothing in your sizes." Mrs. Winter directed them to a table stocked with plain Snipe clothing and shoes. Mrs. Lumpkin helped the smaller children find the right matches and tossed their uniforms in a nearby firepit.

"May I speak to you privately?" Mrs. Winter asked as Owen threw his arms around Ivy.

Alicia and Ivy were right. I was going to suffer plenty.

Mrs. Winter marched me to the other side of the pond and turned, her expression cold. "How could you do this? How could you put me in this position? How could you plan this and lie to me, pretending you weren't planning to do something so incredibly damaging to my reputation?"

"I couldn't just leave them there, Mrs. Winter."

"I made a place for you in my home," she continued.

"They were being treated horribly."

"I gave you a name. I elevated you to the position of a young lady. I offered you an education and a future, at great risk to myself and my family."

"And I paid you back in full!" I cried. "I did everything you asked of me. I smiled and curtsied and fulfilled every social obligation you have asked of me so I could bring honor to the Winter name, to your name. You had a Translator living in your household, and don't tell me that a new dress or a well-hosted party would have done the same for you because I know better. Mr. Winter kept his seat in the Senate in large part to my presence in his home. Don't pretend that this arrangement has only benefitted me. We both gained from it!"

"You forget your place! Do not speak to me in that tone, young lady!" she barked. "If you were not the Translator, it would be easy enough for me to put you out of my house. It still might, if Sebastian Crenshaw has his way and puts this alternative candidate up as Translator. If that happens, you and I will have to have a serious discussion about your future. So I would suggest that you focus your efforts on the Mother Book."

"Sebastian Crenshaw is dead."

She stopped. "What?"

"He was being occupied by the spirit of Miss Morton for who knows how long. She was behind all of his plans for Mary and for Jenny."

"Jenny?"

"My maid. She was a Changeling, too."

Mrs. Winter's gaze narrowed at me.

"I'm sorry!" I exclaimed. "It wasn't my secret to reveal. I was just trying to protect people like me. People who didn't have anyone else trying to help them."

She sighed and dropped to a nearby bench. "So where does this leave us?"

"Well, you should tell Mr. Winter what happened. I don't know if Miss Morton can come back. We ejected her from Mr. Crenshaw's body, but she has the ashes of the Mother Book and she seemed to think she could use them to anchor herself to Mr. Crenshaw permanently."

"The Mother Book, gone?"

I nodded. "I tried to stop her. Jenny stole it from my room and took it to her."

"So you have had quite the evening, haven't you? Thousands of years of magical heritage gone, just like that. The dead rising. Mass kidnapping"

I sat next to her. "Mrs. Winter, I'm taking the Changelings to your uncle's farm in South Hampshire. I would appreciate it if you told your servants to accept these children and to take care of them."

Mrs. Winter straightened. "And why, might I ask, would I be willing to do that?"

"Because if you don't, I'll go to the Senate Inquiry Committee, throw myself on their mercy, tell them everything, and make my confession conditional on nothing happening to me. "

For a moment, Mrs. Winter looked supremely offended, but then her face relaxed into an expression of something like pride. "You've learned well from your time with me."

"Thank you.

"I will find a place to hide them in the country until…"

"Until what?" I asked.

She stood, fluffing her skirts. "Well, I cannot simply hide a dozen children indefinitely. They're certainly not going to want to go back to their lives in service, so you're going to have to decide what to do with them, Sarah."

"I know."

"I'm proud of you for what you have done. It was the right thing, even if it causes me trouble for me personally. I cannot support what the Committee was doing. It's the worst sort of barbarism to hurt a child, no matter where they were born."

"So, what are you going to do?"

She shrugged. "I will take Mary back to Lightbourne, to your parents. I will give you a month at my farm to figure out what you're going to do. And then, after that, I will report that you have run off to the continent. You will be entirely on your own. I won't be able to protect you, not given the route I believe you're going to take. I'm not sure I want to."

"I understand," I said, standing. "Please take care of my parents and tell them that I love them."

"And so it seems that our venture together has met its end."

"It would seem so." I curtsied to her. "Thank you, Mrs. Winter, for everything you've done for me."

She offered me the same curtsy, just as deep, almost unheard of to someone below her station.

"Oh, come here, you silly girl." She squeezed me tight against her and patted my back. "Stay safe."

"Thank you, Mrs. Winter." I hugged her back. "Now, I just have to figure out how to get them to your farm. I hadn't thought that far when I stole the McCray's gondola."

"The *Aventurine* is ready and waiting for us," Alicia said. "We just have to walk a mile or so down the shoreline."

"You don't think your family's private airship would be just a little obvious?" Ivy asked. "It's covered in your family seal."

"It's not my family's *only* air ship," Alicia said. "How do you think the McCray company makes shipments all over the county?"

"And how exactly would we convince the people who run the ship that we have permission to send said train south?"

"I had Gavin write them a letter, just in case," Alicia said, pulling an envelope from inside her wool jacket. "The conductors will take us to the McCray shipping facility in Southhampshire, and they'll provide wagons to take the children to the farm."

We dragged a bunch of newly dressed Changelings down the shore to the *Aventurine.* The children were quiet during this walk, probably wondering if they'd made the right choice tethering their future to a bunch of insane young women. Robert, however, took the time to chat to Alicia, who stumbled… repeatedly. Owen held Ivy's hand the entire walk, which was an interesting development, but given the way she glared at me when I grinned at her, I wasn't going to be teasing her about it any time soon… probably the next day, if we lived that long.

Fortunately, the novelty of a giant floating train seemed to spur the children on board. Mrs. Lumpkin followed them like a mama duck, telling them not to touch anything or sit on anything.

"Wait, you said the Coven Guild keep records of who approves air ship travel," I said, turning to Alicia. "You can't do this."

"You know, you spend a lot of time telling McCrays what we can and can't do." Gavin stepped out of the shadows, his expression quite serious.

A thousand apologies and explanations came to my lips, but all I could do was say, "I told Alicia not to tell you."

"She didn't tell me anything except that I needed to anchor the *Aventurine* near the Winter's Home tonight as soon as possible, and you appear to have spontaneously collected a dozen children who seem intent on dismantling the observation lounge."

"I'm not who you think I am," I told him. "My name is Sarah Smith. I was born in the Warren to a Snipe couple, and up until last year, I served as a maid of all work at Raven's Rest."

"Oh," he said his hands falling away from mine. "I knew you were hiding something, but I thought it might be a history of insanity in your family or that you might have a strange birthmark."

"It's a little more than that," I conceded. "I'm sorry that I lied to you. I was afraid that if people found out who I was, the Coven Guild would punish me for having magic."

"I understand why you did. I'm not happy about it, but I can't imagine what you've been through and what sort of strain you've been under. You performed admirably, all things considered."

"Please don't say that when performing admirably means tricking you. I hated doing that, but I had so much to lose," I said. "And these children, they're like me. Snipes born with magic. And they were going to be used as soldiers in a fight they had no business fighting. I had to help them."

He nodded. "I know. And when it came down to it, you refused to enter into an official relationship with me based on a lie. I appreciate that, Cass- Sarah."

"I really wanted to say yes. So badly."

"I can't say whether this changes how I feel about you. I still like you very much. In some ways, I have all the more reason to adore you, but I haven't had time to process it. I respect what you're trying to do, though. It's not right to use children that way."

"Thank you. You're taking a great risk helping us. I hope you realize that."

"I do," he said, a small smile returning to his lips. "I wouldn't do this for just anyone, you know. In terms of courtship gifts, this is considerable."

"I wish that I could go back and give you a different answer," I said.

"The discussion isn't over," he said, taking my hands. He bent his head and kissed me gently on the lips. "Simply tabled for now until your covert espionage is done with."

"And your sister forgives me," I added.

"And you prevent the collapse of magical society."

"And your mother stops hating me."

He cringed. "That could take a while."

"Very comforting, Mr. McCray."

"I try to be… Miss Smith."

17

UNMOORED AND UNCERTAIN

I stood on observation deck of the *Aventurine* watching the nightscape roll by. The moon cast a blue light over the hills. I could smell the heather on the wind and tried to breathe as much of it in as possible. I would miss that scent so much when we landed, wherever it was we were landing.

I had no real plan. I'd lost most of my resources. Oddly enough, I felt better than I had all year. I wasn't lying to anyone anymore. I was fulfilling the purpose my magic had given me. Gavin knew who I was, and he'd taken such a risk to help us. Mrs. Winter knew all of my secrets and wasn't holding them against me.

"What are the children doing?" I asked Ivy and Alicia as they joined me on the floor.

"I believe they are emptying the kitchen compartment of all of its contents," Alicia said. "They found the jellies and the candy. Apparently, they weren't allowed sweets at the facility because it would distract them. Mrs. Lumpkin is in despair at the amount of sugar being consumed."

"Oh, let them enjoy themselves," Ivy sighed. "I get the feeling that there weren't many after dinner puddings at the training facility."

"It's very clear who the soft-touch parent is going to be in this little family," I told them. "Those children will have you wrapped around their fingers by the time we reach the farm."

"You're assuming that they haven't already," Alicia snickered.

"So, here we are, heading south on a stolen ship full of children, whom we have also technically stolen. Somehow, I always knew our friendship would come to this," Ivy said dryly.

"Don't forget about the cranky cook," Alicia added.

"If it ever becomes too much, if you ever want to go back home, I'll understand. It's different for me. I don't have much to go back to, but you two, you could have safe, normal lives. No one besides Mrs. Winter knows that you've helped me, and she's certainly not going to tell anyone," I said.

"Never," Ivy told me, seriously. "Before you came into my life, I was afraid of everything and everyone. Afraid of wearing the wrong thing, saying the wrong thing. Afraid of not being liked. Afraid of being mocked. And now, I realize how stupid that was, how much time and effort I was wasting, just trying not to make anyone angry. I've changed, Sarah. I've not afraid anymore. I don't care if someone likes me, as long as I know I've done the right thing. That's an amazing gift."

"And I can use my magic. I'm alive, apparently, because of you two. You don't know what that means to me. Where you go, I go," Alicia said. "Besides, you have my hover ship. It would be irresponsible not to come with you."

Ivy sighed, "What are we going to do with all of these children?"

"Take care of them. Hide them. Teach them about their magic. Help them figure out what they want to do with their lives. Help them figure out if they want to help us hunt down Miss Morton or Mr. Crenshaw or whoever she is now," I said.

"The girls with mostly acceptable marks are going to instruct a gaggle of untrained magical children?" Ivy muttered.

"Oh, well, don't forget the time we'll have to spend unteaching them whatever terrifying skills the facility was teaching them," Alicia added.

"It's not going to be easy, but we did the right thing," I told them, propping my chin on the railing and staring into the distance.

"What are you thinking about?" Ivy asked.

"Just something that Jenny said about the Book. That no matter what she did, the Book wouldn't respond to her after that first initial contact. She tried and tried, but the Book was just dead to her. And I have to wonder how her life would have turned out if the Book had just left her alone. Would she still be working as a maid at Miss Castwell's? Or would she have gone bad no matter what? Did the Book engage with her to try to light a fire under me, or was it honestly trying to reach out to someone new in case I continued to lollygag about in school? Or did the Book recognize right away that Jenny was... What's a nice way of saying destined to be a big bag of megalomaniacal insanity?"

"Those are some very deep questions about very difficult topics," Ivy told me.

"None of which we are likely to resolve tonight," Alicia added. "We may never know how this situation may have turned out with this variable or that variable, and it would drive us mad to try to guess. We should focus on what we know. Our world is changing. There are other Changeling children. We saved them from an awful situation where they were going to be used for terrible things. We bested an undeniable evil and got away without any of us getting hurt. And now we're going to rest and recover until our next bout with that same evil because it will be back, and we need to be ready."

"Agreed," Ivy said. "This little holiday was no holiday at all. We need to rest if we're going to face Miss Morton again. We should think of more pleasant things."

"Like Owen Winter?" Alicia asked pertly. "Don't think I didn't see that kiss before we boarded."

"What?" I turned to Ivy. "How dare you kiss my cousin without permission!"

Ivy buried her face in her hands, peeking out between her fingers.

"It was a rather remarkable kiss," I observed.

Ivy squealed lightly. "It was."

I laughed, which prompted giggles from my friends.

"I take it back. I don't know why I'm friends with either of you," Ivy said, shaking her head.

"Well, given the way Robert was looking at Alicia earlier, we may be teasing her soon enough," I said, making Alicia spluttered.

"What! I didn't — he — jellies!" she exclaimed, her face going bright pink even in the moonlight.

We cackled, for once not caring how loud we were or who heard. For a few moments, it was nice to indulge in silly girlish talk about boys. It felt good to laugh in the middle of all this chaos. Our laughter died down, and we watched our joined light slip over the ground below us like quicksilver.

The year, or possibly years, to come were going to be difficult. We would be in danger. We would be living without the comforts and courtesies we were used to. We would be without guidance and without parents, but with my friends at my side, I was not afraid.

DISCUSSION QUESTIONS

1. How have Alicia and Ivy grown since the first book? Would they have reached that stage without Sarah's friendship?

2. Are Sarah's efforts to befriend other girls mercenary or kind, or a combination of both?

3. If you were Jenny's position, what path would you want your life to follow?

4. What do you think success means if you aren't using it to lift up the people around you?

5. Was Sarah brave for trying to protect her friends from the final confrontation at the training facility, or foolish for not relying on the resources and people available to her?

6. Is it inevitable for YA heroines/heroes to re-order the world around them?

7. If you had a floating gondola, where would you go?

ACKNOWLEDGMENTS

Thank you, as ever, to my agent, Natanya Wheeler, for her endless support for this series. To Darcy, thank you for being the inspiration for Sarah. And you were right about the bad guy. I am very grateful for the support of Jeanette Battista, Kathleen Jackson, Jenn Mason, and Anna Yeatts. To Paul Goat Allen, thank you so much for your support and patience through the writing and editing process. IMMERSION. And thank you to Emma Sancartier, without whose *Monsters You Should Know*, I wouldn't even know that hollowhorns exist. Or don't exist. I really hope evil carnivorous unicorns *don't* exist.

ABOUT THE AUTHOR

Molly Harper worked for six years as a reporter and humor columnist for The Paducah Sun. Her reporting duties included covering courts, school board meetings, quilt shows, and once, the arrest of a Florida man who faked his suicide by shark attack and spent the next few months tossing pies at a local pizzeria. She is the author of the Jane Jameson series, the Half-Moon Hollow series, the Mystic Bayou series, the Southern Eclectic series, and the Society and Sorcery series, as well as several standalone titles of romance and women's fiction.

Be sure to check out https://www.misscastwells.com/ for more information on the Houses, when the next book in the Sorcery and Society series is coming out, and fun fan goodies.

Molly also writes adult paranormal romance, adult contemporary romance, and women's fiction:
   https://www.mollyharper.com/

facebook.com/Molly-Harper-Author-138734162865557

twitter.com/mollyharperauth

instagram.com/mollyharperauthor

ABOUT THE AUTHOR